RIGGED GAME

BROOKSDALE #2

J.D. UNDERWOOD

For M, R, and L.

RIGGED GAME

By J.D. Underwood

1

The Monday morning sun split the greyness that saturated the spare bedroom. A groan came from a lump under a blanket on the bed. Curled up in a ball under that blanket, was Bec. She knew she had to get up and get on with the day's chore: have it out with Phil, but the vodka courage was gone.

Bec heard her sister, Jen, burst out of the other bedroom, "I'm going to be late for work." The sound of curtains being flung open soon followed.

Bec opened the bedroom door and winced at the sunlight. Shouldn't have had so much wine, or maybe it was the vodka?

Jen added coffee grounds to the coffee-maker, then flicked on the switch. "Help yourself to whatever but don't make a mess. I'll be back around five," said Jen with a piece of toast dangling from her mouth.

Bec felt ashamed of herself and her hangover. "Wait," she said. "About last night..."

Jen grabbed her teacher's bag and moved toward the door. "Don't worry about it."

"No, I was angry. I didn't mean all of what I said."

Jen's free hand went to her hip. "I know what you meant. You're my sister, and I forgive you. You can stay as long as you need to."

Somehow Jen's nonchalant attitude made Bec feel even worse. How did her life jump the rails like this? She bit her bottom lip but couldn't meet Jen's gaze.

Jen opened the door to leave, then stopped. "You have to call Phil and end it properly. For your own sake." She closed the door and was gone.

Bec's head throbbed. She knew Jen was right. On the seven-hour bus trip from Brisbane, Bec had thought exactly the same thing.

The front door banged open, making Bec jump with fright. "Forgot my phone!" Jen called with a red blush upon her cheeks. Slam! Out she went, rushing off to work at Brooksdale High School.

Relax. Nothing to worry about here, Bec chided herself as she downed a cup of coffee. She went into the bathroom and, stripping off, noticed her reflection in the mirror. Mercifully, the swelling around her eye had gone down.

She pinched at her hips and thighs. Phil always said she should 'get some work done' there. Now, Bec looked at herself as a new woman. She smiled in what seemed like the first time in six months. Phil could go to hell for all she cared. She was out. Done. Finished with him, his manipulative ways, and his violent outbursts. She was free to be who she really was: Rebecca Williams and no one was going to tell her how to live her life.

With new found freedom warming her heart, she stepped into the shower before the water had warmed up letting the cold take her breath away. It felt good. She fought to control her breathing as the water rushed over her sensitive areas. Her thick, blonde, shoulder-length hair flattened against her neck. Gathering it up, she began massaging her hair with a two-in-one shampoo and conditioner. *Perhaps I'll go back to brunette.* The hot water came through and Bec darted backwards out of the shower spray. She laughed out loud, excited by the physical sensation and emotional freedom she had found.

Fifteen minutes later, Bec emerged refreshed, clean, and wrapped in a towel. She went through to the kitchen, checked her phone, then put it down. Still nothing from Phil. *Should I call now?* Looking at the clock, she saw it was eleven-thirty. *Phil would be busy with work and in no mood to be disturbed. Better to wait until twelve-thirty, when he had lunch.*

She toasted a piece of bread, looked for Turkish feta cheese, but found only sliced. *This was country New South Wales, after all. Guess they don't have real cheese in the boonies.*

Bec looked around Jen's flat. It was meticulously tidy. She strolled into Jen's bedroom. There was a dresser against the wall and Bec smiled – it was the dresser her father made for Jen when she turned five. Her father, a woodworking enthusiast, had made one for Bec, too. She wondered what had become of it and felt sad that she didn't know.

Above the dresser was an enlarged, framed photo of the Pyrmont Bridge in Sydney. Bec's breath caught sharply in her chest. It was her photo. It was taken just before her mother died.

Bec had been working for a marketing company in Sydney and had taken a few days off to visit her mother. There hadn't had much time for photography since joining the marketing company, so she took some time out to indulge her passion. She had taken a little excursion along the river, and this had been the best photo of the day. She had the photo printed and framed and gave it to her mother before going back to work. Not long after, her mother passed away.

Bec went to her backpack and pulled out her Nikon D810. She had bought the camera not long after Phil convinced her to focus on the social aspect of being an entrepreneur's spouse. It was the last thing she had bought with her own hard-earned money – making the camera invaluable. It was a professional-level camera and she had saved hard to buy some quality lenses. She dreamed of putting on an exhibition in Brisbane, but she never got beyond a couple of field-trips before Phil reined her in with his demands of what a 'good woman' should be like. Turning the camera over in her hands, she suddenly felt sick. Her father's camera and lenses were still at Phil's. She'd had no time to pack them. Shit. Now I have to call him.

Feeling the need for some vodka-courage before the phone call, Bec rummaged around the kitchen for last night's bottle. She found it in the recycling bin, with barely a dribble left in the bottom. Jen will definitely notice an empty vodka bottle. She grabbed her backpack, camera, purse, wool cap, and sunglasses, and headed out the door for her first excursion in Brooksdale.

It was a gorgeous day despite the cold. The air was clear and fresh, not at all like city air. But it was dry, not like Brisbane, which had a salty humidity, just at the edge of your senses.

Bec snapped photos as she walked along. At the first bridge she came to, Bec went out half-way and took a photo along the Black Rock River. The trees were plentiful and they gave the town a forested look. Several willow trees bent over the bank and dipped their tendrils into the slow-moving waters. Brooksdale was a beautiful place, Bec decided.

As she continued her way North, she snapped photos of trucks laden with construction gear or farm equipment such as tractor tyres. Maybe she could make a photo-essay of rural life in New South Wales.

Every second vehicle she saw was a ute and every other was a four-wheel-drive. The Australian ute was a vehicle whose beauty was in the eye of the beholder. It was like the American pick-up truck, except less truck-like and more car-like. The cabin was similar to a sedan, whereas, the rear was a tray for carting building equipment, motorbikes, or any other big toys.

With utes, there was but one choice: Ford or Holden – a choice made for life.

A hundred meters or so ahead was the liquor shop Bec and Jen visited last night, Louis' Liquor. Bec ducked through the barn-like doors and entered the shop. The radio was playing golden-oldies country music: Sim Dusty and John Williams. As she walked down the aisles, Bec noticed that over half the shop was devoted to beer. There was an impressive selection of bourbons, rums, pre-mixed drinks, and finally the wines. Bec found the same merlot she had last night and cradled it in the crook of her arm.

Next was the vodka. She browsed the aisles, found a bottle she liked, checked her purse, then put the bottle back. She would need to be careful until she found a job.

"Oh, excuse me," said a male voice after he bumped into to Bec. She stumbled a step and the man reached out a hand to steady her.

"How about you watch where you're going?" complained Bec as she shook her arm free of the man's grasp.

"Whoa! No need to bite my head off. What have you got there anyway? Merlot? Not bad. A bit cheap, but it'll do for your average barbecue."

Bec's eyes narrowed and she looked the man up and down. He was dressed in a fine, dark grey business suit, with a flashy red tie. It was the first business suit she had seen in Brooksdale. He was slender, and his eyes were a clear blue. He was attractive, she had to admit. Maybe Brooksdale would turn out okay after all.

"Isn't it too cold for a barbecue?" Bec retorted.

"Never too cold, even for townies like me." The man grinned and extended his hand. Bec hesitated, then took it. His grip was firm but he didn't squeeze too hard. "Name's Steven James. Local businessman."

"Rebecca Williams. I'm staying with my sister for a few weeks."

"Oh, on holiday? Not much to do around here except drink and do laps of the town." He grinned and continued, "Looks like you've got the drinking sorted out."

Bec laughed with him then turned her gaze to the vodka. Steven said, "Ah, Vodka. I can recommend this one." He bent down and picked up the bottle from the shelf that Bec had just replaced. He handed it to her.

Not wanting to seem cheap, Bec took it from him and went to the checkout. Steven went with her. He had a six pack of a craft beer Bec had never heard of before. At the counter, the clerk scanned the bottles. Bec picked through her purse, checked the price, looked in her purse, then paid with her credit card. Worry about it later.

Steven had followed her out. "It was nice meeting you, Rebecca Williams. I hope to see you around."

He waved and went to the car park where he got into a white Mercedes Benz and drove off. Maria headed back towards the flat. One drink then I'll call Phil, Bec told herself.

2

Monday, four-thirty and time for the teachers at Brooksdale High to get to the Youth Centre. The sun was still shining but low in the sky as Ryan walked with his friend and Math Teacher, Mark Strathfield, to Brooksdale High's staff car park.

The Youth Centre Committee met on Thursday afternoons from five o'clock. Today they were discussing Michael Brooks's offer to purchase the land occupied by the Youth Centre - land Ryan's father had donated to the Brooksdale Shire before his accident.

"Hey, there's Jen," said Mark. They walked over as Jen waved.

Ryan got along well with Jen and he was pleased to see her. He said, "We didn't see you this morning."

"My sister arrived late last night and we had a bit too much wine. I came in just before class."

That was unlike Jen. She was one of the most organized and professional people Ryan had ever worked with. Mark slapped Ryan on the back, "Tell us more about this sister of yours. Is she single? Stud here is ready to get back on the horse, so to speak." Mark chuckled and Ryan felt a sharp pang of embarrassment. He could always count on his good friend to humiliate him.

"Oh really?" said Jen with a sparkle of mischief in her eye, "I thought you looked a lot fitter as you walked across to see me. You been working out?"

Ryan plunged his hands into his pockets, "Yeah, Jerry and Tony convinced me to take extra Brazilian Jiu-Jitsu classes over the summer. It's good fun."

Jen replied, "Well you look a hundred per cent better than you did this time last year. I'm glad you've moved on from Tammy." Jen became serious and added, "But I'm not sure my sister is ready for dating. She just left her boyfriend."

Ryan nodded with understanding and Mark nudged him on the shoulder, "Don't worry my friend. This weekend we're heading out for drinks and you can be my wingman."

Jen looked from Ryan to Mark and said, "Ryan be your wingman? What happened to Katrina?"

Turning his palms upwards and shrugging his shoulders like a kid making an excuse for not doing his homework, Mark said, "It didn't really work out. You know how it goes."

Shaking her head, Jen returned her gaze to Ryan. "How're things at the Youth Centre?"

What was there to say? Michael Brooks and his pack of wolves had captured votes on the shire council and put down an attractive offer for the land. This town cared more about money than its youth. Ryan replied, "It'll work out. We're meeting from five."

"Then you'd better going," said Jen as she got in her car, waving as she drove off.

Mark said, "Things that good, eh?"

"It's up shit creek," replied Ryan. He felt hamstrung by

the faceless bureaucracy presenting the proposal to sell the land on which the Youth Club sat. Every letter and every document he read from the council was written in passive voice - this thing was being done by no one in particular. And there was no one to argue against, just a committee that would hear people's concerns. Complete bullshit. The real kicker, the piece that hurt the most, was the council had no intention of relocating the Youth Centre, or the skate park, or the playground. Just bulldoze it for property development. Didn't people realize that young people are an investment, too?

Mark clasped Ryan on the shoulder and said, "Hey man, keep Friday night clear okay? We're going out and if Jen's sister is as hot as Jen, it'll be a fun night," said Mark.

Ryan assured Mark that he would do so, then got in his own car, an old Ford F-150, and headed for Brooksdale Youth Centre for another meeting on saving it.

BEC WOKE UP WITH A START. Sprawled on Jen's sofa, she had a headache the size of Uluru. She heard a key fumbling in the front door and sat up – a little too quickly. Her hand went up to her head as she recovered from her dizzy spell.

Jen came in through the door and called out, "I'm home. I picked up some things for," Jen froze as she walked through to the living room and saw Bec. "What happened?"

Bec blinked away the fuzziness in her vision. I do not need this now. "Look, Jen. I..."

"What's that empty bottle there?" Jen strode across the living room floor and picked up the bottle of wine Bec bought earlier in the day.

I hope she doesn't notice the tequila.

"Bec, you can't drink this much! You'll kill yourself."

"Jen you're overreacting. It's not what you think. I just had a little celebration."

Holding an empty wine bottle in one hand and putting her other on her hips, Jen adopted a teacher-stance. "A celebration? By yourself? Do explain."

Bec stood up, thought better of it and sat down again. "Well," she began, "I went out to replace the wine we drank last night, and I took some gorgeous pictures of the town. It really is a lovely place. You did well coming here.

"So anyway," continued Bec, "I took a great photo of the river and the town and set it as my background on my phone. I deleted Phil's background photo, then deleted all of Phil's photos."

Breathing a sigh of relief, Jen put the bottle up on the kitchen counter. "Well, that is a step in the right direction. Did you call Phil? Has he tried to call you?"

"I need to get him at the right time. If you knew Phil, you'd understand." Bec picked up her phone and checked for messages. There was one from Phil:

Where u at?

SUDDENLY FEELING ANXIOUS, Bec showed Jen the message. Jen said, "So you've been gone for two days and the jerk finally messages you. You did the right thing leaving. Now you can call him and end it properly."

Bec walked through to the kitchen and let the water run. She splashed her face with water and drank from cupped hands. Not classy but it worked. The haze of alcohol parted and was replaced with anxiety around confronting her ex.

She couldn't just end it with Phil now. It was more complicated than that. Besides, she still had to get her father's camera gear back. Bec needed some breathing room - change the topic.

"Jen, that photo of the Pyrmont Bridge. Did Mum give that to you?"

Jen folded her arms and looked directly at Bec. Perhaps that question wasn't as well placed as Bec originally thought. Jen said, "After the funeral, I had to go through her things. I liked that photo. It reminded me of her and of home."

Guilt prickled Bec. Jen had been there at the end, had organized the funeral, made countless phone calls to friends and family, and packed up their mother's belongings. Bec wanted to tell Jen that she wanted to be there but things with Phil and his business and - it was complicated. The words caught beneath a broth of emotion and guilt about being a reckless daughter. So Bec did what anyone feeling guilty does: she confessed. "Jen, I left Dad's camera gear at Phil's."

"You what?" Jen pointed a finger at Bec, "How could you do that? That's all we have left of him. That's what got you into photography in the first place."

Bec tried to deal with the situation by adding humour. "It's better than carting around a lathe and jigsaw."

Jen's eyebrows creased. "You're unbelievable - making jokes at this time!"

A flash of retaliatory anger swept through Bec, "Hey! You don't know what it was like living with Phil. I just wanted to get out of there, okay."

Bec's head throbbed and she sat on a stool at the kitchen counter. "I'll just ask Phil to send the stuff over." Bec said it as much to give herself hope as to get Jen off her back. What chance did she really have of getting her father's photography gear back without seeing Phil one more time and then one more time after that? Nil.

Sitting down next to Bec, Jen put a hand on her sister's shoulder. It was soothing. "Call him. Now. Don't put it off because it will just get more and more difficult."

Jen was right, of course. It would only get more difficult the longer she waited. And the longer she waited, the more booze she'd drink and the more anxiety she would feel. She took a long drink of water and picked up her phone, dialling Phil's number.

On the fourth ring, he picked up. He sounded angry. "Becky? Where the hell are you?"

Bec looked at Jen and Jen nodded encouragement. She replied, "I'm staying with my sister."

"Your sister? Gene? Come home. I'll pay for the bus. Do you know how embarrassing it is for me to keep answering questions about where you are? I have to tell people that you've gone on a trip visiting family."

This was it. Her chance to be assertive. Bec replied, "My sister's name is Jennifer. And no, Phil, I'm not coming home. I'm staying with Jen for a while. I want you to send the rest of my stuff." The phone went quiet. Had she over-stepped? Asked too much or not enough? Tentatively she asked, "Phil? You there?"

He replied, "Yeah, yeah I'm here. You caught me in the middle of sending an e-mail. Listen, I'll come down to your sister's and pick you up. Where did you say she was? Bingsdale or something?"

Bec's posture changed, she hunched forward with fatigue and rested her head on her hand. She replied, "No, Phil. I'm not coming back. Just send my stuff."

"You're not coming back and you want me to send your

stuff. Don't do this to me, Becky. You know I've got a business to run. I don't have time for your games."

Bec felt a reassuring hand on her back. She straightened her posture again, "No. You hit me, Phil. Send my stuff or I'll go to the cops."

That should get Phil's attention. He was in the wrong, not Bec. She had to remind herself of that fact continually. He replied, "Don't do it to yourself. You think they'll believe you? I'm a respected member of the business community. Besides, it was your fault. You know how I get when I'm stressed out. You know not to press my buttons."

He was right. She did know what he was like when he was having a bad day and she usually stayed well out of his way, but the other night she just pushed it too far.

No. Getting hit is not my fault.

She found her balance and tried to act confidently, "Phil, you hit me. That's not right. Now send my stuff. It's in the very top of the wardrobe."

"Ok. Whatever. Look, I won't send it, I'll deliver it. I'm busy this weekend, but I'll come down next weekend - last Saturday in June. Message me the address."

And with that, he hung up. Bec looked at the phone. Her hand shook. That bastard had done it to her again - made her think his actions were her fault. Jen moved in front of Bec and asked, "Well?"

"He's coming here."

3

Friday night and the Black Rock Pub was packed with locals out to enjoy the start of their weekend. The car park and street were lined with Ford and Holden utes with tall UHF Radio aerials mounted on bull-bars and heavy mudguards with the RM Williams logo on. Inside, Ryan and Mark were met with the sound of sizzling meat and loud conversations.

The two friends pushed their way to a table in the dining area. Ryan breathed in the grill-smoke-filled room with pleasure.

"Thanks for driving, man," said Mark. "Looks like we beat the girls. Fancy a beer to get started?"

"Thanks, but I'll just have a ginger ale."

Mark strode up to the bar. It was new and gave the impression of cheap functionality. It was covered in bar mats advertising Tooheys beer and some craft beers from South Australia.

Ryan watched his friend chat casually with a woman wearing a slim white dress while ordering the drinks. Ryan wished he had Mark's confidence with girls.

Ryan spotted Jen through the crowd searching for the boys. Her brunette hair was up and she looked like she had come straight from school. Ryan stood and waved to get Jen's attention and noticed a beautiful blonde woman walking behind Jen. He stared for a moment. Her jeans showed the curve of her hips and her blonde hair was loose and hung down around her neckline. Realizing he was staring he sat down as a wave of self-consciousness washed over him.

Jen flashed a broad smile when she reached the table. She pulled her sister by the hand. "Hi, Ryan!" Jen chirped, "Glad you could make it out. This my sister, Rebecca."

Standing up, Ryan reached across to shake Bec's hand. He was struck by her gentle smile and her deep coffee-coloured eyes. She's beautiful, he thought.

Realizing he was staring again, Ryan forced himself to move around the table and pull out a chair for each of the ladies.

"Well, I wasn't expecting silver service!" said Bec with a light laugh that put a smile on Ryan's face.

"All part of the Brooksdale experience," replied Ryan as he took his seat and did his best to keep his gaze at eye-level.

By way of introduction, Jen said, "Brooksdale's very own Ryan Anderson here is the best English Lit Teacher in New South Wales."

Bec leaned forward slightly, "Is that so? I always enjoyed English Literature at school. I think it's so important to learn how to express ideas clearly."

It was refreshing to hear someone else state enthusiasm for English. Normally people said something like, "Oh? That must be interesting," and changed the topic.

Ryan asked, "What do you do, Rebecca?"

Jen spoke for Bec, "She's in the market..."

"Photography," said Bec. "I've just moved from Brisbane where I did some work in marketing, but my heart is in photography."

Bec and Jen looked at each other and laughed. It was music to Ryan's ears.

Mark returned to the table with four drinks. He must have seen the ladies come in and had ordered for them. A suave move thought Ryan. Mark said loudly, "A house white for Jen, and I figured since you were sisters, you'd like your individuality, so a house red for..."

"Rebecca - call me Bec."

Mark sat down next to Bec and handed Ryan's ginger-ale over to him. Bec teased, "Not drinking?"

Mark answered for Ryan, "He takes his role as the designated driver very seriously. No alcohol will pass those lips tonight."

Ryan replied, "Teachers need to be role models in the community, not just in the school-house."

"Haha! Ryan, you're pushin' the proverbial uphill on that one," said Mark and he raised the glass. The others at the table raised their glasses in response and the first drinks for the night were underway.

A cute, if somewhat shapely, waitress took their orders and dashed off. Bec and Mark began chatting, so Ryan and Jen shuffled closer. "Looks like those two are getting on well," said Jen.

"Who doesn't Mark get along with well?"

"True. So how's the Youth Centre coming along?"

Ryan lowered his voice, "Okay, we've got about fifteen regulars coming in now and the Billy Cart Bash is coming up. We've got a couple of teams entered."

Jen shook her head. "That's all good, but not what I meant."

Ryan rubbed his chin with his thumb and nodded. "About the only thing we can do is get a petition signed, but with only fifteen regulars..." he shrugged in defeat. It was a hopeless cause.

"Bec used to be in marketing," said Jen and she put her hand gently on Bec's shoulder, drawing her attention away from Mark, "Hey Bec, Ryan needs some help with something."

Ryan gulped down a mouthful of ginger ale and nodded. "Yeah, umm... I'm trying to keep the Youth Centre up and running, and..."

"Oh come on Ryan!" Jen said, "It's more than that. It's a Youth Centre, skate park, maker-space, and all-around good place to hang out."

Bec smiled and leaned into the conversation. "A community-minded guy. I like that. Tell me more."

It was the safety line Ryan needed. He spoke with passion about the Youth Centre. His years volunteering there, the kids who had come in and out over the years, the ones who made it to University, or just kept out of trouble. Now it was all coming to an end - unless they could do something about it. When he had finished telling the story, Bec had a serious expression on her face and Ryan worried he had bored her. To his surprise, she said, "Okay, I'm in."

Mark drained his beer and tapped his glass. To Ryan, he said, "Your turn, Mr Community. I'm off to the loo."

Ryan took everyone's orders and went up to the bar. As he slipped in-between tables, he considered Bec. He had been taken aback by her easy-going nature. Clearly, she was intelligent. Maybe it was time for him to get back into the dating scene, as Mark had so often said.

At the bar, Ryan got served quickly. The bartender was a

former student with whom Ryan spent many afternoons a week tutoring in the youth centre.

"Hey, Mr Anderson. What can I get ya?"

Leaning against the bar, Ryan replied, "Brian, you can call me Ryan now. You know that."

"No Sir. You'll always be Mr Anderson, now what can I get you?

While he waited, Ryan looked back to the table. What he saw made him straighten. A man had taken Ryan's seat next to Jen. He could only see the man's face side on, but that was all the view he wanted. It was Steven James – one of the most annoying people in Brooksdale.

The drinks arrived and Ryan carried them back to the table. He placed the drinks down and Steven said, "I'll have gin and tonic thanks – no ice." He didn't even look at Ryan.

Jen tried to smile politely. Ryan replied, "I'm not your waiter and you're in my seat."

Steven twisted in the chair, "Ryan Anderson. Good to see you. Good to see you."

Jen interjected, "Steven just popped over to say hello. Where are you sitting, Steven?"

Steven grinned, "Well, it looked like there was room for me here. Does anyone mind if I stay at your table?"

Yeah. Ryan minded, but he bit his tongue and pulled a chair from a neighbouring table, dragging it along the ground and placing it on the corner of his table. Steven was involved in the purchase of the Youth Centre land, so Ryan didn't want to make things worse. He decided to sit passively and let the night play out - let Steven puff himself up and take a fall.

Mercifully, the food arrived when Ryan was in the middle of his thoughts. Greek Salad for Bec, Lasagne for

Jen, Prime Rib Steak for Mark, and Chicken Casserole for Ryan.

"Will there be anything else?" asked the waiter.

Steven called out, "Yes. Filet Mignon and a bottle of champagne for the table. Glasses for everyone."

Fancy. Who does this guy think he is? Ryan thought.

The waiter raised a single eyebrow and walked away. Steven adopted a relaxed, yet confident position in his chair. He started talking about his business: Champion Gym and property development. Ryan tuned out.

Mark returned from the bathroom, "Well if it isn't Steven James."

"Oh, Mark. Nice to see you, too. Pull up a seat and join us."

"I never un-joined."

"Never mind, never mind. Sit down. I ordered champagne."

The bottle and glasses arrived. Steven poured a glass for the ladies, but not Ryan or Mark. The fillet Mignon arrived next and Steven looked settled for the long haul.

Mark shrugged, exchanged a glance with Ryan and continued as if nothing had changed.

To his dismay, Bec and Steven seemed to be getting along well and Ryan found it hard to enter the conversation. His thoughts brewed and soon turned to the renovations on his house. A granite kitchen counter-top awaited installation.

After finishing his casserole and trying not get angry or flustered with Steven, Ryan downed his ginger-ale and said, "Well, excuse me. I should get home. I'm in the middle of a big renovation and want to get an early start tomorrow."

"Oh, you're a handy-man?" asked Bec.

"I just like working with my hands."

Steven giggled, "Working with your hands by yourself sounds suspicious. It's always better with someone else. Haha!"

Ryan was used to smart-alec students but from an adult? Ryan wanted to make a cutting reply, but he buried it, not wanting to cause a scene. That was just like Ryan. How many times had Tammy flared up in anger because of his unwillingness to share his true feelings - his frustrations - with her? "Maybe I'll see you at the gym," said Ryan. "We should roll."

Mark leaned over, "I thought we were having a big one? Come on. Don't bail out now."

Rubbing his stomach, Ryan said, "I'm just not feeling too well and I need an early start tomorrow."

Without waiting for a reply, Ryan nodded farewell to Bec and Jen, wished Mark good luck, and left. On the drive home, he replayed the events of the evening. His thoughts kept coming back to Bec and he realized why Steven had flustered him so much: Ryan was jealous.

4

Bec awoke with a headache on Saturday morning. "I have to stop doing this to myself," she said out loud. The curtains were open and a dull light came through. It was overcast, but no sign of rain. Bec went to the kitchen and gulped down a Panadol with a glass of water. She saw a note from Jen:

Popped out for a coffee with a friend. Be back before lunch.

BEC LOOKED AT THE CLOCK. Just before ten. Bec figured she'd have about forty-five minutes to get herself tidied up and non-hangover-looking. Jen had been on her case recently about the amount of drinking she'd been doing. Her phone buzzed. A message from Steven.

Want to do lunch? Pick you up at 11:30

DID she want to go on a date? Bec wasn't entirely sure if she was ready to start dating again. She felt vulnerable and, if she were honest with herself, still in love with Phil. Then again, a date with another man might be just the thing to help push Phil from her heart. Steven was an attractive guy and seemed interested in her. What harm could a coffee date do?Bec responded:

How about brunch. Pick me up at 10:45

STEVEN ARRIVED in a white A-class Mercedes Benz. Bec saw him through the window of Jen's flat. He tooted the horn, so Bec went out onto the street. She waved at the car and the driver's window rolled down revealing Stephen. "Hey good looking!" called Steven through the open window, "Get in and we'll grab some brunch."

As Bec slid into the passenger seat, she caught Steven checking her out, which gave her some confidence. She was wearing her slim-fit jeans and a tight-fitting winter coat. *Good choice.*

As soon as she closed the door, Steven sped off down the road, took a corner a bit too fast and headed toward Main Street. "I'm taking you to a café that overlooks the river. It's not much by big-city standards, but it's the best this little place can do."

They made small talk as Steven sped North on Main Street. He weaved between the slower moving traffic until he turned down a side street that took them to a knoll right next to the water. On top of the knoll was a quaint café with floor to ceiling glass walls and a stellar view of the river. An iron scroll sign read, 'River View Café and Tapas Bar.'

Steven took Bec's hand and lead her through to a table right by the window. He called out, "Service!"

Bec suppressed a smile when the waitress behind the counter gave the slightest of eye-rolls. A big-city attitude would not win friends in Brooksdale.

The waitress sauntered over, swinging her hips as she approached. "Get you something?"

"How about some decent service? I'm a paying customer and shouldn't have to wait a life-time to have my order taken," replied Stephen.

Sensing conflict, Bec pushed the conversation forward, "Can I get a cappuccino? I could murder for some caffeine right now. And the toasted chicken avocado sandwich sounds wonderful."

The waitress smiled kindly at Bec and scribbled down the order. Steven's eyes narrowed. He flipped through the menu then pushed it aside. "Flat white and a salmon salad."

Steven locked eyes with Bec and said, "You look good today. I have to admit, I was so pleased to find such a beautiful woman in Brooksdale. "I sensed some class about you the moment I saw you. You're not a country girl, are you."

Bec smiled. Flattery could work wonders, even if it came at the expense of the locals. She fluttered her eyelids and rebuffed, "Brooksdale isn't all that bad you know."

Reaching across and taking her hand, Steven said, "This place should be grateful to have people like you and me."

Smiling, Bec felt a little uneasy at the flattery. There was something a bit off about it. "I don't know about that. I'm really just visiting."

The waitress brought their coffees and sat them on the

table. Steven glanced at the waitress, "I'll take my coffee after my salad, thank you. Rebecca?"

Bec looked at the waitress, who was biting her lip. Bec smiled, "Thank you. Now is good."

Without a word, the waitress picked up Steven's coffee and walked away only to return five minutes later with the toasted sandwich and salad.

Bec and Steven ate and he regaled her with stories of running businesses in a small town, his friendship with Michael Brooks, and the importance of good local governance. Bec nodded dutifully and smiled in the right places, but she rarely gave information about herself – she wasn't ready for that yet.

Bec's phone buzzed in her bag. It could only be mother-hen-Jen checking on her. Bec glanced at the clock. It was approaching eleven-forty. She finished off the last piece of her sandwich and coffee. "I need to head back now. I've got some things planned with Jen."

Steven looked put out and rubbed his hand across his forehead. "Why don't you have another coffee? We can talk some more. I haven't finished telling you about the newest property development in town. It's a really exciting project – a ton of money to be made."

For a moment, Bec worried that Steven wouldn't take her home, but she didn't want conflict with this man, either. Conflict gave her anxiety. Better if people just got a long. But people don't 'just get along,' so Bec decided to assert herself. "No. I really need to get back once you've finished your coffee. If it's too much trouble for you, I can walk."

Caught in an ego-trap, Steven replied, "Of course it's not too much trouble! A real man always picks up his date from where she wants to be picked up and drops her off where she wants to be dropped off. I don't even want the rest of this coffee – not very good."

Ten minutes later, the Mercedes pulled up alongside the block flats where Jen and Bec lived. Steven dropped Bec off at Jen's apartment. Steven said, "Sorry about the place. The coffee and food were pretty ordinary. I'm going to complain to the owner – I know him, you know."

Steven was quite harmless, Bec decided. Perhaps a little insecure, but harmless enough. She thanked Steven, and as she was getting out of the car, Steven said, "I'd like to take you out on a real date. Dinner. How about Thursday night?"

Bec hadn't really thought that far ahead, and caught in a bit by surprise, replied, "Um, sure. Pick me up at six?"

"Done. See you Thursday."

Steven drove away, leaving Bec wondering if she had made the right decision. Steven was cute enough, had plenty to say, and certainly wasn't boring. Yeah. A second date would be fine. If nothing else, it would help her move on.

5

B *ang. Bang. Bang.* Ryan bashed a stake into the dry, hard ground. It was a sign encouraging people to come into the Youth Centre and sign the petition against the budget cuts. The *roll-clunk* of skateboards on the concrete skate park sounded behind Ryan as he worked. It was mid-afternoon on Sunday and the sky had cleared of all cloud. Still no sign of rain.

"Hey community guy. So, this is how you spend your Sundays?" Ryan spun around. It was Rebecca Williams. His heart beat a nervous rhythm. She continued, "Jen told me you'd be here. I came to see what I could do to help."

Unsure of what to do, Ryan looked about. "You can grab that piece of board and move it over there," he said. Bec laughed - delightful sound. She looked vibrant in a wool cap and long winter coat. The cold of June turned the tip of her nose red, and it was the cutest thing about her.

Bec said, "I meant help with the online stuff. Social media, a website, photos. Like the modern world."

"Oh, yeah. I don't really have any of that yet."

Bec unslung her camera. "Well, I'm gonna fix that for you. Stand by the skate park and I'll get some photos.

Ryan stood awkwardly in front of the half-pipe while the skaters rolled by.

"Ryan. You have to relax and look happy."

He shoved his hands in his pockets and Bec told him to take them out. He tried to lean on the half-pipe, but he felt unnatural.

One of the skateboarders came over. "Hey Mr. Anderson. What's happening?"

It was Arkell Green, a Year Eleven student in Ryan's class. His father worked at the meat-packing facility and his mother ran a small coffee shop in town. He was one of the Youth Centre's success stories. A year ago, he was close to dropping out of school. Now he played representative football and his grades improved every term.

Ryan introduced Arkell to Bec. As Ryan talked, Bec snapped off a few shots.

"I think I got what I need here," she said. "Mind if I look around?"

BEC TOOK a few more shots of the skate park, the playground, and the outside of the Youth Centre building. It looked more like an old brick-veneer house than a Youth Centre, with orange brick at the bottom at the walls and white weatherboard reaching up to a corrugated-iron roof. She took a few shots from a low angle, but wasn't happy with any of them.

Bec took a few photos of Ryan working. Those shots turned out better. She had to admit, he was a well-built man. His broad shoulders and winter coat gave him a chiseled look and, as he swung the sledge hammer against the sign-post, she was reminded of the old black and white images of masculinity from 1920s construction sites.

Around the side of the building, Bec saw three half-built billy-carts. They didn't look like much – just a rough timber frame with some old bicycle wheels attached. She was about to turn away without taking a photo, then thought it might be a good idea to get some pictures. Imagine if one of these carts actually won a race at the Billy Cart Bash. It would be a triumph for the little guy! What a story. Bec snapped a few shots at interesting angles and made a mental note to return regularly and capture the progress of the carts.

Bec walked into the youth centre. A little plaque at the entrance gave recognition to Thomas Fletcher for donating the building, the Brumfield family for donating the furnishings, and Gareth Anderson for donating the land. Bec wondered if there was a family connection for Ryan.

The interior walls were covered with posters of bands, films, and one wall was devoted to graffiti. There was a kitchenette, tables and chairs for studying, a TV and PlayStation, as well as a row of bookshelves filled with comics, graphic novels, and books. Two reverse-cycle air conditioning units pumped hot air into the room.

Two students, a young man and a young woman, sat at the tables. Their books were open and they were testing each other. Bec introduced herself. The girl spoke first, "I'm Sally and this is Adam." They seemed like nice kids, obviously dating.

Bec asked if she could take some photos and the students agreed. While she took photos, Bec asked, "So does everyone study here?"

"No, not everyone," replied Adam. "Some kids watch movies, others play video games. It's mostly good."

Bec said, "Doesn't anyone smoke, or sneak in alcohol? That's what I would have been doing at your age."

Adam and Sally exchanged a look and Bec suddenly felt uncool.

Sally said, "There's a few trouble-makers that try some stuff, but there's always an adult about with the keys. 'No adult, no open' as Mr. Anderson says."

Adam continued, "Yeah. I think the town should trust us a bit more. Kids have to make mistakes to learn."

Bec noticed the two were holding hands under the table. She smiled and thought back to her own teenage romances. Young people did have to learn for themselves, but it was good there were grown-ups around to pick up the pieces.

Bec went outside and saw Ryan again. "I've got enough to get started on a basic website. Can you e-mail me some details for the site? I'll start some social media stuff, too."

Ryan smiled and said, "Sure, but I don't have much of a budget to play with. Everything we get goes to paying bills."

"Cheap it is then," said Bec.

She gave her e-mail to Ryan and he said, "We could meet sometime and talk through this website."

That sounded like a good idea to Bec. Another coffee with a good looking local wouldn't hurt either way. She said, "I could use the local knowledge. Let's do it."

"How about Thursday evening?"

She had a date with Steven on Thursday night, but she didn't want to tell Ryan that. "I can't then. Wednesday?"

Ryan said, "I've got JiuJitsu on Wednesdays. Tuesday?"

"Sure, see ya then." Bec left the park. It was cold, but she felt warm inside. She didn't plan on being in Brooksdale for long, but while she was here, she might as well help. And besides, having something to do kept her from worrying about Phil.

6

At six-thirty on Tuesday evening, Ryan said goodbye to his mother and drove to Jen and Bec's flat. Mare's tail clouds streaked the sky in a blaze of orange caused by the setting sun. On Tuesdays, Ryan dropped off cooked meals for his mother so she didn't have to cook for a few days – and to make sure she was looking after herself.

As he drove through the streets of Brooksdale, he thought fondly of Bec. She seemed to have some drive and determination about her. He knew she had just left a bad relationship, and he himself had recently recovered from a divorce. "Don't be foolish. You're both vulnerable now," said Ryan out loud. He pushed the thoughts of romantic liaisons out of his mind.

JEN FUSSED ABOUT TIDYING UP. "Ryan's going to think we live like animals!"

Bec cleared the laptops and mess of papers off the table.

"Relax. You've been friends with Ryan for ages, right? He'll be fine. It's like having a brother over for dinner."

Jen put her hands on her hips. "No, it's not like that. Besides, Ryan's bringing dinner."

That was part of the deal. Ryan does dinner, Bec does the website. *A pretty good deal for Ryan*, thought Bec.

A solid knock on the door filled the flat. Bec swung the door open and Ryan stood there in blue jeans, a brown double-breasted winter coat, and scarf. On Sunday he was the construction worker, on Tuesday the academic.

Ryan interrupted her thoughts, "May I come in?"

Bec took the bags of food from Ryan, stepping back as she did so.

"Wow. You two have this place looking really nice," said Ryan.

Jen bustled out of the kitchen and replied, "No! It's a mess. I've just been so busy lately that it's hard to keep up with the work."

Ryan laughed easily, good humour in his eyes. He hung is coat and scarf then went to the kitchen. "I'll heat up the food. Don't get too excited. It's just beef casserole."

Bec said, "Anything someone else makes is good for me."

Ten minutes later, the trio were sitting down with full plates of a delicious beef casserole. Bec poured wine for everyone and started to eat.

Bec slipped a spoonful of the casserole with a hearty chunk of beef into her mouth. Tender and flavourful, it broke apart in her mouth. This man could actually cook. "Ryan," she said. "This is the best casserole I've had in a long time."

Ryan flushed slightly at the compliment. He looked cute. In reply, he said, "It's a mainstay at my place. So, Rebecca, how're you finding Brooksdale?"

"Please, call me Bec. I like it so far. I wasn't expecting people to be so open. You know, small towns have a reputation."

Jen added, "Yes, and she has already found a date."

Ryan raised his eye-brows then rubbed his chin with his thumb. "Fast work."

Bec felt heat rise in her cheeks and she shot daggers at Jen, who added, "With Steven James."

Ryan put his fork down and coughed.

"Another glass of wine?" Bec didn't wait for an answer and filled everyone's glasses.

The rest of the meal passed in small talk. Bec poured more wine, but Ryan refused, citing his two-by-two rule. Bec shrugged and continued to drink. *Less than a bottle tonight,* Bec told herself.

Ryan said, "I'll make coffee." He went to the kitchen and banged around looking for coffee-making implements.

Jen rolled her eyes and grinned, "Ryan, I'm afraid we've only got a simple coffee maker. The coffee is in the top cupboard."

"I can live with a basic coffee maker, but this coffee? Jen, you'll get better flavour if you grind your own beans."

Jen giggled and Bec smiled. The mood had lightened again. Jen said, "Ryan here is our resident coffee expert."

"That's right," replied Ryan. "Despite what people say, you can get good coffee in Brooksdale. The Flat Rock Café has a great selection and they'll grind beans for you."

Ryan brought three steaming cups of coffee to the table. Bec sipped hers. "Wow! Is this really the same coffee I've been drinking?" The coffee was as good as any cafe she had been in.

Ryan chuckled.

"Well, you two have work to do. I'll clean this lot up," said Jen.

WITH THE TABLE CLEANED OFF, Ryan sat shoulder to shoulder with Bec as she showed him the work she had done so far on the website. He felt stiff and uncomfortable. The mood had changed. He realized he was a little jealous of Steven James. That sly politician-of-a-businessman had gotten a date already, and that rankled Ryan. Perhaps it was true what they said - good guys finish last. At least Ryan knew he was a good guy, even if he finished last.

Bec pointed to the screen, "This is what I'm thinking. A blog and a landing page. We do a little advertising on social media, send people here, they sign up, and we send them update and reminders to sign the petition. We can even do an online petition."

"It's that simple?"

"Pretty much, but you're the word-smith, Mr. Anderson. You have to write the words and I'll put them in."

They spent the next forty-five minutes filling in pages on the site. Ryan told the story of his father, at the time a successful business man who donated the land the youth centre was on. His connection to the Youth Center ran deep and the memories were all he had left of his father.

"That's a pretty amazing story," said Bec. "Where's your father now?"

Ryan kept his eyes on the screen. "He passed away not long after he donated the land.

"Oh, I'm sorry." Bec put her hand on Ryan's shoulder. More words floated through his mind, but he hadn't talked about his father for so long, that the words cracked, split, and crumbled like a poor concreting job.

Bec did a fine job laying out the website with information and history. Ryan was impressed with Bec's level of professionalism, or perhaps he was just a simple country boy. In any case, With the website filled out with the history of the youth centre and social media accounts set up, Ryan felt it was time to leave. He thanked Bec and Jen for their time and walked out.

As he got in his Ford and looked back up at the flat he had just come from, he felt a twinge of loneliness.

7

A bitterly cold wind blew on Thursday night when Steven arrived to take Bec out on their second date. The gum trees waved in the breeze and Bec felt a chill run through her body as she left the apartment. Jen looked disapprovingly at her. "What?" said Bec, like a disgruntled teen.

"I don't know that dating Steven is a good idea. You've just broken up with Phil, you're drinking a lot..."

"You're not my mother, Jen."

"No. I'm your sister and I'm worried."

"At least I'm dating." *Slam!* The wind took the door as Bec closed it. Jen probably deserved a slammed door anyway. Who was she to pass judgement on Bec's dating decisions?

Steven greeted her with a smile and a bouquet of flowers. "Tonight, we're breaking out of Brooksdale. I've got reservations in Gum Flat Ridge."

Steven sped West along the highway. Dance music played on the car's audio system. "You like dance music?"

Bec replied, "I don't mind it. What I really like is electric blues."

"Haha, I don't think I have any of that old stuff."

Steven pulled off the highway and drove through Gum Flat Ridge.

"Have you been to Gum Flat Ridge before?" Steven asked. Why would she have been to Gum Flat Ridge? Bec shook her head and Steven pulled into a parking lot. They walked to the riverside restaurant. Steven put his arm around Bec as they walked in. Bec slipped out from under his arm and followed the waiter to their table. She immediately ordered a wine and Steven followed her. "Nice place," Bec said.

"Yeah, I've been here a couple of times now. It's been a great date place."

Bec brushed her hair over her ear and drank some wine. Steven seemed confident - she liked that. But there was something else. Something of a smooth-talking salesman or politician about him that just didn't sit right. Was it a certain masculinity he was compensating for?

Steven pulled a black case out of his breast pocket and slid it across the table. "For you," he said. "A token of my admiration."

Surprise! A gift on a second date. What would he want in return? Bec waved the case away, "You don't know me well enough for this type of thing. I can't accept it."

"Of course you can. I insist. In fact, you'd hurt my feelings if you refused."

Bec took another drink of wine and picked up the case. She opened it to reveal a silver bracelet. The silver links gleamed in the light of the restaurant and Bec knew she couldn't accept it.

"Put it on," said Steven.

"Really. This is too much-"

"Put it on."

Shit. Jen was right, thought Bec.

Bec slipped the bracelet over her hand. She was reminded of the gifts Phil had given her, then demanded she wear them. They weren't gifts, they were symbols of ownership.

Steven said, "I thought it would go well with your blonde hair and dark brown eyes. You're very beautiful, you know."

Bec tried to smile. She still had to ride home with this guy. "Thank you, but I'm actually a brunette."

Steven didn't seem to hear. The salad arrived and was soon followed by the main. Bec had cioppino and Steven a red sauce pasta. He talked on and on about his work, about Brooksdale, and about the exciting new property development that he was involved in, and his work on the town council.

Bec said, "Do you know Ryan Anderson?"

Steven laughed, "Yeah, sad story that one. He actually thinks he's doing a good thing for the town by saving that Youth Centre. But what else can you expect from a bleeding heart? Oh, I'm sure he is smart enough. But look how he has decided to spend his life - teaching! I mean, what's the point? Real change happens through business and politics."

A smug smile spread across Steven's face, which rankled Bec. She felt the need to defend Ryan. She countered, "Actually, I went to the youth centre the other day to take some photos. I thought it was a great place. A bit cold, but it is winter."

Steven drained his wine then licked his upper lip. "You went there? I'm surprised you didn't get mugged. It's a hang out for teens and an excuse for parents who should be taking better care of their kids."

"What I saw was teenagers studying. Have you been there?"

"Me? No way. I've driven past it plenty of times and that's enough for me." Steven leaned forward conspiratorially. "Did you know that Ryan Anderson's father topped himself? Dodgy business dealings caught up with him."

A rush of thoughts hit Bec. Poor Ryan. To lose his father in such a horrible way. Then, how could Steven sit here and talk of working *for* Brooksdale while criticising a man who had given so much of himself to the community? She was sure this date had been a mistake.

Bec rubbed her stomach and bent over slightly. "Oh. My stomach! I think I need to go home. I'm not feeling well."

"Oh. Bad ciopinno, huh?" Steven quickly finished his meal, wiped the corners of his mouth with his napkin, and called for the bill. As they left, he put his arm around her back. She stiffened slightly, but she still needed to get home.

On the drive back to Brooksdale, Bec remained quiet. Steven had the dance music turned up and seemed absorbed in his own world. When Bec got out of the car, Steven said, "When can I see you again?"

Bec put her arm over stomach, "I don't know. I need to get to the bathroom. Message me later, okay?"

She rushed into the building and climbed the stairs. Once inside, she breathed a sigh of relief. "What a jerk."

It was ten o'clock. The lights were on and Jen's bedroom door was closed. Bec went to the kitchen and made herself a vodka and lemon. Jen's door opened and a sleepy-looking Jen stood in the doorway with hands on hips.

"Jen," said Bec. "You were right. It is far too soon for me to be dating. I'm officially on holiday from men - permanently!"

8

Bec reminded herself to breathe deeply. Everything would be fine. She was in a public place. She just had to assert herself. Saturday. The last Saturday in June and Bec had to confront Phil today. She sat with her back to the window in a quaint coffee shop off Main Street. It had deep-brown timbers and brass fittings which gave it a Victorian steam-punk feel. Bec wished she could relax and enjoy the atmosphere.

The past week had been a fuzz of tequila, wine, hangovers, and Jen's nagging. All that punctuated with some work on that beacon of light in the distance - a job interview at Paul's Photography. The job was for an assistant photographer - below Bec's experience level. But it was the first step in rebuilding her life. As Bec's body tired of the booze assault, her mind formed a post-Phil plan: photography was her thing, so make photography *her* thing. All she had to do was kick Phil from her life.

Beep. Beep. Bec was startled by her phone. There was a new message from Steven.

Saw you go into the Flat Rock Cafe. I'll buy you coffee.

"Oh shit," whispered Bec. Steven had messaged her a few times since their date on Thursday night and she had politely declined his offers for more. He obviously couldn't take the hint.

Bec looked out the window and was horrified to see Steven's Mercedes pull into the curve and parked in front of the Flat Rock Café. Bec watched anxiously as he got out of the car and walked into the shop. The bell tinkled as he opened the door.

He wore gym clothes and looked like he had just gotten out of the shower. He saw her and smiled. "Hey! How're you doin'? I'll get you a refill."

Bec said, "No, that's fine."

"Hey, they do a great cheese cake here." Steven sat down and Bradley the barista came to take Steven's order of a soy latte and two cheese cakes. "I'm really looking forward to this. I just finished a work out and it was great. Nothing like working out in your own gym. And mine is a hell-of-a-lot better than that other place run by Tony Carpenter - it is a real shambles. The town needs a pro-gym."

The cakes and coffee arrived and Bec said, "Look. I'm sorry, but..."

"You don't like cheese cake? C'mon, who doesn't like cheese cake?"

The bell tinkled and Bec stiffened. It was Phil. He looked around the café like predator, scanning the environment for his prey. He saw Bec and strode towards her. "What the hell is this?" Phil demanded.

Steven turned in his chair to face the new-comer and Phil scowled at him. Steven said, "Hey. Back off, man." Phil took off his coat and slung it over an empty chair.

Phil said "I need to talk with Becky, alone. I bet she didn't tell you she was already in a committed relationship." Steven looked open-mouthed from Phil to Bec. Phil continued, "She's just using you to make me jealous."

Steven stood abruptly, stumbling on the leg of the chair and Bec noticed his hands were shaking. A red flush showed in his cheeks. Steven glared at Bec and said, "I should have known!" He walked out, leaving Bec alone with Phil.

Bec's heart pounded with nerves. Phil knew how to own a situation and get his way. It's what made him financially successful, but there was hell to pay when he didn't get his way. Phil was handsome, too. Fit and a good dresser. He had mastered the rugged city look; square jaw with a day's worth of stubble, a slim-fit shirt that showed off his angular torso, and short cino's that revealed muscular calves. He sat down where Steven had been sitting moments before.

Bradley chirped, "Hello. What can I get you, sir?"

Phil waved the enthusiastic young barista off. His eyes settled on Bec. "What're you playing at Becky?"

Be assertive. Bec held Phil's gaze. "I left you. I'm not coming back. I want the rest of my things."

Phil's hand went to his hip. The other rested palm down on the table. "Cut the crap. You belong with me in Brisbane. I've got a plane ticket for you." He reached into his breast pocket, pulled out the ticket, and slapped it down on the table.

"No Phil. I'm not going. Did you bring my photography equipment?"

Phil's top lipped curled in derision. "Is that what this is about? You want to chase that photography dream you've been whining on and on about? Why the hell can't you just say that? Do you know how much shit I've had to put up with since you've been gone? Neighbours constantly asking, 'Where's Becky? I haven't seen her around.' And that nosey bitch Jacinta from next door. She's been spreading the word that you looked terrible, that you'd 'run-into-a-door'. Unbelievable." Phil shook his head and exhaled after this outburst.

Bec retaliated, "You hit me, Phil."

"You look okay to me. Besides, it was your fault."

Breathing deeply, Bec fought to control her anger and fear. She said, "My fault? That's the problem Phil, you never take responsibility..."

He thumped the table with his hand and the plates clinked from the vibration. "Here we go! Always going on with 'I need so and so. Why can't you do such and such.' You should be thankful I'm willing to take you back."

RYAN PULLED in to the curve outside of the Flat Rock Café. He was out of coffee beans and needed to pick some up on his way home from the gym.

The bell clanged as he walked inside and the aroma of coffee was a delight. A loud voice immediately caught his attention. He saw a man sitting with Bec and she seemed distressed. The man raised his voice, "I came all the way to this shit town to get you, and all you want to talk about is your crap photography shit!"

The man abruptly stood up and his chair crashed backwards. Bec stood, too. The man reached forward and grabbed Bec's chin, as if he were inspecting livestock at an auction.

. . .

Bᴇᴄ ᴊᴇʀᴋᴇᴅ her head back and pushed the man's hand away. She backed up against the glass window and felt fear pulse through her nerves. Tears welled in the corners of her eyes. *No. Not now. Don't cry.*

"Oh, for God's sake!" said Phil, and he ripped his hand way from her face then clutched her wrist. "You make me mad and look what happens!"

Phil's voice had become louder and louder. Now he slammed his hand against the window, right next to Bec's head, and pressed it there. She was trapped.

"Hey, calm down!" Bec's eyes focused beyond Phil and hope swelled inside her chest. It was Ryan. He had walked up behind Phil and put his hand on Phil's shoulder.

Phil's hand dropped to his side and the muscles in his jaw flexed. Bec had seen that look before and she flinched uncontrollably as Phil shoved her down into the chair. He slapped her. Hard.

Eᴠᴇʀʏᴏɴᴇ in the shop turned to look to see wear the sound of the slap had come from. It had taken Ryan by surprise. Who would have though that someone could slap a woman like that?

In the midst of Ryan's shock, Phil spun around and threw Ryan's hand off his shoulder. A fist came swinging through the air, aimed at Ryan's face. Ryan saw it coming and stepped back. The fist sailed harmlessly by, but Phil wasn't done. He shoved Ryan with both hands.

Ryan's Jiu-Jitsu training took over, and later, when he thought about it, he would be surprised at how easy it had been to deal with Phil's reckless aggression.

Using the momentum of Phil's push, Ryan threw Phil to

the ground. A table and chair got knocked over, but Ryan pinned Phil down, locking Phil's arm and shoulder and pushing his face into the floor.

Bec rushed forward, "Let him go! He was just angry at me." Later, Bec would wonder why she felt defensive of Phil, when Ryan had clearly been on the receiving end of physical violence. But there it was.

"Ryan. Let him go. You'll hurt him."

Looking up from his kneeling position on the floor, Ryan said, "I want his word that he's done throwing punches." He looked at Phil, "You hear me? Are we done?"

Phil gasped. He was out of breath because he was still struggling, ineffectively. "I'm gonna kill ya!" Yelled the struggling Phil.

Bradley called out, "Don't worry Mr. Anderson. I saw the whole thing. That man attacked that girl, and when you went to help, he turned on you. Want me to call the cops?"

At that, Phil stopped struggling, "Okay. Okay. I'm done. I'm done, damn it!"

Ryan said, "Call the police Bradley."

"No. No! Don't do that. He was just angry. It's been a tough break-up for both of us. Just let him go," said Bec in a shaky voice.

Ryan hesitated. He looked at Bec, saw the tears in her eye and the red mark where this prick had hit her. Why wouldn't she want her attacker arrested? Ryan looked to Bec for confirmation, but appeared genuinely concerned for Phil. Against his better judgement, Ryan released Phil.

Phil rose slowly, coughed, and brushed his clothes off. He glared at Bec, "You see what you've done? This is your fault and now we're really done. I'm finished with Rebecca Williams."

He stepped forwards, Bec moved away, startled, but Phil only picked up the plane ticket he threw down on the table earlier.

With that, Phil stalked out of the café with his head held high.

9

Bec sat in the passenger seat of Ryan's F-150 and her hands were still shaky. They stopped outside Jen's flat and the side of Bec's face tingled with heat from Phil's slap. She refused to touch it as if that would deny Phil the results of the pain. Bec still couldn't believe Phil hit her in public. And she still couldn't believe she had rushed to his defence when Ryan intervened.

The world appeared grey and cold to Bec. The lack of rain had left the median strip brown and cracked. Why did she notice this now? It's not like the grass shrivelled and died over night. The trees, too. She noticed them sway with cold winter wind as if they were grasping at the last drops of moisture carried by the air.

"You want some help to get out?"

Ryan's voice brought her back to the human world. She shook her head and reached for the door handle, but her hand didn't feel like she owned it.

"I'll walk you to the door," said Ryan.

"No. You've done enough." Bec's voice sounded flat and

empty. Too embarrassed about her behaviour, she didn't look at Ryan as she got out of the vehicle.

RYAN INTERPRETED Bec's distance as anger, or disappointment. He cursed himself for not getting involved sooner. He should have done something as soon as that asshole grabbed her, but the suddenness of it had taken Ryan by surprise, like when you see something for the first time and your brain needs a moment to catch up with your eyes. Ryan promised himself he would not fall short next time.

Bec got out of Ryan's old F-150, slammed the door, and went inside Jen's flat without looking back. Ryan waited for a few minutes to make sure she was inside and safe, then drove home annoyed with himself.

INSIDE THE APARTMENT, Jen brewed camomile tea while Bec sat on the sofa, tears streaming down her face. "I was stupid enough to think he'd just bring my things and let me go. I'm such an idiot!"

"He's the idiot, Rebecca. Not you. He's the abuser. You can't think you're anything less because of him."

Jen's words made sense, but thinking it and feeling it were two very different things. The tea brewed, Jen brought two steaming cups over to Bec and sat down next to her on the sofa. It was good to have a sister like Jen, who simply listened as Bec sobbed and talked in a swirling mess for what seemed like hours but was really only fifteen minutes.

Bec felt drained, as if her emotions were the last hints of moisture evaporating from barren soil. But with those emotions, so to her attachment to Phil seeped away, and somewhere deep inside, Bec knew that soon she would be ready to truly move on.

Nursing the cup of tea in both hands, Bec breathed deeply, "Everything happened so fast." She shook her head in chastisement of herself. "I'm a real idiot. I didn't even say 'thank you' to Ryan. I know it sounds weird, but my reaction was to worry about Phil! Can you believe it?"

Jen put an arm around Bec and let her talk.

"I even yelled at Ryan, even though it was Phil who threw the first punch. You know, I don't think Ryan even hit back. The two of them just seemed to fall. I should have said 'thank you' or something. Ryan must think I'm a real psycho." The tears started to flow again.

Jen rubbed Bec's shoulders. "I wouldn't worry about Ryan. He's a good guy. He'll understand that you were just in shock about the whole thing."

As the sun sank and the shadows grew longer in the living room, Bec gradually regained her composure. She could just make out the golden-red of the sun sliding behind the dusty horizon and she decided that as the sun went down, so to would her feelings for Phil. She would not allow herself to wallow in self-pity any longer.

10

It was Monday and the coldest time of year – mid-July. The electric heater in the classroom ticked furiously as it warmed up. Ryan was looking forward to this lesson: British Literature, an elective for Year II, which meant students were generally motivated to be there. Generally.

As he wrote up class notes on the whiteboard, his thoughts drifted to Bec. He hadn't seen her for a few weeks, since that day in the Flat Rock Café. Ryan wondered if she was avoiding him.

Of course, it wasn't entirely Bec's fault. Ryan had been busy on the weekends with the youth centre. The website was published, the petition was nearly done, and he would need to face the local council to present his case for funding. He was pondering over his main points and ideas, when students filed into the room.

Ryan Anderson really enjoyed teaching this particular group of students, and it was a great way to start a Monday. He loved pulling the words off the page and making the problems that the characters faced real to his students. These ones were interested, asked questions, and challenged each others' ideas – as long as the class-clowns didn't ruin things.

Sadly, not every student who chose the course saw the value in participating sensibly. Tyler Brooks and his two friends, Bayden and Foster, were not in the class to learn about Shakespeare or Chaucer.

Ryan taught at Brooksdale High School. It was a state school that enrolled students from Year Seven to Year Twelve. Ryan had worked there for six years and loved it. He was a Brooksdale boy, born and bred.

The stream of students slowed to a dribble, then stopped. Ryan closed the door and was secretly thankful that Tyler, Bayden, and Foster hadn't come in.

"Today we're looking at *Romeo & Juliet* Act 1 Scene 5, the party scene where the young lovers meet and have their first kiss." Ryan's voice rang clear, and the students's heads all faced him. He heard few whispers then some giggles floated forth. It seemed romance could still capture an audience. Ryan smiled. This was going to be fun. He continued, "We're going to decide if love at first sight exists or not. Raise your hand if you believe in love at first sight."

A little more than half the class raised their hands, boys and girls. Some grinned at each other and Ryan stored the information in his teacher-memory. In the world of hormone-charged teenagers, those love-struck smiles could turn to tears within a week. Ryan could find himself counseling some heart-broken Romeo and Juliet.

Ryan called on one of the students to explain their answer, "Sally, what makes you say you believe in love at first sight?"

"She's already found it!" A boy called out, but it was in good humour. The only result was a blushing Adam Lee, Sally's boyfriend.

Sally pursed her lips as she considered her answer. "I think sometimes you just know when you're in love. Especially teenagers. We don't have all the hang-ups and prejudices that our parents do, or our teachers."

That drew a laugh from the class and Ryan chuckled, too.

Another student, Keysha, chimed in, "Yeah, but Sally, you can't say that there is only one person in the whole world for you."

Arkell leaned forward in his chair and added, "Yeah. Like, as if that one person in the whole world would be in the same small town anyway."

Ryan allowed the conversation to continue, but was worried that Adam hadn't joined in. Perhaps the topic was too close to home. Ryan liked seeing his students think and express their ideas. After all, that was what literature was about. Serious conversations, though, lead to uncomfortable feelings.

The classroom door burst open and a loud voice said, "That's so stupid!" Laughter followed and in walked Tyler, Bayden, and Foster as if they owned the whole school. They walked straight passed Ryan and were about to take their seats, still having their conversation, when Ryan stopped them.

"Boys, that's not the right way to enter a classroom, especially when you're late." Ryan's voice was nonchalant, yet carried authority. "Go back outside and try again."

The class was stone-cold silent. Tyler and his buddies hovered at their desks for the briefest of moments before swaggering slowly back out the classroom.

The room seemed to breath a collective sigh of relief and the three juveniles re-entered quietly, went to their desks, and sat down. Confidence when in front of a class was paramount. Ryan's thoughts drifted to Bec. *Perhaps I just need to get out of my own way.*

He moved on with the lesson. "We'll take a look at an abridged version of the scene. The important thing is not to get hooked up on understanding every word, or even every line. As long as you get a sense of the overall idea, you'll be fine."

Ryan stood in front of his desk and read for the class. After a few lines, he stopped and explained what was going on while the students scribbled notes on their abridged scripts.

Keysha asked a question, "Wait, Romeo gets to the party and he's in love straight-a-way?"

Arkell replied, "Crazy! And didn't they pop some pills before going? You know, Mercutio and that Queen Mab thing? They partied hard in Shakespeare's day, huh?"

The class laughed and Tyler called out, "You'd know Arkell. I seen you down on the corner buyin' some baggies. Haha!"

The mood changed like a thunderclap. Arkell thumped his desk. He was a strong young man and the sound silenced the room. He swiveled in his chair and glared angrily at Tyler, "You wanna go, white boy?"

"Stop!" Ryan raised his voice.

Tyler had a grin on his face and sat with his legs splayed out wide, as if he were at home watching TV. Bayden and Foster sat with their chests puffed up trying to look tough.

Tough guys, huh? Galahs more like, thought Ryan.

It was a scene Ryan had seen many times since Tyler came to Brooksdale High. If it wasn't for Tyler's father, the teenager would have progressed through the disciplinary system and calmed down, or been moved to another school. But that wasn't likely to happen.

Maybe Janice will be a stronger Principal.

After getting everyone's attention, Ryan's voice returned to that of calm authority, "We're a class and we don't insult each other." He looked at Tyler. "And we don't threaten each other with violence." He looked at Arkell. "Now. We were just talking about how quickly Romeo fell for Juliet. In addition, Romeo was love-sick for Rosaline only a few hours earlier."

This brought disgusted looks from a lot of the girls and chuckles from the boys. Tyler started tapping his pen loudly on his table.

Ryan continued his narration of the scene and so did the tapping. "Tyler, please stop tapping your pen; it's distracting me and the rest of the class," said Ryan.

Tyler wore his best innocent face and replied, "Oh sorry Mr. Anderson. I was just wondering, since there's drugs and alcohol and sex in Shakespeare, are there homos, too?" Tyler grinned and leaned further back in his seat.

Ryan knew better than to take the bait. Instead, he said, "Love and desire are elements of the human experience regardless of gender preferences. Study literature and you can learn more."

Tyler rolled his eyes and sighed, "Whatever."

Ten minutes later, Ryan had finished his reading and it was time for the class to have a short discussion before writing their thoughts down.

Sally started, "I don't think this is love at first sight. Romeo is on a high from whatever Mercutio gave him AND he's crashing his enemy's party. Bad time to make life decisions."

There was some back and forth before Keysha asked, "How 'bout you, Mr. Anderson? Is love at first sight real?"

Ryan knew the standard answer. The one any teacher could rattle off, but that wasn't Ryan. He valued his relationships with students and believed that he had to show some vulnerability if the young adults in his care would ever trust him.

"Let's separate 'love at first sight' from 'true love'. I don't really believe in 'love at first sight' as such. Perhaps, 'attraction at first sight' is a better way to think of it."

Tyler scoffed and called out, "Me and me boys just go for the lovin' and we're real practiced now. Haha!" High-fives between Tyler, Bayden, and Foster followed.

Ryan couldn't help himself, "Well, what you three do in your free time is up to you. We don't judge in here."

That broke the class like hot water poured into a cold glass. A crack of laughter and claps ensued. Tyler and his two friends flushed red and sunk down in their seats.

Ryan's voice quickly restored order, "Now that leaves 'true love.'" Ryan felt a twinge of anxiety roll through his stomach, as if he were confessing a transgression. Most of these students knew that Ryan was divorced.

"I have to say," said Ryan. "I believe in 'true love.'"

There were some whoops and cheers from the students. Ryan leaned forward and put his hands on his desk, "But," his voice rang clear, "True love can trap you as well as free you. So be careful with your hearts."

The bell rang and school noises flooded the room and hallways as students moved on to the next class. Sally and Adam were the last leave. They seemed to hover a moment, then Sally nudged Adam.

Ryan said, "Is there something I can help with?"

Sally kept her eyes on Adam and Adam kept his eyes on

the floor. Adam said, "Thanks for the lesson Mr. Anderson." He dashed out with a flustered Sally right behind him.

11

The staff room at Brooksdale High thrummed with conversation on Tuesday lunchtime. Two reverse-cycle air-conditioning units pumped hot air into the room with a gentle gushing of air. A group of teachers stood hunched at the kitchenette that ran along one side of the room, while others sat with legs crossed at the tables in the centre of the room.

Ryan sat with Mark and a History Teacher, Donita, in a corner of the room. Each of them had a coffee in one hand and a sandwich in the other.

Donita said, "Adam Lee seemed withdrawn yesterday in class."

Ryan replied, "In English, too. It's unusual for him."

Mark joined the conversation, "He's probably just having girl problems. Not uncommon, you know." Mark grinned and winked at Donita playfully as he continued, "Speaking of which, there is a decided absence of girl trouble in your life at the moment, Ryan."

Ryan felt heat rise in his cheeks. "I'm happy with how things are going, actually."

"And how are they going? Musty old books and back-breaking renovations on your house." Mark leaned back in his chair and spread his arms in mock frustration as he spoke, "Then there is the wrestling. With other men. That's no way to find a girl." Mark was grinning broadly now.

Donita said, "Hey, that wrestling part doesn't sound too bad." She laughed and drained the last of her coffee. "Time to get back to work boys."

Donita stood up and patted Ryan on the shoulder, "And good luck with the girls, Ryan."

After she was gone, Mark said, "Donita's hot, man. And she's single. You should ask her out."

Ryan replied, "I don't know. Work relationships and all. It never works out well."

Mark's grin faded and he said, "How would you know? You haven't had any."

Ryan had no comeback for that. Despite his protestations of Mark's womanizing ways, Ryan did feel lonely. Mercifully, the conversation was interrupted by the Principal. Janet Heartford walked through the crowd of teachers to where Ryan was sitting.

Janet was in her late thirties and this was her first school as principal. When she took over, there had been some grumbling, but Ryan suspected it was because Janet was so young, which caused jealousies to flare. So far, Ryan had found her to be personable and competent. Janet wore a standard of uniform of grey suit with a white blouse. Professional.

Janet spoke, "Ryan, can I have a moment of your time?"

Mark interjected, "Sit here if you like, I was about to head off to class anyway." Mark slipped through the crowded staffroom and disappeared out the door, leaving Ryan to face Janet alone.

Janet sat next to Ryan and got straight to the point, "I had a call from Michael Brooks, Tyler's father. He claims that you allowed another student to threaten his son and that you humiliated Tyler in front of the whole class."

Ryan exhaled audibly. This had not been the first time Ryan had called Tyler out on poor behaviour and earned a complaint from the father. Ryan explained what had really happened in the class: Tyler's tardiness, rudeness, and Arkell's response to Tyler's insulting comments.

Janet nodded her understanding and said, "I didn't think Tyler was a complete victim here."

"Do you want to me call Michael Brooks and explain what happened?"

Janet replied, "No. I'll handle it. He was talking about starting an investigation into discrimination against Tyler."

Ryan's jaw clamped tight. Janet continued, "Don't worry. There are no grounds for such an investigation and you're not the only teacher who has to deal with Tyler Brooks and his father. But, it would be better to document any future incidents and let me handle correspondence with the family."

Finished with the conversation, Janet got up and mingled amongst the staff before the school bell signaled the end of lunch. In a matter of seconds, the staffroom emptied, leaving Ryan sitting alone.

He finished his coffee, cold now. *Be damned if I'll let myself be bullied by that Michael Brooks.* Anger and frustration swirled inside his head. Didn't these people realize education was the most important thing a child could receive? Didn't they realize teachers had to be academics, counselors, and police officers all at the same time?

Ryan left the staffroom and headed for the English Department Office, clenching and unclenching his fists all the way. The more he thought about the accusation against him, the angrier he got.

In the office, Ryan sat in front of his lap top. He opened his e-mail, clicked 'New message', and found Michael Brooks' e-mail address from the School Administration folder, and began to type.

After the first few sentences, Ryan stopped. A line he often told his students when they were fighting with a friend came to the front of his mind: Don't *send that message when you're angry.* Time to follow his own advice.

The office phone rang. *Saved by the bell.* It was Chris, the Deputy Principal.

"Ryan, I've got a photographer here about the school photos next Wednesday. The regular guy double booked a wedding on that day so he sent his new assistant over. We need someone to show her around and you don't have class. She's in the reception area."

Ryan hung up the phone cursing Chris. Giving photographers tours of the school was not in Ryan's contract. Still, Chris wasn't a bad guy and Ryan didn't mind helping the guy out – especially if it distracted him from Michael and Tyler Brooks.

12

W hen Bec's boss asked her to take care of the school photo shoot at Brooksdale High, she said 'yes'. Bec had been at Paul's Photography for a couple of weeks and he was trusting her with a major job.

At first she was thrilled to have the responsibility. Then the reality of what she had agreed to settled like mud after a flood. As she pulled into the Brooksdale High visitors' car park, a wave of nerves rippled through her stomach. She pulled a half-pint bottle of vodka from her backpack on the driver's seat.

She put the bottle back in her bag unopened.

You're going into a school for goodness sake!

The past two weeks had gone well for Bec. She had picked up a job at Paul's Photography. The pay wasn't great, but it meant she could help Jen with the bills, and having something to do meant she had to cut back on the alcohol.

She felt that she had turned a corner. A warm, gentle feeling of security and progress infused her days. She even returned to being a brunette.

Bec got out of the car and looked at the school. Its concrete buildings were typical of nineteen-eighties school architecture. It could have easily been a prison. No doubt there were students who felt so.

At reception, a woman in her sixties, with her hair tied in a bun and wearing glasses on the end of her nose with a beaded chain securing them around her neck, greeted her. "Yes, can I help you?"

Bec stepped forward hesitantly. "My name is Rebecca Williams. I'm the photographer."

The woman looked at Bec over her glasses. "You wouldn't be related to Jen Williams, would you?"

Country towns. "Yes, I'm her sister. Do you know her?"

The older woman's straight face broke into the slimmest of smiles. "There's not a teacher in this town I don't know. I might add that Jen Williams is one heck of a teacher, so you'd better be one heck of a photographer." The smile broadened and the woman reached across the desk to shake hands, "I'm Delores Mayfield."

Delores' grip was firm but friendly. She continued, "Sign the visitor's book while I call through. Mr. Anderson is supposed to show you around this afternoon. I'm sure he's got a tour all worked out for you." Delores grinned as she picked up the phone.

Bec's nerves intensified. *Anderson?* The name sounded familiar. *Ryan Anderson.* A little panic fluttered up Bec's throat. Bec hoped her voice didn't waver as she replied to Delores, "Oh, I don't want to be any trouble. A quick look at where the photos are taken will be fine. It should only take fifteen minutes or so."

Delores said, "Right. Fifteen minutes. I'll mention to Ryan that you're in a hurry."

Bec signed in. Her hand shook slightly. To cover her

anxiety, she looked around the school's entrance, at the trophy cabinets and past graduating class photos. There in the top left was a face she recognized: Ryan Anderson, Brooksdale High Football Team, 2005. He was younger, but that was him all right.

RYAN PICKED up the phone in the English Department office. "Ryan? The photographer is here," said Delores. Then added in a hushed voice, "And she's a looker."

Ryan ran his hand over his close-cropped hair. Delores was the heart of the school: the unofficial counsellor. Many a student and a teacher had accepted tissues and a cup of tea from Delores Mayfield in a time of emotional crisis.

"Thanks Delores. I'll be right down."

A few minutes later, Ryan walked into the reception area. Delores called out, "That's Rebecca Williams over there. She's Jen's sister."

Ryan was momentarily taken aback.She looked different. Her hair wasn't blonde. She was wearing a grey double-button blazer and trousers that accentuated the curves of her hips. Delores was right, Bec was a looker.

"Hi Rebecca."

Bec spun around, "Ryan! It's great to see you again. Thank you so much for showing me around."

Ryan lead the way through to the gym, which doubled as an auditorium. Bec said, partly to relieve her nerves, "Only a one-man escort for me?"

"We're not as flash, or as dangerous, as your big-city schools."

Bec expected to see graffiti, broken windows, teenagers chewing gum in the hallways, and young lovers tonguing in the corners. Instead, the hallways were clean, no one loitered, there wasn't even the smell of cigarette smoke.

As they walked through the double doors to the gym, Bec stole a moment to look Ryan up and down. *He definitely works out.*

The doors banged closed and Ryan said, "Well. This is where photos are usually taken. Last year, Paul set up some scaffolding against the stage, then curtained off a corner for the portrait photos. The photography students help out with set up."

Bec shivered. It was cold in the gym. Ryan said, "Here. I'll take your stuff." He reached out clumsily to take Bec's camera gear and they brushed hands. It was a gentle touch, warming.

Handing her gear off to him, she said jokingly, "Do you always take your dates to a cold gym?"

Ryan held on to the camera bags as Bec slipped on her coat. He replied, "If I'd have known it was a date, I'd have made sure the heater was on!"

Bec pulled out her light metre and walked around. She called out, "Can I get the lights turned on?"

"Sure, but they take about ten minutes to warm up. Why don't I take you for a little tour while we wait?"

"Is this where I get to see the students doing time in 'study hall?'"

Ryan pointed playfully at her, "That's where you'll be going if you're not more respectful to teachers."

Bec laughed and she forgot all her anxieties as she followed Ryan out of the gym.

"This is the IT Lab," said Ryan as they walked past a modern looking room with wide glass windows. Jen could see videos playing on some computer screens. On others was software she didn't recognize.

Bec said, "Nice for some to watch videos at school."

Ryan looked at her and grinned, "Things have probably changed since you were in school. Those guys will be watching an instructional video then trying to make something of their own."

Bec's hands went to her hips, "Are you calling me old?"

"No. You don't look a day over forty!"

Now Bec folded her arms. "That's because I'm not even over thirty."

They walked on down the corridor and outside into the sun.

Bec considered what to say next. Ryan seemed to have forgotten about the Flat Rock Café, but surely he hadn't. There was also the fact that she had been distant and hadn't properly thanked him for his help.

She stopped walking and said, "Listen. I'm sorry you had to get involved with my personal affairs back at that café."

Turning around, Ryan faced her and he seemed a little surprised that she'd brought it up. He said, "Glad I could help. That guy seemed like a real jerk. Not to mention violent. Better off without those people."

"I know, but – "

"Hey. It's been more than ten minutes. I'd better get you back into the gym so you can do your thing. Delores said you were in a bit of a rush," said Ryan as he consulted his watch.

Feeling relieved that the incident was behind them but unwilling to end her time with Ryan, Bec replied, "We don't have to hurry. I'd like to scout some places for class photos. I don't know if you've done them here, but at my school we'd take a class photo in some interesting place, you know, like the weights room, or something."

"Weights room it is!"

For the next thirty minutes, Ryan walked Bec around the school. She saw the weights room, art room, science labs, and manual arts shop. A bell signalled the end of one class and the beginning of another. Students streamed out into the hallways, and just as suddenly, disappeared into classrooms as if a clowder of cats had been scared out of hiding, then skittered away into new hidey-holes.

She noticed that students seemed to respect Ryan. They weren't shy to say hello and when he told a group of boys who were getting a bit rowdy to settle down and go to class, they did.

"Well, it's the last class of the day, so I'd better get you back to the gym," said Ryan.

"And this not-a-day-over-forty-year-old was just starting to feel young again."

After finishing at the gym, Ryan lead Bec back to reception and, with a wave, left her to sign out of the visitor's book.

Delores looked over her glasses at Bec and said, "Well that was a bit longer than fifteen-minutes."

Bec did her best not to look up from the book as she answered, "Yeah, Ryan gave me the grand tour." When she looked up, Delores was watching her with a knowing smile.

Delores said, "Well, I guess we'll see you here next Tuesday."

13

Ryan wanted to finish grading his British Literature class's essays before the weekend. He rushed through them and when he write that last grade in red pen, the office clock read four-fifty-five.

Ryan's grading from white to blue belt started at five-thirty. Ryan was excited, yet worried. Some of his students also took classes at Tony's gym. What if he failed the test? The whole school would know!

As it was Friday, he could have two celebratory drinks if he passed. He never had more than two drinks these days. Not since recovering from Tammy leaving him. He rushed out of the office and down the corridors in a walk-run-shuffle, into the staff parking lot, and jumped into his faithful F-150.

As he eased his beloved and well-used Ford through the carpark towards the road, he spotted Jen making her way to her car. He made a detour and called out, "Hey Jen!"

Jen had her head down and was digging in her bag for her keys. She looked up and smiled when she saw who it was. Ryan said, "Coming out for a drink tonight?"

"I don't know. I've got a stack of papers to grade. I might if Bec is up for it."

Ryan glanced at the clock on the car's dashboard, five o'clock. "Well, I hope to see you both out. Can't stop and chat now. I've got my grading for Blue Belt at five-thirty. "

"Five-thirty? Ryan, it's five-fifteen now. You'd better hurry."

Damned clock! He'd have to fix the clock – that a hundred other things in his truck. Ryan waved to Jen and sped out of the car park, his focus shifting to the grading he was about to miss.

Brooksdale High sat atop Chuckwood Hill, which the locals often called 'Chalky's Hill'. Every morning, students trudged up the hill towards the school while bus kids waved and jeered from the windows of the busses that came in from the surrounding villages and farms. The gym was in the South-East corner of town and it usually took ten minutes to get there from school, but Ryan had to get his gi on and he wanted to warm up. No chance of that now. If he didn't get stuck at the lights, he'd be barely on time.

Ryan flew down Chalky's Hill on Black Rock Road, which didn't level out until it hit the bridge across the river. The truck bounced as it transitioned from hill to flat.

C'mon. Gi'me green!

There were only a handful of traffic signals in Brooksdale, and one of them was on the intersection of Black Rock Road and Main.

The light was green, Ryan spoke out loud, "Green baby. Stay green."

Closer now. The light changed to yellow, Ryan braked to take the corner and his brakes squealed embarrassingly. At least it served as a warning for anyone crossing the road.

The F-150 rocked as Ryan steered it around the corner,

making a tight right-hand turn as the traffic signal turned red.

"Yeah!" Ryan thumped the steering wheel in triumph. Five minutes later he pulled into the gym's parking. His truck's clock still read 5:00.

"Damn, Ryan, you cut things fine today!" said Jerry as Ryan stepped onto the mat.

"Sorry. Had some extra work to do at school – last minute."

Tony, the chief instructor and owner of the gym walked over. He was built like a front-row rugby player but moved like a dancer. "We get that people have lives," he said. "Paul is going up against Maria when she is done with her aerobics class. You and Jeff are going first and you'll help out for the grappling section."

There were four tests today, Ryan, Jeff, Paul, and Maria, who was grading after she had finished teaching an aerobics class. Maria was Tony's wife and business partner. Tony always said if it wasn't for Maria, the place would have been bought up by Michael Brooks – and that would have been a disaster.

All of the people grading today were going for blue-belts. On the benches around the training area sat a few spectators. Both Paul and Jeff's girlfriends were there.

As Ryan nodded to greet them, a pang of loneliness hit him. No girlfriend, no wife, no mother. Well, he did have a mother, but...

Alongside the mats, sat some other students who had come to watch the grading. Class normally started at six, but these keen white-belts wanted to see what they were in for. Ryan took his place on the far right-hand edge of the line of students and the test began.

. . .

Bec had dinner under way as Jen walked through the door into the apartment. "You want a drink?" asked Bec, keeping her eyes on the teriyaki chicken sizzling in the frying pan. "There's a bottle open and a glass for you on the counter."

Jen threw her keys into the fruit bowl on the table, as she hung up her coat by the door. Picking up the bottle of wine on the table, Jen poured herself a glass. "This is half-empty."

"Half full, sister. And don't start on me. I've been good these past weeks."

Taking a sip of her wine, Jen said, "I haven't seen you drink vodka for a while, so I guess that's an improvement." Jen really knew how to throw a back-handed compliment.

Bec splashed some wine into the pan, and stirred. The sizzle and warm scents of cooking filled the apartment.

Jen said, "Saw Ryan this afternoon. He invited us out for drinks."

At the mention of Ryan's name, Bec felt a little heat come to her cheeks.

Ryan struggled to keep a close guard under Jeff's mount. This was the grappling section of Jeff's blue belt test. It was Ryan's job to pose as an opponent for another person's test, then someone else would be Ryan's opponent in his own grading test.

Ryan struggled to retain some freedom of movement under Jeff's aggression. Ryan could feel the friction of his gi against the surface of the blue mats and sweat dribbled into his eyes. At Tony's MMA Gym, a prospective blue belt had to grapple for two rounds of five-minutes each. Round two was nearly over.

Ryan had dominated the first round, but Jeff was rolling hard in the second. Ryan thought he felt his opponent lose balance. He thrust upwards with his hips and Jeff slid forward, but instead of falling, Jeff spun around, caught Ryan's arm and fell backwards, getting a textbook arm lock. Ryan tapped, but not before he felt a twinge in his shoulder.

As Ryan walked off the mat, he rolled his shoulder to see if there was any serious pain. He went to the freezer and pulled out an ice-pack, then waited for his grading.

"So, HE WAS MARRIED." Bec asked as she served up dinner. Bec wanted to know about Ryan Anderson from Brooksdale.

"Yeah, to a local girl. Ryan's a local boy, too. Been here all his life, except to go to college in Armidale."

The sisters sat down to eat. Bec raised her glass, and toasted, "A toast. To single life!"

Jen smiled broadly and clinked glasses with Bec, "To single life!"

They drank and giggled. Bec hadn't felt this good since she didn't know when. The job, her sister, finally getting Phil out of her system, being interested in men again. All of it moved in the right direction. She savoured the warmth of the used furniture in the apartment. The smells of life, delicious and in contrast to her old life in Brisbane, couldn't have been more pronounced.

"I'll message Ryan. Tell him we'll meet him out," said Jen.

Bec crossed her legs and looked her sister in the eyes, "You haven't dated anyone since I've been here."

Jen poked her chicken with her fork. "I've been busy. You know, looking after my sister!"

"Ouch. That's low!" Bec leaned forward, put her elbow on the table and rested her chin on her hand. "Seriously, though, you haven't had any male friends over. How about Mark?"

Jen raised her eye brows, "Mark! He's the biggest playboy in Brooksdale. I wouldn't..."

"That's my point. You need to get back on the horse so to speak." A cheeky grin settled Bec's lips as she saw Jen's cheeks redden.

"I think I'll message Ryan. Ask him where he's going out to tonight," replied Jen, clearly dodging the subject.

SWEAT ROLLED down Ryan's forehead. His gi was wet with sweat and he was nearing the end of his own blue-belt grading test. He felt the grading had gone well so far. Until now, that is. Ryan always struggled with defence against bear hugs.

Jeff now played Ryan's attacker, and he was going at it hammer and tongs. A couple of times Ryan failed to break out of the hug and was left flailing like a lamb in a petting zoo desperately trying to escape the excited grip of a nine-year-old kid.

Tony said, "Let's see your rear bear hug escape again."

Jeff moved behind Ryan and whispered, "Drop your weight early."

Noted. As soon as he felt Jeff rush towards him, Ryan dropped his weight, grabbed Jeff's legs and threw him to the mat, finishing off with an arm lock. Jeff tapped and Tony nodded. Time for grappling.

Ryan knelt opposite Jeff. He leaned forward and slapped Jeff's hands the way boxers bump gloves before the fight starts. They stood up and started vying for a dominant grasp on each other's gi.

Ryan was particularly good at takedowns. He shot for

one now, caught Jeff, and brought him down with a thud that knocked the wind out his opponent.

Ryan took advantage of the situation and went for a choke, but Jeff was no slouch. Ryan felt alive as he and Jeff rolled on the mats, straining and fighting for dominance, struggling for a grip on sweaty bodies, thinking about the next move. He knew Jiu-Jitsu was more about technique than strength, but there was something primal in the fight.

Jeff, a barrel-chested, fourth-generation farmer, was by far physically stronger than Ryan. But Ryan's technique was better, having had some extra coaching from Jerry. Tony called five minutes, and Ryan felt the strength go out of his shoulder like air escaping a balloon. *Damn. Just one more round to go.*

The second round started and Ryan's shoulder throbbed. Ryan succeeded in another quick take-down, but Jeff was too strong, and Ryan's shoulder burned with pain. Ryan tried desperately to pass Jeff's guard and get a choke on that tree stump sized neck. To do so would mean a quick end to the round and good chance at passing the test.

Ryan's gi fell open and draped the two wrestlers; Ryan on top, Jeff underneath. Ryan felt himself lifted and flung head-first over Jeff's head.

Breaking the fall with a roll, Ryan sprung back to his feet. His sweating chest heaving as he sucked in oxygen. He grinned at Jeff, who nodded then charged at Ryan.

No doubt the two white-belts thought they were two glorious warriors in the throws of a magnificent struggle. In reality, they looked more like two tumble weeds blown together, bumping into anything and everything in their path.

Jeff slipped around Ryan and grabbed him in a rear bear hug, no doubt trying to work Ryan's weakness. He was slow, so Ryan had time to drop his body weight and grab Jeff's foot and pull.

They crashed to the mats. Ryan spun and Jeff's heel was exposed. Ryan went for the heel hook and got it. He tapped Jeff out with six seconds left on the clock.

The two men, breathing heavily from the exertion, with their gi open, man-hugged and slapped each other on the back.

Tony said, "Well that was as good as KI boys!"

"ANOTHER BOTTLE?" asked Bec as she drained the last mouthful from her glass. Jen stood up and wobbled slightly. She put both hands on the table to steady herself.

"No, if we're going out, we should lay off a little. How about coffee?"

"Sure, I'll make it." Bec walked into the kitchen and switched on the coffee maker. Jen went into the bathroom. Bec waited until she heard the lock click shut, then rushed over to her backpack with a coffee cup in hand. She pulled out the bottle of vodka, and added a shot of the clear alcohol to her cup, then went back into the kitchen. A little extra buzz wouldn't hurt tonight.

By the time Jen came out, Bec had two steaming hot coffees sitting on the table.

"Mmm, that smells good," said Jen dreamily.

RYAN WAITED ANXIOUSLY on the benches at the side of the training area holding a pack of ice to his injured shoulder. Paul sat next to him with a pack on his knee and Jeff sat on the other side. Paul had just finished his grading with Maria.

They had to wait until the end of training to get the results of their test. It was Friday, and training finished at seven.

Paul, also injured, grinned and said to Ryan, "Together we'd make one whole man."

"Yeah." Ryan looked at Paul's knee. "Maria do that?"

"Yeah."

Ryan and Paul chuckled and slapped each other on the back.

Tony called an end to class and all the students sat in a line along the edge of the mats. It was time to celebrate, or wallow in self-pity.

Tony began, "Tonight, we've got some promotions. Maria, congratulations."

Applause from the students and spectators. Tony continued and the same happened for Paul, then Jeff. Ryan waited anxiously. He had read the message from Jen earlier about meeting up for a celebratory drink, but he didn't know if he'd be celebrating or not.

Finally Tony said, "And last, but not least, Ryan."

A small cheer went up since some of the white-belts were also Ryan's students at school. Ryan couldn't keep the smile from his face.

14

S ully's Sports Bar, the other pub in town, was a ten-minute walk from Brooksdale Gym. On a Friday night, the place was packed with workers from the farms, meat works, and other supporting businesses that form the economic engine of a rural town.

Sully's was one of the newer buildings. It had a dedicated dining area that was separate from the bar with cheap carpets that handled spilled drinks and other liquids associate with a night out. There was an open space for live bands and dancing at one end and poker machines that blinked enticingly to patrons at the other.

Ryan was physically tired, but felt relaxed and had a pleasant sense of achievement. He was happy to be out and spending the evening with his friends from the gym. Paul's girlfriend, Missy, came along with her friend, Angela, which rounded out the party nicely.

"Shame Tony and Maria couldn't make it," said Missy, as the group slid into their bench table in the dining area.

From where they were seated, they had easy access to the bar. This was important on a Friday night, as the wait staff would be busy, and if drinks were needed in a hurry, the best option was to go up to the bar yourself.

Jerry said, "There was a time when Tony would have been the first one with a beer in his hand. I tell you what, though, that gym has really turned around since Maria arrived on the scene."

Beers arrived, then steaks. The hum, broil, and sizzle of cooking meat blended nicely with the footy playing on the TV screens around the dining room.

"Git that protein into ya, Ryan," said Jeff with a big country grin. The meat was juicy, and after a hard day at school followed by the grading, was just what Ryan needed.

"How's the youth centre kids doing for the Billy Cart Bash?" Jeff asked Ryan.

"Not bad. We've got three carts this year. Still need a couple of wheels. If you've got any old bicycles to donate, we'll take them off your hands."

"You think you'll beat Fletcher Hardware?"

"We'll give it a good shot. But those guys have got the resources and the knowhow."

Angela moved a little closer to Ryan. "I think it's wonderful what you do at the Youth Centre. And building those carts gives the kids such a good experience."

Smiling at the compliment, Ryan suddenly felt self-conscious. Was Angela making a move on him? Nervous excitement ran up and down his nervous system in anticipation of more attention from the good-looking Angela.

Angela continued, "Missy tells me you're a bit of a handyman around the house." She leaned forward to catch Ryan's answer. Paul had warned him earlier that Angela had recently become single and was looking to start dating again. Ryan knew her ex – Bryce Tremblay. A mountain of a man.

Ryan's imagination plotted through the events of small-town drama. Angela gets with Ryan, Angel's ex beats up Ryan. Angela goes back to ex. Great outcome.

Jerry chimed in, "Ryan here is not just a hand-ee-man. He is a craftsman. He has done wonders with that old place on Granville Street."

Ryan lifted his glass to his mouth, sipped, and said, "Gives me something to do in my spare time. Tomorrow, I'm starting the bathroom."

Jerry didn't let off. "Well, that is one good thing about bachelorhood – free time!" He raised his glass and the men at the table joined in, toasting, "Bachelors!".

After the toast-in-jest, Angela pursued her line of questioning, "What are you going to do once you've finished doing your place up?"

Ryan became thoughtful and rubbed his chin. "I think I'll sell and try to buy Mum's old place."

Angela smiled and leaned back, as if satisfied with Ryan's answer. The waitress came and took away the empty plates. Ryan saw Jen and Bec walk into the dining area. He stood and waved to them. Bec saw him first, smiled, and returned the wave. *Her smile was beautiful,* thought Ryan. It felt fresh and warm.

Jen slid in next to Jerry, and Bec next Ryan. Introductions and congratulations were made. Bec ordered a *Screwdriver* and Jen shot her a glare. "Fine, I'll just have a house white," said Bec.

Ryan re-told the drama of the blue-belt grading. Bec watched him as he spoke and he was occasionally interrupted by Paul or Jeff.

. . .

BEC HAD a nice buzz going and she enjoyed being out. She looked Ryan over. His hair was ruffled and the top two buttons of his blue, collared shirt were undone, revealing a muscled chest. Bec liked this version of Ryan. Actually, she liked the teacher version, as well.

The drinks arrived and Bec sipped her wine. She bumped Ryan's shoulder and he flinched. She asked, "Injury?"

"Yeah, nothing too serious, though."

Bec touched his shoulder and she could feel the muscle under his shirt. She said, "I don't know what you men see in fighting. Rolling around with another guy. Waste of time if you ask me." Bec smiled.

Ryan played along, "There's all types of fun to be had rolling around." He picked up his beer and sucked down a big gulp. Bec matched him and soon her glass was empty. *Finally. I'm relaxing around men again.*

"You ready for another?" asked Ryan.

"Make it a *screwdriver,*" she whispered. Ryan took orders from everyone else and went to the bar.

With Ryan at the bar, Bec looked about her and took in the casual ambience of the establishment. She hadn't been in this type of place for at least a year. Despite herself, she felt relaxed. There were no pretentions here. Loud rumbles of male laughter came from the bar and a Lee Kernaghan song came on.

Bec's eyes glanced over Ryan's body as he leaned on the bar waiting to get the drinks. He was fit. Bec felt a movement by her side. Angela had slid closer to Bec and brushed against her shoulder. Angela said, "New to Brooksdale are you?"

Bec could smell the cheap perfume on Angela. "I've been here a little while now."

Angela drew back a strand of hair over her ear and said, "You're new."

Bec's hackles went up. She smiled and asked, "What about you? A local born and bred?" She wanted to say 'in-bred' but that would have been rude.

"Yes, and I know what's what around town. Ryan, for example. He's just gone through a divorce." Bec was surprised that Angela would share something so personal so soon. It made her weary.

Ryan came back with a broad smile on his face and drinks clamped together in his hands. The talk turned to football, then cricket, then the cold winter. The drinks and the talk swam together. Someone else put a drink by Bec and she sipped on that, too.

When both her drinks were finished, Bec got up to go to the bar. Out of the corner of her eye, she noticed Angela move closer to Ryan and start a conversation with him. *Popular guy,* thought Bec. She felt glad there would be more opportunities to meet him at the Youth Centre when she went back to photograph the billy carts.

She should have been looking where she was going. As she approached the bar, Bec tripped on a chair leg and fell into a thirty-something man with two-day's stubble and red-flannel shirt. She spilled his drink, whisky, and it soaked into the Bunderberg Rum bar mat.

"You all right there Miss?" the man asked. He had a strong rural accent.

Bec righted herself. "Oh, I'm so sorry. Let me get you another."

"In this part-a-the-country, the man buys the lady a drink. I'm Bryce, by the way."

He extended a hand. Bec looked into a broad, square-jawed face. Her hand disappeared completely in his and she suddenly felt a desire to flee from this over-sized human. This man didn't smile. His voice was commanding, he was freakishly big, and he looked brutally strong. She had to get out of the situation without causing a physical altercation. Womanly charm was her only defence.

"I'm Bec. If you're buying, I'll have a *screwdriver.*"

Air burst out of Brice's lips like a truck's air brakes. "Tell me the name of a real drink."

Composing herself, Bec said, "Vodka."

"Vodka shots it is!"

Too late. Bryce ordered two vodka shots for Bec and two for himself. While they were being made, Bec looked back over at her table of friends. Ryan was engaged in a conversation with Angela, Jen was flirting with Jeff, and Jerry was laughing with Paul. No one had noticed her predicament.

Bryce asked, "Not from around here, are ya?"

"No. I spent the last year in Brisbane."

"Thought I could hear a bit of the city on you." He looked at Bec out of the corner of his eye.

The shots arrived. "Ready Bec from Brisbane with a city accent?"

Bryce faced her and she saw that his nose was crooked and had a scar over his left cheek bone. A half grin twisted his lips.

Bec said, "After these, I'm going back to my table. My friends are over there." She pointed out her table, but Bryce had downed the first shot.

She shot her first drink and felt the alcohol plummet into her stomach. Suddenly she wished she hadn't drank so much at Jen's flat. *When will I learn?*

Bryce asked, "They your friends?" He gestured with a nod of his massive head. "I know Jerry. Copper. Good man. Fair. And that other guy, Ryan Anderson. Went to school with him. Good guy. That girl he's talkin' to, Angela. She certainly has her hooks in."

Bec barely had time to look before Bryce did his second shot, but Bryce was right: Angela and Ryan had certainly hit it off.

A twist of frustrated disappointment burst into Bec's mind and she downed her second shot. Bang! Bec thumped her second shot glass down on the bar and said, "Fancy another?"

That twisted grin split Brice's face again. "All right Miss, but it's your round."

"BEC JUST WENT to get one drink, didn't she?" Jen asked. She looked around, suddenly worried. The others looked too.

Angela spotted Bec first, "She's over there. Oh God, it's Bryce." Angela shielded her face with her hand and Ryan hoped Bryce didn't think he was hitting on Angela.

When Ryan saw Bec at the bar with Bryce, he stared and felt his heart sink. Bec and he had been getting along so well. How could things have changed so quickly? Bec was all over Bryce.

Ryan struggled to comprehend. He certainly found her attractive and interesting to talk to. The flirty comments and the gentle body contact were fun, too. What happened?

Jerry called across the table, "Ryan. You've been nursing that beer for a while now. You ready for another?"

Ryan looked at the glass in his hand. "This is my two-beer limit. I think I'll finish this and head home. Get an early start on the bathroom."

He lifted the glass and drained the last of the beer, leaving traces of white froth in the glass. As Ryan left the dining area, he looked back over his shoulder and saw Bec give Bryce a drunken hug.

THE VODKA SHOTS went straight to Bec's head. She slipped off her stool and fell into Bryce. He caught her with little effort and sat her back on her perch.

"I think I'll get a wine and go back to my table." Her words slurred and she had trouble holding eye-contact with Bryce.

The big man said, "I think you're done-in, Miss. I'll walk you back to you're friends."

He didn't need to. Jen arrived with a look that shot daggers at her sister.

"I think my sister and I are ready to go home."

Bec raised her voice, "I'm fine!" She tried to stand up, but fell. Bryce steadied her.

Jerry came over. "Evening Bryce."

"Evening." Bryce nodded politely and added, "Didn't mean no harm, Jerry. Just having a few drinks."

Jen said, "It's not your fault, Bryce. She was drinking at home before she came out."

Jerry and Bryce supported Bec between them and walked her out of Sully's and into a taxi.

None of them noticed as a black Hyundai Sonata rolled down its driver's side window and snapped some photos of the embarrassing scene.

15

Saturday morning. Bec awoke to the sound of the front door slamming shut. Sprawled on the sofa, the sun shone on her face, and she was still dressed in her clothes from last night. Her mouth felt as dry as a flat rock sitting in the sun next to a pool of water. Bec wanted that water more than anything right now.

She tried to move, felt sick, and closed her eyes again. Her head ached mercilessly. The sweet and sour hint of vomit caught in the back of her throat. She forced herself onto her feet and lurched across the living room to the nearest receptacle – the kitchen sink. She dry-heaved.

Bec turned on the tap and shoved her mouth under the cold stream of water. She didn't drink. She just let the water run in and out. Her hair fell into the stream of water, too. She didn't care.

After splashing water on her face, she felt a little better. The living room was a mess. Stale vomit stained the carpet next to the sofa. It looked like a mud puddle that had dried quickly after morning rain in summer.

"Jen. Jen!" Bec croaked for her sister. Jen would know

what had happened last night. Bec tried to recall the events of the previous night. She remembered having a good time with Ryan. She was pretty sure he had returned her flirting. Then Bec remembered that snooty local girl, Angie, or Anna. Something like that.

"What happened next?" she asked herself, as if hearing a voice would trip the memory switch. "I went to the bar. Big guy grabbed me." The residue of fear she initially felt when she first saw Bryce bounced back and she frantically tried to piece together the next event.

"Shots!" she said a little too loudly. "That big guy must have got me drunk." She put her hand to her head to ease the headache, but her head felt crusty.

Bec rush-stumbled to the bathroom and looked in the mirror. Dried blood was caked on the left side of her face. When she saw it, she shuffled backwards, slipped on the rug, and fell.

Flailing for a handhold to steady herself, Bec's fingers caught the towel rail, but it was no match for her downwards momentum, so it ripped out of the wall. Bec fell heavily on the tiled floor. She bounced on her backside. It hurt the same as being punched.

The worse-case scenario entered Bec's mind. She added two and two and got six. Jen wasn't here. That meant they didn't come home together. Bec had a cut on her head. That meant someone struck her. A wild-looking man got her drunk. That all meant...

Her heart pounded, she could hear her pulse in her ears, and her head felt all the worse for it. Her hands shook. "Get a grip Rebecca Williams," she said.

Steeling herself, Bec pressed her hand to her lower abdomen and groin, feeling for bruising. She checked her clothing for any rips, tears, or stains. Nothing.

Momentary relief flooded through her, but the fear and shock of losing so much memory of the night overcame her. Bec curled into a ball on the bathroom floor. She pulled a bath towel close to her and sobbed gently.

"Bec! My goodness. What happened?" Jen stood in the doorway of the bathroom holding a bag of groceries. Bec looked up at her from the floor through half-open eyes. She had fallen asleep.

Jen put the bag down by the door and rushed to Bec's aid, helping her to sit up. "Oh, you stink!"

"Yeah. Thanks. Where were you?"

"Where was I? I was out getting food to cook for my drunkard sister." Jen let Bec's hand drop and raised her voice, "And what the hell happened in here? Vomit in the living room, the kitchen tap running like river, and my bathroom trashed!"

Bec put her hands on the vanity for support and turned her head to look at her sister. She felt her chest constrict and said, "You left me! I didn't know if something had happened to you, or me. I didn't know how I got home. I didn't know if someone had – "

"Had what? Attacked me? Attacked you? I was the one who had to pull you from the taxi and rag you into the apartment. Clean your mess. You were wasted." Jen shook her head, turned and walked out of the bathroom.

Somehow the truth had a way of hurting. Bec called after Jen, "What about that big guy, huh? He forced himself on me!"

Jen spun on her heels. "Bryce? He and Jerry – you do remember Jerry, don't you? Well Bryce and Jerry carried you out of Sully's and got a taxi for you. For us. Bryce even gave the driver ten bucks for our fare because he felt bad."

Bec raised her eye-brows. "Jerry? Not Ryan?"

"You really don't remember? Ryan left about the same time you started doing shots with Bryce." Jen picked up the groceries and went through to the kitchen.

Bec called out after her, "Then what happened to my head? There was blood all over me this morning."

Jen was packing food into the refrigerator and her voice sounded distant as she replied, "There *was not* blood all over you. I cleaned you up a bit when I got you inside." She slammed the refrigerator door shut. "You fell over on the stairs and hit your head. It was your own silly fault."

Bec looked at herself in the mirror. Her eyes were blood-shot, her hair a tangled mess, and Jen was right, of course. There wasn't blood all over her, just a dried line of blood over the cut, which was only about a half-inch long located just below her hair-line. It was backed by an angry red mark that would soon turn blue and purple. *It wouldn't be the first time I've had to cover a bruise.*

Bec peaked out of the bathroom. Jen fussed in the kitchen, so Bec ran the shower. The hot water worked its magic and washed away the hang-over fog and the feelings of uncertainty.

Wrapped in a bathrobe and towel, Bec came out into the living room and was greeted with the delightful sounds and smells of sizzling food. Well, delightful if she didn't have a hangover. "Jen, I'm not sure I can handle grease," said Bec in a weak voice.

Her sister didn't look up from the pan. "Your fault. Not mine."

"Any coffee?"

"You know how to make it."

What to do? The living room was still a mess, so Bec started cleaning up. She bent over and picked up a blanket on the floor and her head swam. *It is my mess.*

She kept going. First the floor and the dried vomit. As she cleaned, Bec began to feel better. She came across her back pack and thought of the bottle of vodka tucked safely away there – in case of emergency. *Maybe later tonight, when the hang-over has passed.*

Bec caught herself. What was she thinking? Was she really *that* dependent on alcohol? Did that make her an alcoholic? Bec made a promise to herself – *No vodka tonight.*

Jen called out from the kitchen, "Brunch is ready!"

16

Saturday afternoon found Ryan slamming shut the door of his Ford and driving to Fletcher's Hardware. He had spent the day working in fits and starts. Getting some tiling done, then making a coffee. Moving some tools or timber around, then icing his injured shoulder. He had found it hard to concentrate on the work at hand – installing a new bathtub and vanity.

In this absent-minded state, he tried to move a length of timber, jerked at the pain in his shoulder, and put a piece of wood though the mirror he planned to install with the vanity. The last thing he needed was seven year's bad luck.

Saturdays were for dinner with his mother at her small apartment. As long as he didn't mess around too much, he could buy a mirror from Fletcher's, get the mirror home, pick up some flowers, and be at his mother's before six.

As he drove, Ryan could see heavy, pregnant clouds building on the horizon and he could smell the rain on the wind. It smelled like water sprinkled on dust.

Ryan checked the time in his truck, but the hands of the clock just twitched in place. *Damn clock.*

.   .   .

BEC AWOKE GENTLY. Like riding an escalator up from the car park to the womenswear section in a department store, she left the land of slumber and transitioned into the land of the awake. She rolled off her bed and walked out into the living room. The cleaning and the sleep made her feel refreshed. Jen had papers spread all over the table and a held a red pen in her hand.

"How long was I asleep?" asked Bec.

Jen kept her eyes on the papers in front of her, "A few hours. It's nearly four."

Looking around, Bec noticed the apartment was clean. A flash of panic burned in her chest. Where was her back-pack? She went to the sofa and found it sat on the opposite side. She put her hand inside the bag, being careful not expose the contents, felt the cool glass of the vodka bottle, and relaxed.

If Jen found out...

To cover her movement, Bec pulled out her wallet. She said, "I should fix that towel rail I broke."

"Mmm," replied Jen.

"You know where I should I go?"

"I know a place you can go," replied Jen flatly.

"C'mon Jennifer. I messed up pretty bad last night, but I'm trying to make things right. It hasn't been easy, you know."

Jen put down her pen and looked at Bec. "I know. It's just... Why can't you do things the normal way?"

"You think I don't ask myself that question? So how can I get this towel rail fixed?"

Jen picked up her pen and returned to grading papers.

"Fletcher's Hardware would be my guess. You can take my car if you want. Don't crash it, though.

A smile crept onto Jen's lips and Bec knew she'd come around. "No thanks. The walk will be good for me."

RYAN PULLED into Fletcher's Hardware. Streams of people pushed trolleys filled with bundles of firewood in preparation for the coming cold snap. *Next job should be the fire place.*

He pulled his brown overcoat up around his ears and went into the store. Fletcher's Hardware had been operating in Brooksdale for as long as Ryan could remember. His mother had told him that his father was about to do a business deal with Marcus Fletcher, then owner of the store, but that Ryan's father had died before closing the deal.

Not long afterwards, a young Michael Brooks bought a share in the business and eventually bought the Fletchers out.

Brooks transformed the store into a large warehouse style store, and it now enjoyed brisk business; even if the quality of the products and service wasn't quite what it used to be.

Ryan pulled a trolley out of the rank and wandered down the long aisles. Flyers advertising the upcoming Billy Cart Bash sat in racks near the entrance. Ryan grinned as he walked by. *This year the youth centre is going to win.*

He felt like a kid in a toy store. He couldn't resist browsing the power tools section, lusting over the new drills, circular saws, and tile cutters.

He meandered, looking over products his brain invented a need for. He couldn't help but stop and look at the variety of wheels and bearings. If only the youth centre budget would stretch to buying some new bits and bobs for the carts.

His wallet kept him honest, though.

Ryan got back on task and picked up a tub of grout, then turned up into the bathroom section where the mirrors were.

Coming down from the other direction was Bec. She wore a woollen hat and a black parka. Her tight-fitting jeans showed off the athletic curve of her hips and legs.

Ryan smiled and raised a hand in greeting, but was careful not to show too much enthusiasm – he was still sore from last night and felt both embarrassed and jealous.

Bec returned his greeting with a curt wave. Ryan wandered if she was embarrassed to see him and decided to stay focused on browsing the aisle. To his surprise, a voice said, "Hi Ryan. I'm so glad I ran into you!" It was Bec. She was at his shoulder.

Ryan couldn't suppress his smile as Bec continued, "The towel rail in Jen's bathroom broke. Flimsy thing it was. Anyway, I came in to get a new one but I really don't know what I'm looking for."

"Oh, Sure. Do you want glue-on, or screw-in?"

"Anything with a screw is good." Bec grinned.

Ryan pushed his cart over to the relevant section. He attempted to reach for a bathroom rail off the shelf with his injured arm, winced and swapped arms.

Bec said, "Shoulder still giving you trouble?" She remembered. *Maybe last night wasn't a complete write-off.*

"Yeah. A week of rest should fix it." With his good arm, he pulled down a white, plastic towel rail. He said, "This one should do the job. No need to spend too much."

. . .

BEC REALLY WAS happy to see Ryan. As soon as she walked into the hardware store, she realized she was out of her depth. She couldn't even find the bathroom section and had to ask some pimple-faced teenager.

When she saw Ryan in his heavy coat and work boots, her heart lifted.

As he helped, he chose a suitable product, she lightly touched his elbow and felt him stiffen. Was he angry with her about last night? She decided to take a risk.

"Ryan. Look, I'm sorry about last night. You know. Getting back into the single-scene and all. I guess I just – "

"Hey, don't worry about it," said Ryan, and he gave her shoulder a gentle squeeze. "Let's get this towel rail. It needs to be screwed in. Can you do that?"

"To be truthful, I don't even know if there is a screw-driver in Jen's place." Bec sensed Ryan relax. Maybe it was because he was on familiar ground talking about home improvements.

Ryan rubbed his chin with his thumb. "I'll tell you what," he said. "I'll fix the towel rail if you help me choose a bathroom mirror."

There was no hesitation in Bec's reply, "Done!"

FORTY-FIVE MINUTES LATER, Ryan was in Jen and Bec's bath-room. His cordless drill whirred loudly. He was happy to help the girl and for the chance to see more of Bec, but last night still needled his feelings. And he was going to be late for dinner with his mother.

Regardless, he was here now, and he didn't intend to make moral judgements about anyone's behaviour. He put the last screw in and tested the rail with a firm hand grip. *Not bad.*

Ryan walked out and stood in the bathroom doorway. Jen was at the table marking papers, Bec was in the kitchen. Ryan asked, "Do you have a broom and dust pan?"

Bec looked up and smiled, "Sure. I'll get it."

Jen raised her eye brows and her gaze followed Bec's movements for a moment, then she went back to grading papers.

"Where's the mess?" Bec asked.

Ryan pointed to the dust that had fallen on the bathroom floor and Bec pushed past him, brushing her hips against him as she did so, "I think I can manage some dust."

Ryan watched as she knelt down and swept up. She moved quickly in a no-nonsense way and was done in a moment. She looked up and Ryan was worried that she had caught him checking her out. He said, "It'll hold, but there are a couple of holes showing where the old rail got pulled out."

"That's okay. Just as long as it holds a towel," Bec replied.

Ryan packed his tools away and went into the living room.

Jen said, "Thanks for doing that."

"No problem."

"Did she tell you how it broke?"

Ryan shrugged and said, "Something about not being very strong."

Jen gave a snort then added, "Someone was far too drunk last night."

The needle in Ryan's thoughts twitched. "Did you guys stay out much after I left?"

Bec came out of the bathroom holding the dustpan and broom. She said, "I already apologized for last night. No need to say more."

Jen pushed her chair back and crossed her legs. She

said, "Well, as it happens, we went home not long after you. Vodka shots are not Bec's friend. Right Rebecca?"

Bec had disappeared behind the kitchen counter. The rubbish bin lid clanged and she called out in a droning voice that mimicked children at school, "Y-e-s M-ii-ss Wil-lia-mz."

The needle stopped twitching. In fact, it fell out and Ryan felt relieved. But anxiety returned as he realized he wanted to ask Bec out on a date. He hadn't asked a girl out since college.

Bec popped back up from the rubbish bin and asked, "You want to stay for dinner? I'm doing a Thai green curry."

Ryan looked up at the clock in the living room. It was just after six. He was already late for his mother's. He wanted very much to stay for dinner, but his mother didn't have many visitors. Besides, he would see Bec on Tuesday for school photos. He said, "Thanks, but I have a date with another woman."

"Oh, uh. Okay, then," Bec said.

Jen laughed and said, "I think it is great that you have a dinner date with your mother every Saturday."

17

Tuesday morning was cold. There had been some rain on Monday – barely enough to wet a spider's lips, but enough to make Tuesday one of the coldest days of winter so far.

Ryan stood in front of his Home Room Class reading the morning announcements. There were twenty-three Year Eleven students in Ryan's Home Room. Today was school photos. Usually it was a day of disrupted classes, over-excited students, too much make-up, and the ubiquitous odour of hair-spray.

Today was a little different. Ryan was looking forward to seeing Bec.

Spoke to the class, Ryan announced, "The Year Eleven whole-class photo is at twelve-thirty. Individual photos will be immediately afterwards. I'll be there to speed the process along."

There was a groan and a whine, "But that's lunch break. How come we don't get lunch? Do we get a longer break?"

"No. So make sure you're on time to the group photo and don't mess around with the individual photo."

The student who had spoken sunk low and leaned back in his seat to signal his dissatisfaction with the situation. The bell rang and everyone moved out to start another day of teaching and learning.

BEC FRANTICALLY RUSHED around the school gym. As Ryan had promised, several students from the Year Eleven Art class had arrived to help set up. Bec would have been lost without them. She had to remember to thank Ryan for organizing their help. She smiled and looked forward to seeing him, even if it was rushed.

One student was particularly keen and Bec made a point to remember his name: Adam. He asked a lot of questions about the cameras and settings Bec used. Bec wanted to explain more, but time was short. No sooner had the tall tripods and ladders been set up, then the first class arrived: Year Nine.

Bec's helpers went off to their first class of the day. Bec caught Adam just before he left and said, "I'd be happy to show you around the photo studio sometime. Make sure you come in, okay?"

Adam thanked Bec and rushed off to class. The noise of rowdy teenagers filled the gym and Bec wondered how she would ever get the adolescents to do the same thing at the same time. Mercifully, there were a couple of teachers assigned to each year level. Time to earn that pay check.

AT TWELVE-TWENTY-FIVE, Ryan dismissed his Year Ten English class. He stuffed his papers and laptop into his bag. He wanted to get to the gym to say hello to Bec before the Year Elevens arrived.

Ryan skipped down the stairs, his feet bumping over the steps like a drummer tapping out a military tattoo. He didn't go back to his office. No time. Instead, he went out into the courtyard intending to take a short cut to the gym. He reached the side-door of the gym and was about to push through when he heard a thump like a watermelon hitting the concrete.

Ryan looked around and saw Adam Lee sprawled on the ground with Tyler Brooks standing over him, leg cocked back as if about to kick a soccer ball. Bayden and Foster stood behind Tyler. They were just around the corner of the gym.

"Hey! Get out of it," yelled Ryan and ran over to the boys.

Tyler regained his footing and casually strolled away, calling over his shoulder, "You can thank me later, Adam."

Ryan reached the scene and helped Adam to sit up. "You okay?" Ryan asked.

"I don't need any help," said Adam and he shook Ryan's helping hand away. Blood flowed bright red from Adam's lip. Ryan looked Adam over, but he insisted, "I'm okay Mr. Anderson!"

Turning his attention to Tyler, who by now was on his way to the lunch hall, Ryan called out, "Tyler Brooks. Take yourself to the office. We'll talk there."

Tyler turned, a big grin on his face, "Whatever Anderson. I didn't do nothin'. I ain't goin' to no office!" Bayden and Foster laughed loudly and jeered at Ryan.

A wave of anger rolled through Ryan. He went after Tyler with long, deliberate steps. Ryan caught up just as Tyler reached the glass double-doors to the lunch hall. He reached out and put his hand on Tyler's shoulder. "Tyler Brooks, come to the office. I saw what you did and you're not getting away with it!"

Tyler spun around, slapped Ryan's hand away, then launched into a two-handed shove. Ryan stepped to the side and Tyler, suddenly without an object to push, stumbled forward.

The wave of anger passed and coolness returned to Ryan's head. Tyler was still a kid, after all. "Tyler, this isn't going to help. Let's walk over to the office together and you can tell me what happened on the way."

Tyler stood with his fists clenched. Foster and Bayden were on Ryan's left, in front of the doors to the lunch hall. They were big lads and if they decided to attack, Ryan wouldn't have much of a chance. A crowd started to form at the windows of the hall. The lunch duty teacher arrived. It was Mark.

"Away from the windows!" Mark shouted. "C'mon, get back to lunch." He burst through the doors to where Tyler stood off against Ryan.

Bayden looked at Mark and said, "Let's go Tyler." Foster echoed Bayden and began to walk away. Tyler hesitated and shot Ryan one last glare before stalking off.

Ryan exhaled and the tension left him. Mark asked, "What happened? It looked like Tyler was about to throw a punch at you."

Ryan rubbed his jaw with his thumb, "Would have been easier if he had." He filled Mark in on what he had seen.

"Best get it all down in writing and e-mail Janet. Knowing the Brooks family, she'll be hearing from the father soon enough.

Mark went back into the cafeteria and Ryan went back to Adam, who now sat at the back of the gym in solitude, head back with toilet paper stuffed against his cut lip.

"What happened?" Ryan asked.

Adam kept his eyes averted as he answered, "Just tripped. Tyler was helping me up."

Ryan stood directly in front of Adam, but Adam still wouldn't look at him. "That's a lie. Tyler hit you. All you need to do – "

Adam looked at Ryan, anger in his eyes. "Don't tell me what I need to do! I tripped. That's all." His head dropped and Ryan heard a gentle sob. Ryan pushed a little more, but Adam wouldn't budge. He was scared, and with good reason. It was Adam's word against three others; Ryan hadn't actually seen the punch. It burned Ryan that this had happened. People had to stand up against bullies. For the sake of the victim and the bully.

After leaving Adam with Delores at the nurse's station to ice his swollen lip, Ryan went back to his office to type up his incident report for Janet.

18

R yan dismissed his last class and went back to the English Department office. His thoughts running a mile a minute from the incident at lunch. As he walked, he was hyper-alert to the sounds around him. Running in the corridors, a surreptitious swear word. Yelling from the playground.

"Hey Ryan," said one of his colleagues, Lewis. "Check your e-mail. Janice called while you were in class. Said to tell you."

RYAN,
Thank you for the e-mail. Come in to see me before you go home.
Janice

RYAN RUBBED his chin with his thumb before closing his laptop and left the office.

. . .

A GAGGLE of older students came out of the gym as Ryan went in. Bec was stood by the backdrop for the individual photos. Her head bent over her camera as she reviewed the shots she'd just taken.

She wore a pair of professional looking slacks, blouse, and jacket that accentuated the curve of her hips. She looked athletic. It was a look Ryan found appealing and it jolted him out of his pensiveness.

A tinge of nerves fluttered in Ryan's gut and he nearly walked back out. Should he do it now? He was supposed to be on his way to see Janice, not asking Bec out on a date. Anyway, what would he say? And there was the fact that Bec had just gotten out of a bad relationship.

Too late. Bec looked up, saw Ryan, and smiled that wonderful smile that lit up a room.

Ryan walked over, "Hi. Busy day?"

Idiot. Of course it was a busy day, thought Ryan.

"Yeah. But it went surprisingly well. You've got some great young people here. I thought you were coming in with the Year II class."

As she talked, Bec packed her camera away in a soft-lined case.

"Sorry about that. There was an incident with a couple of students," replied Ryan.

"Mmm." Bec started wrapping cables up and packing them into boxes.

Ryan asked, "How were the helpers this morning?"

Bec started to pull down the back drop where the individual photos were shot. "Really good. One in particular, Adam, I think his name was. Seemed really into photography."

Ryan began helping Bec pack away the equipment. He was glad to hear Adam stood out.

"Careful with that! It's getting old and the clips are worn," warned Bec.

Doing his best to be gentle, Ryan glanced at Bec. She moved confidently, as if she had worked a lifetime with the equipment. Ryan laid the folded backdrop on the floor and accidentally knocked a lighting stand. It rocked and Bec rushed over to steady it.

"Watch what you're doing. This stuff is not cheap, you know," chided Bec.

"Right. Sorry. Um. What are you up to after you finish here?" *Stupid!*

Bec went back to collapsing the equipment. She said, "I'm going to upload all the photos to the studio computer, go home, and have a drink." She stopped and put her hands on her hips. "Can you carry some of that stuff to the van?" Bec pointed to the folded backdrop sheets.

Ryan picked them up easily and walked out to Bec's work van. Bec followed him with a suitcase full of camera gear in each hand.

They did two trips like this. On the last one, when they were loading the last of the equipment, Ryan asked, "Um. So, I was wondering if – "

Bec was half in the van, trying to fit some cases in so they wouldn't fall. "Just a sec," she said. She extracted herself and looked into Ryan's face. "You were saying?"

"Yeah. So, I was wondering if, you know, if you wanted a better job done on the towel rail."

Bec arched her eye-brows and tried to suppress a smile. "That's all you wanted to ask? About the towel rail? It's fine. You did a great job."

C'mon Ryan! You can do this!

Absent mindedly, he rubbed his cheek with his thumb and said, "That's good. Just checking."

He kicked at a pebble and sent it skipping across the car park. Bec said, "Well. I need to get going."

"Yeah. Sure. Um. Are you going to the Billy Cart Bash?"

"I don't know. Seems a bit young for me. And it's the same day as my birthday, so you know, celebrating and all." Bec got in the car. She looked through the window at Ryan.

She probably has a ton of friends to celebrate with, thought Ryan gloomily - and he wasn't one of them. Trying to look positive, He waved and said, "That's a shame, well, safe drive."

She waved and drove off, leaving Ryan standing alone in the car park. *You bloody idiot, Ryan,* he thought. He had just told Bec it was a shame she was born on the same day of the Billy Cart Bash. Could he have said anything dumber? Probably not. Feeling foolish and defeated, he slowly walked inside the building to Janice's office.

19

Bec arrived home at four-forty in the afternoon, placed her laptop and cameras on the table, then turned the heating on. She shivered as the air conditioning unit coughed cold air before the warm air came. Next, she turned on the gas heater, instantly sending warm air radiating out. Satisfied, she went to the kitchen, poured herself a glass of red wine, and sat down to work.

She had intended to transfer the photos from the cameras to the computer at the studio, but she was tired. She needed a drink and the apartment was empty; Jen was probably still at school.

Bec plugged the camera into the computer and started copying the photos. A little bar appeared on her screen indicating that the image transfer was in process. She leaned back in her chair and raised the glass to her lips. *What a day!* She thought back to Ryan's awkward attempt to ask her out. He seemed like the kind of guy you settled down with: two kids, a dog, and a white-picket fence. She wasn't sure if she wanted that. She had just gotten out of a hole, and Ryan could well be another trap. A good trap, but a trap none-theless.

There was a knock at the door. Bec put the glass down gently.

She could just pretend that no one was home. Another knock. This time more forceful and followed by a voice, "Hello? I'm from Smith, Hall, and Townsend Realtor's. Can I come in?" Bec recognized the name. Smith, Hall, and Townsend had a shop front on Main Street not far from Louis' Liquor.

Bec called out, "Just a moment!"

She went to the door and hooked the security chain on, unlocked the bolt, and opened the door a fraction. A well-built, middle-aged man in a grey suit and a man-bag slung over his shoulder stood outside. His hair was greying at the edges and was cut short, military style. He smiled at Bec. He had a look about him that bespoke professionalism. It reassured Bec.

"Hello," he said. "Peter Watson. Property Manager with Smith, Hall, and Townsend. May I come in?" He passed Bec his business card through the door opening. Bec inspected the card then unhooked the chain, and swung the door open. "What can I do for you, Mr. Watson?"

"Oh, just a routine inspection," said Mr. Watson and he walked through without waiting for a verbal invitation. "Mind if I take some pictures for the owner?"

Again, he didn't wait for permission. Out of his man-bag, he pulled a Canon EOS 70D.

Bec smiled awkwardly and said, "You take your job seriously."

Mr. Watson snapped of a few shots of the living room and replied, "Yes, of course. What could be more important than people's homes?"

The man moved through the apartment methodically. Clearly he had done this thousands of times. Bec stood with her arms folded as Peter Watson took photos of nearly every surface. He saw the glass of wine and said, "Happy hour?"

"Yeah. It was a tough day."

"I know what you mean. Do you have guests over regularly? Parties? That sort of thing?"

Bec wasn't expecting that sort of question. Its suddenness took her by surprise, but Peter Watson's confidence assured her and she replied, "No. I'm really just staying with my sister, Jennifer."

"Staying long?"

"Just a few weeks while I help my sister with a few things."

When he finished, Watson shook Bec's hand with a firm grip, thanked her for her time, and left. It was an odd sort of visit, but they did things differently in the country, didn't they?

Bec peered through the curtains, which gave her a view of the street below. She saw Mr. Watson trot across the street and get into a black Hyundai. She put his card down on the corner of the table and checked her computer. The file transfer was complete, so she took a long drink from her wine glass.

Jen came home thirty-minutes later to find Bec in the kitchen, knife in one hand, wine glass in the other.

"What's all this?" Jen asked as she hung up her coat.

"Pan-fried chicken and couscous."

"Fancy! What's the occasion?"

"Oh, you know. Just had a good day."

Jen sat down at the table and cast an eye over the mess of cameras, computer, and cables on the table. She started to tidy up.

Bec noticed, rushed out to the table and started packing away. "Careful, careful. That's work stuff. Can you keep an eye on the chicken instead?"

Jen stepped back, hands in the air. "Okay, Okay."

Bec packed her gear away and inadvertently knocked Peter Watson's card onto the floor, under the table. She sat the laptop and cameras on the floor next to the sofa and went back to the kitchen. Jen's fussing and incessant tidying could really get to Bec at times. Perhaps it was time to look for her own place.

"Here, have a glass of wine," said Bec and she poured a glass for Jen.

"Just a small one. I'm grading papers tonight."

"You can grade papers any time. Tonight, let's have a girl's night in!"

Jen handed the spatula to Bec, who resumed her position as cook. Jen said, "It's a bit early in the week, for me. I'll have one with dinner."

"Oh, come on, Jen. Live a little."

Jen pulled out a folder of papers and sat them on the table. She said, "Did something happen today?"

Bec cleared her throat, put a serious look on her face and said, "Ryan asked me out today. Well, he tried to."

"Ryan? Ryan Anderson?" Jen went back into to the kitchen and gave Bec a hug. "Tell me EVERYTHING," Jen squealed. The girls sat down at the table to eat their dinner. "Mmm!" Jen exclaimed, "This chicken is good." That put a smile on Bec's face. She ate the couscous and took a mouthful of wine to wash it down.

Bec recounted the details of the day. Jen grinned wide-eyed and interjected with, "No!" or, "He didn't?", and "Poor man." A twinkle of mischief lit up Jen's eyes. "You should ask *him* out on a date."

"What!" Bec put her glass down and leaned forward. "If he wants me, he'll have to man-up and ask *me*." Bec thumped her fist on the table in mock anger. "Besides, I'm just not sure I'm ready to commit to anything. I'm hardly independent at the moment, and I don't even know if I want to settle in Brooksdale."

"It's a bit premature to be talking about settling down, isn't it? Ryan might not be looking for anything serious either."

That was a point Bec hadn't considered. She had just assumed he Ryan was a level-headed country boy. "Do you think he's just after a fling? Is that what people think of me?"

Jen leaned back in her chair. "No. But as far as I know, you're the first woman he's shown interest in since his divorce."

Bec got up "You want ice cream?"

She scooped out ice-cream into two bowls and thought over what Jen had said. It had been so long since she was with a caring guy. Placing the ice-creams on the table, Bec said, "You're right. I'll message him. But if he screws up the date, he's canned!"

BEC: *Hey, want 2 do dinner 2morow night?*

RYAN: *Hi. Can't. BJJ. Thursday night?*

BEC: *Can make time. Pick me up at 6.*

. . .

RYAN: *OK. Dress warm and bring your camera.*

BEC SHOWED the message to Jen with delighted anticipation. Ryan seemed like a decent guy and that's exactly what she needed right now - some stability. A least she hoped he was stable.

20

"Well I'm ready," Bec said as she sat at the table. Jen was in the kitchen noisily chopping vegetables - preparing a meal for one.

It was Thursday evening and the clock showed five-fifty-five. Ryan was due to pick Bec up at six. She looked longingly at her backpack on the floor next to the sofa. An unopened bottle of tequila sat in the bag. Bec rung her hands, then said, "I think I'll have another coffee. You want one?"

"No, and don't drink so much coffee. You'll spend half the night peeing."

As Bec made yet another coffee, Ryan sprinted out to his car which was parked at Brooksdale High. He ripped open the door of his Ford and revved the engine, and speed off down the road - late again.

"Damn that Brooks!" Ryan shouted, as he thumped the steering wheel several times.

Ryan had just gotten out of a meeting with Janice about

the incident with Tyler on Tuesday. Adam still insisted that he had tripped and Tyler had merely offered assistance. To make matters worse, Tyler claimed that Ryan had assaulted him outside the lunch hall.

Tyler's father had submitted a formal complaint and the school was obliged to investigate. At least Janice had managed to dissuade Brooks from pursuing legal action. Now Ryan had a week of leave-with-pay while the investigation took its course. Ryan tried to look at the bright side. *I'll have the week to put the finishing touches on the billy-carts.*

Ryan flew down Chalky's Hill. He hit Black Rock River Bridge and the old Ford's suspension bounced and rocked.

"C'mon! Gi'me green," Ryan pleaded as he looked at the lights ahead. They changed to orange, then red just as he reached the intersection. For an instant Ryan thought of cutting around the corner, but his foot slipped across to the brake and the truck came to an embarrassingly screechy halt.

A family of four, a Mum, Dad, and two little kids, rugged up against the cold, stepped out from the shadows and crossed the road. Ryan exhaled loudly. He could well have hit that family. *I need to calm down. Get my head in the game.* He breathed deeply, like Tony had taught him to do. The light turned green and Ryan turned right on to Main Street. He kept to the speed limit and thought about Bec's warm smile. He knew he was going to be late, but he hoped she would forgive him.

"IF I CAN'T HAVE coffee, How about wine?" Bec asked Jen.

"Alcohol before a date leads to bad decisions," replied Jen.

True enough, thought Bec. The apartment smelled filled

of sweet chicken stir-fry. Jen turned off the gas and slid her meal from the pan to her plate.

Bec looked at the clock. Six-fifteen. "He hasn't sent you a message?" Bec asked Jen.

"Nope, nothing." Jen sat down at the table. "Look. Ryan's a good guy. He wouldn't stand you up. Something's happened. Maybe a parent came in and he's been tied up."

There was a knock at the door. "Hello?" It was Ryan. Bec looked at Jen and put her finger to her mouth. She didn't want Ryan thinking she had been waiting at the door for him.

Ryan knocked again and called out, "Hi, sorry I'm so late."

"Coming!" Bec replied. She flashed a grin at Jen, then swung the door open. Ryan stepped into the apartment. He was wearing a pair of slim-fitting blue jeans that pulled tight around his thighs and calves. His wool coat was dark-brown and gently covered the triangle of his shoulders to his waist.

"Sorry I'm late. I got caught up at work with Janice, the Principal."

Bec replied, "Oh, no problem. Jen and I were chatting away and I barely noticed the time." Jen nodded in agreement.

Bec grabbed her parka and wool hat from the coat stand by the door.

"Don't forget your camera," said Ryan. Bec grinned. This guy knew her already. She picked up her camera bag and they were off.

RYAN OPENED the passenger side door for Bec. She looked good, as if she were going to watch a college football game. Ryan liked the casual look.

He was excited to be out on a date and a bit nervous. When they got to his truck, he remembered the passenger side door was a bit sticky. He dashed ahead of Bec and opened the door for her.

As Bec stepped up into the seat, she said, "I wasn't expecting a chauffeured service."

Ryan chuckled and replied, "I'm the full package." He trotted around to the driver's side and hopped in. "I hope you like Spanish," he said.

"I'm intrigued," she said, as they drove off, turned north onto Main Street and made their way through the middle of town. The street lights cast a yellow hue over the shop fronts. On the northern edge of town, Ryan pulled off Main and headed towards the river. At the end of the road sat a beautiful glass building, the River View Café and Tapas Bar.

"Dinner here and you might get a photo opportunity."

"Are you my muse?"

Ryan grinned, enjoying the riposte. "No, something better."

Inside the café was a long bar that served a variety of coffees, teas, cocoa, and alcohol. Along the far wall was a floor to ceiling glass wall that overlooked the river. There was a row of tables along the glass wall. One table had a 'Reserved' sign on it. There was no need for the sign, because Bec and Ryan were the only customers at that moment.

BEC COULDN'T KEEP her eyes off the river. Upstream, where the river narrowed, were some rapids. Further downstream, where the café was perched over the river bank, the water widened out in gentle ripples. Bec felt enchanted by the change in the river. The lights of the café and the moon glittered across the black water like ribbons of pearl, floating across black velvet. Automatically, Bec pulled out her camera and started shooting, but the glass reflection ruined her shots. Bec stepped through the door and onto the balcony. It was chilly outside, but she barely noticed. She took a few test shots to get the camera settings right, steadied herself on the railing, and lost herself in her work.

Ryan joined her on the balcony. She looked at him and said, "Model for me?"

Ryan leaned against the railing, put one hand in his pocket and one on his hip. "How's this," he asked with a cheeky grin.

"A bit clichéd. And you look wooden. Lean on the railing. Pretend you're the captain of a boat and you're surveying the ocean." To Bec's amusement, Ryan obliged. He bent ninety degrees at the waist and wore a serious expression on his face. Bec's eyes traced a quick line over his physique. She bit her bottom lip and raised the camera to her eye. Ryan looked good in this light, in this place, in this moment.

The spell broke when the waitress stuck her head out the door and said, "Your food is on the table. Just wanted to let you know, before it gets cold."

Bec and Ryan looked at each other and laughed. They linked arms and walked back inside. The warmth of the café felt like a furnace blast after the cold outside.

The food began to arrive; lamb sausage, spiced pork, cheeses and vegetables, and some tomato and seafood dish Bec couldn't identify. Bec delighted in it all. "Why haven't I heard of this place before?"

"I don't know. May haps it's the local touch," Ryan replied in an exaggerated country accent.

Bec and Ryan chatted easily for over an hour. She told

him about her father and how it was he who got her into photography. She also told Ryan that Phil had yet to return her father's camera and equipment. In return, Ryan told her about his parents. That his mother lived alone in an apartment and that his father had died young. Ryan spoke matter-of-factly and Bec didn't push him for details. As the plates emptied and the conversation slowed, Bec found her gaze wandering to the bar.

Ryan said, "Let me get dessert." He stood and went to the bar.

While he was gone, Bec checked the photos on her camera. She fidgeted and tried to keep her thoughts focused on the images before her. Some were actually pretty good. Ryan was quite photogenic.

With two hot chocolates topped with marshmallows and cream, Ryan sat back down and placed one drink in front of Bec. She could have squealed in delight. "I haven't had one of these in ages. How did you know?"

"I asked Jen."

Points for planning, thought Bec. She liked that Ryan added this personal touch, bu she was annoyed with her sister for conspiring with Ryan.

At eight-thirty, Ryan said, "Well, time to finish up. School tomorrow."

"The school-boy needs his rest."

Ryan chuckled and pulled out his wallet.

Bec rushed to pull out her purse She didn't want to owe Ryan a meal or any other 'niceties.' She tried to pay for the meal, but Ryan wouldn't let her. "Not on your life, Rebecca Williams. I asked you out, therefore, I take financial responsibility."

Despite her reservations, Bec kind of liked the old-fashioned thought, but hope Ryan didn't expect something in return. She checked her thoughts. Ryan didn't strike her as that type of guy. As they walked out of the door, Bec looped her arm through his and she felt happy.

Ryan said, "I'd like to take you out again."

"Do I get to share the financial responsibility?" Bec leaned into him in a playful manner.

"Ha! I was thinking you could take full responsibility."

She pulled away from him and giggled. "Oh, and here I was thinking you were the 'full package'.

Ryan chuckled, chased after her and wrapped an arm around her waist. She could feel the strength in his arms. Luckily, she had no intention of escaping.

"In all seriousness," said Ryan. "How about Saturday evening, pick you up at five-thirty?" Ryan told her to dress warm and bring a camera, then he drove her home.

21

Ryan stepped out of the shower. It was five o'clock in the evening on Saturday and the winter sun threw its last rays up against the sky in defiance of the coming night. As Ryan dried himself, he looked about with pride at his handy work. The bathroom was finally finished. Sadly, Tammy had never appreciated his skill with tools and often complained about how much time he spent building things. Bec, on the other hand, seemed interested whenever he talked about a renovation project.

He sincerely hoped that she would enjoy the tour tonight. He was taking her on a drive and a walk on a historic section of town and there were sure to be lots of photo opportunities. He thought back to their last date and began humming a tune his father used to sing and got back to his renovations. With the bathroom finished, the only job left was the master bedroom and en-suite.

BEC GLANCED ABOUT THE FLAT. She had a bottle of tequila in one hand and her backpack in the other. She heard the toilet flush and stuffed the bottle back into her backpack. *God! I'll be 28 next week. I can do this without a drink.*

Jen came out of the bathroom and said, "It's nearly five-thirty. You should get ready to go. I can't see Ryan being late twice in a row."

Bec put her wool coat on, looked at her sister and said, "What am I doing, Jen? I don't even know if I'm ready for another relationship and I'm going out with the type of guy you marry and settle down with."

"You had a good time Thursday, right? So, go out and see how it goes. Ryan's a good guy. If you were going out with Mark Strathfield, then I'd be worried, but it's Ryan."

Bec pulled her backpack to her chest and held it protectively with both hands. "What if I hurt him? I'm hardly a model of stability right now."

Jen reached out and took one of Bec's hands. "Ryan is an adult, he'll be fine. Just go and have fun."

A knock at the door interrupted their conversation. It was Ryan. "Good evening ladies."

He was dressed in a simple chequered shirt, and a heavy wool coat. Every bit the educated woodsman. He extended his hand and Bec took it. As she walked out the door, Bec looked back at Jen who mimed clapping her hands. Bec felt like a teenager again.

RYAN AND BEC drove north on Main Street. Ryan had tried a new aftershave and he worried he had used too much since Bec hadn't said very much, but when she took his hand, he relaxed.

Snow began to flutter in the sky in front of the car. Bec said, "I thought is didn't snow in Brooksdale."

Looking at her with a sideways glance, Ryan replied, "It snowed in 1986. This stuff doesn't count. It will melt as soon as it touches the ground." He gave her hand a gentle squeeze.

"What surprises do you have for me tonight, Mr. Anderson?"

"A town tour."

"I didn't know Brooksdale was big enough."

"Ha! You'll learn yet," replied Ryan, enjoying the banter.

The oncoming traffic lights glinted in Bec's eyes, giving her a playful look. The traffic slowed and came to a halt near the intersection with Black Rock Road. Red flashing lights illuminated the scene ahead. The traffic crawled forward. A police car was parked at the intersection and Ryan spotted Jerry with his notebook out, writing down the details of two cars; a new-looking Mercedes SUV and a black Hyundai Sonata.

"You know them?" Bec asked.

"I know the Police Officer, and I've a pretty good idea who owns the Mercedes – not too many of those in Brooksdale – but I don't know about the other car."

Bec peered at the scene. A man got out of the black car with papers in hand. Bec recognized him.

"That's Peter Watson," Bec said.

"Who?"

"Peter Watson from Smith, Hall, and Townsend."

Ryan shrugged his shoulders. "Don't know him. I bought my house through Smith, Hall, and Townsend."

The traffic started moving again and the accident passed rearwards. Bec said, "Maybe he's new to town, like me." She smiled at Ryan.

He glanced at her, smiled, and said, "Not surprising, the

newbie having a fender-bender there. Dangerous bit of road that one."

BEC LOOKED at Ryan as he whipped the steering wheel around and parked the truck. She imagined those arm muscles working under the layers of winter clothing. They had arrived at Uriah Brookes' House. Lamp light filled the windows of the old red-brick home with a calming, yellow glow. Smoke floated out of two chimneys and disappeared into the night. Bec pulled her coat close and took out her camera. "This place is gorgeous. Why haven't I heard of it before?"

"You have to pay more attention to your environment."

Bec shoved Ryan playfully. They laughed and linked arms. In their winter coats, they looked like two marshmallows squished together.

"Stop here," said Bec. She took the lens cap off her camera, snapped off a few shots, adjusted her settings, then stepped off the gravel path onto the lawn. The grass was crisp underfoot, like walking on cracker biscuits - result of the dry winter.

Bec got herself into a low position with her camera and spent time adjusting her shot through the viewfinder. Absorbed in this task, her life disappeared out of focus.

Brooks' House was a two-storey, red-brick building. It was the first brick home built in Brooksdale and the town took its name from the man who built it, Uriah Brooks. Today it belonged to the Brooksdale Shire Council and was managed by the Historical Society of Brooksdale. They had done a wonderful job restoring the old home. At night, the front was lit by two flood lights which, to the photographer's eye, cast interesting shadows across the facade and created beautiful depth.

Ryan called out, "Do you want me to get one of you?"

"I'm good."

"Do you want to get one of me?"

"No," replied Bec. "A couple more and I'll be done."

Bec shot about ten more photos then walked back to Ryan, who by now was reading the information sign.

"Welcome back," he teased.

"Got to do what I've gotta do," replied Bec.

As they went in, Bec saw posters for the Billy Cart Bash. The Youth Centre team was on one of the posters, but there was scribble over it. She stopped and took a closer look. 'Poofters' had been scrawled across the image of the Youth Centre's Team. Ryan stopped and ripped the offending poster from the notice board. He looked at the scrawled word in thick black marker and shook his head before folding the poster neatly and sliding it into his pocket. Bec could tell the vandalism had hurt Ryan's feelings, and that he was trying not to show it.

Ryan lead the way to the reception desk. "Hi Angela," Ryan greeted the attendant, who raised her eyebrows when she saw Ryan. Bec had a feeling she'd met this woman before, but couldn't place it.

Ryan took the folded poster out of his pocket and handed it over to Angela. He said, "Someone's been causing trouble."

Angela looked at the defaced poster and shook her head. "Those damned kids!" she said, "They just can't leave stuff alone. I don't know how you teachers put up with it."

Ryan replied, "Most of them are pretty good given half a chance, but there's always a handful that ruin it for the rest."

Ryan paid the entrance fee and they went into the drawing room. It was warm; the kind of warmth that only a wood fire can provide. Bec loosened her coat and took off her wool cap.

"What's the story behind this place?" Bec asked.

"It's an interesting one. There was a dispute over land between Uriah Brooks and Jeremiah Brumfield." Bec listened as she walked around the room. The floorboards creaked under foot and the walls were lined with book-shelves, filled with leather-bound books. Ryan continued, "Brumfield built a cabin here first, but Brooks insisted he filed his claim first."

"Sounds like the stage is set for a good ol' feud."

"It was no joking matter, especially as there was a girl involved."

Bec stopped and looked at Ryan. "A love story, too?"

"Of sorts. Brooks and Brumfield were in love with the same girl. The two men decided to duel it out. Winner takes all, but the girl, Annie Davis, convinced them to settle peacefully."

Bec's mouth dropped. "How could they just treat a girl like she was something to be traded?"

Ryan held his hands up in surrender. "I know, but I never said it was a happy romance."

"Okay. Okay. Tell the story."

"They play the game Annie Davis set up. Brumfield loses and becomes a recluse. Brooks gets the land and Annie. Brooks wanted to burn down Brumfield's cabin, but Annie wouldn't let him. The rumour was that she secretly had loved Brumfield all along. The cabin still stands and is the oldest building in Brooksdale."

"Huh? Imagine if Brumsfield had won? The town would

be called Brumsfield-dale. Not a good name." Bec grinned, but Ryan failed to see the funny side.

"We'll look around here then go out to see Brumsfield's Cabin."

They walked through the rooms that served as a museum to Brooksdale's pioneer heritage. Bec wondered at the passage of time and the passing of stories from one generation to the next. *Whose voices had been lost in the telling?* she wondered. Did Annie really have a say in the whole duel thing, or was that what people said to justify the actions of their ancestors? There were two other couples wandering through the house.

Ryan lead Bec out the back door and down the path to Brumsfield's cabin. The path was lit with solar garden lights and a row of poplar trees stood guard along either side of the path. Old horse-drawn ploughs and carriages were placed between the trees and added a pioneer feel.

Bec asked, "Are there any monuments to the Aboriginal history in the area?"

"It's something the Historical Society is working on, but progress is slow," replied Ryan.

Voices left out of the story, thought Bec. She snuggled closer to Ryan. "Let's get a photo. Stand beside that plough. I can get the lights and the cabin in the background." Ryan stood where instructed and Bec snapped off a few shots. In the background were two boys, around sixteen years-old. It looked like they were discussing secret boys' business. Bec remembered a time when her cares were simple and each day a new journey.

She called out to the boys, "Excuse me! Could you take a photo of us?"

One of the boys ducked his head and turned away. The other looked at her directly with a scowl on his face.

Ryan turned around. When the boy saw him, he called out, "Mr. Anderson has a girlfriend! Oooo!"

Ryan said, "C'mon Bec, let's get out of here."

The boy called out again, "That's right. Run away. I know ya scared o'me. You're gonna lose the Billy Cart Bash, then you're gonna lose ya job! My ol' man'll see to it!" Bec looked at Ryan and noticed his jaw clenched and his hands were balled into fists.

Clearly she had missed something, but Bec quickly put two and two together and guessed the teen was a problem kid for Ryan at school. Bec said to Ryan, "You shouldn't let him talk down to you."

"Let's get a drink." Ryan walked back to the truck and Bec followed with the sound of childish laughter floating after her.

After an uncomfortably silent drive from Uriah Brooks' House to the Black Rock Bar and Grill, Ryan finally spoke, "Sorry about back there." Ryan felt weak and defeated. He shouldn't have to run away every time he crossed Tyler's path.

They were sitting at a secluded table in the corner of the restaurant area. The TV screens played repeats of the footy highlights of the season so far. There were a few families in the restaurant area and some men and women sitting at the bar, having finished the last shift at the meat-works.

Ryan responded absent-mindedly to Bec's attempts to make small talk. He had trouble focusing his thoughts. The last thing Ryan had expected was Tyler to show up. And who was the other guy with him? It was neither Bayden nor Foster.

The meal arrived, steak and hot chips. Bec had a glass of

the house red and Ryan had a beer. The uncomfortable silence returned as both Bec and Ryan ate. Bec put down her knife and fork with a clang and said, "Look, Ryan. Why did that kid get to you so much? He's just another punk kid. You deal with his kind all the time, right?"

Bec's question pierced the heart of Ryan's feelings. He realized he had been neglecting the most important person of the night and focusing on the least important. Ryan took a deep breath and explained what had happened at the school, the investigation, and his suspension from duties. He waited for Bec to show her disappointment in him, or her disgust. He was a teacher who abused his authority and over-stepped the line. This would be their second and last date.

To his surprise, Bec said, "You've got to be kidding, right? I've seen you at work. Those young people respect you. And everyone I've talked to about you, says you're one of the best teachers this town has."

Ryan felt a tingle in the corner of his eye and he sat a little straighter. He replied, "I should have mentioned it sooner."

"Don't be silly. You barely know me. Maybe you should have told Jen, though." Ryan couldn't help but agree. Bec leaned across the table and took both of Ryan's hands. Relief was replaced with anxiety. Was she going to kiss him? What if he leans in and she leaves him hanging halfway? Or he leaves her stranded in a foolish half-kiss?

Ryan inhaled sharply, leaned in, and kissed Bec gently. Well, she probably kissed him as much as he kissed her. Ryan hadn't felt that type of intimacy for a long time. When they broke away, he grinned sheepishly. Bec looked relaxed and content.

Then he had an idea. "Bec, can I see the last photos you took? The ones of me by the tree?"

Bec raised her eye-brows. "Sure," she said as she pulled the camera out. Ryan flicked through the images on the digital screen until he found the one he was after. He zoomed in. There, at the corner of Brumsfield's Cabin stood frozen in time, were Tyler Brooks and Adam Lee.

22

Bec slipped her finger nail under the tape, being careful not to rip the paper. Ryan exchanged a conspiratorial glance with Jen as they sat around the dining table in Jen's flat. It was Bec's birthday and Ryan was taking her out to see the Brooksdale Billy-Cart Bash.

It sounded silly, but it was a big event for the bush town. Finished unwrapping the gift, Bec looked at the object left in her hands - necklace made of wooden discs. The pieces fit together like the feathers on a dove. It was an understated piece of craftsmanship.

She looked up at Ryan, "Did you make this?"

"Certainly did."

"Ryan, it's beautiful." Bec slipped the necklace over her head and found it surprisingly light. She planted a kiss on his lips and Ryan gushed with pride and a little embarrassment since Jen was standing there.

"We'd better get going," said Bec. More to deflect the attention away.

Ryan asked Jen if she were coming, but Jen declined,

saying she had too many papers to grade. It was just Bec and Ryan.

RYAN DROVE with one thought on his mind: defeat Brooks. Bec's presence made him feel secure and confident and her comment startled him. "I thought the Billy Cart Bash was on the other side of Chalky's Hill," said Bec when Ryan turned down Rock View Street.

Of course it wouldn't be obvious to Bec why they weren't going directly to the race course. Ryan replied gently, "It is, but I have to pick up the billy carts for the youth centre teams. We've got three carts entered." Ryan slowed as he passed his father's old house. Despite the bright cold of the sunny July day, the house appeared dark.

Ryan didn't see the decay of the old house. Instead, he imagined it as it would look after he bought it back from Brooks. His mind saw a full wrap-round bullnose veranda with iron scroll-work decorating the corners.

When they pulled into the youth centre car park, Bec asked, "What's the story between you and Brooks?"

"How far back do you want to go?"

Bec shrugged. "You decide."

This could be a tough question. Ryan didn't want to apear spiteful or vengeful, but was there any other way to feel. He decided to tell Bec the bare details and see how she reacted. Ryan started, "Back when Dad died, Michael Brooks bought the house from Mum. I remember her saying things like, 'Too many ghosts,' or, 'Who would want to buy this place anyway?'"

Bec placed a comforting hand on Ryan's shoulder. Ryan continued, "It was, and still is, a beautiful house. Dad bought two blocks of land. One for the house, and he set one aside for parkland. He put in play equipment and donated the land to the council. At the time, he was successful in business and had no inkling of trouble on the horizon." Ryan smiled weakly at Bec and she nodded her understanding.

Ryan said, "Anyway, Dad was barely in the ground and Brooks started hanging around. He offered Mum a 'fair price considering.'" Ryan snorted loudly. "Mum sold to Brooks. She had no idea what the property was worth. She trusted Brooks. Why I'll never know."

Bec rubbed Ryan's shoulder and said, "If she relied on your father for financial decision-making, I can understand how she would have been an easy target."

Bec was right, certainly, but the hurt of injustice still stung Ryan this many years on. He said, "All Mum could afford was the tiny two-bedroom house she still lives in today. Can you imagine? She traded a beautiful four-bedroom home for a crappy two-bedroom." Ryan scoffed then added, "That man took complete advantage of a grieving woman who was suddenly left with two boys to take care of."

Bec said, "Oh Ryan. I'm so sorry for you and your mother." Ryan shot her a quick glance - determination in his face.

"Don't be sorry for me," replied Ryan. "I'll get the place back *and* keep the Youth Centre going." He smiled.

As Ryan and Bec walked into the youth centre building, Bec couldn't help but marvel at the depth of community spirit within Ryan. He had every right to feel bitter towards Brooks and the town that allowed such a man to dominate it, yet Ryan worked hard to make Brooksdale a better place for the kids.

It was devoid of human activity and cold inside, and Bec could smell fresh paint. Three billy carts sat on the floor. One painted green, one blue, and one red. All the tables and chairs had been pushed back against the walls to make space for the speed machines.

"My money's on the red one," said Bec. "Red goes faster." She laughed and Ryan gave her gentle hug. It felt warm.

The carts had been made from re-used materials. The back wheels were old bicycle tyres – no two from the same bicycle by the looks of them. The front wheels were from wheel barrows.

"Help me wheel them out," said Ryan and he pushed the green cart out first. Bec took the red one. It was heavy and Bec doubted her ability to pick a winner. Outside, another vehicle had pulled up. A white Holden ute. It was Arkell's father, Gene Lewis. With Gene's help, they put two carts into the back of Ryan's F-150, and the third – blue – into the back of Gene's ute.

Ropes were thrown over the load and tied down, then they drove to the course on the western side of Chalky's Hill to do battle.

23

The western side of Chalky's Hill gave its self over to the Billy Cart Bash. Spectators lined a dirt track of one hundred and fifty metres. Because of the lack of rain, the grass was dry and brown. Some council workers had sprayed the track with water to keep the dust down, which turned the dirt to a dirty brown colour. From the air, it would have looked like some giant's skid-mark on the side of the hill.

Shouts of delight and laughter assaulted Bec's ears as she walked through the crowds on her way to the Youth Centre tent, camera in hand. Ryan and the team were beside her: Sally, Arkell, and Keysha. The fun runs were on. Overly-decorated carts cashed their way down the track to the amusement of the audience. Their drivers rolling and bouncing down the hill while the carts crashed out. Soon the real races would start. It seemed to Bec that the whole town had turned out on this sunny, Saturday afternoon for the races.

Prep areas were back from the track under pavilion tents. Even these tents were arranged in a hierarchy with

Fletcher's Hardware at the top, closest to the start line. The Youth Centre had earned a place at the bottom.

As the team neared the Youth Centre prep tent, she heard a shout, "There go the first losers!"

Bec turned her head. It was Tyler, Bayden, and Foster. The boys laughed and pointed at the carts that Ryan and the kids at the youth centre had made. These boys just loved to cause trouble.

Ryan said, "Just keep walking. Don't even look at them."

The team obeyed, but Sally looked daggers at Tyler and a vein throbbed in Arkell's neck.

At the tent, Adam tinkered with a spanner. He was along for support as were a couple of younger students who had helped build the carts and wanted to prove their loyalty and earn a driver's seat next year. Bec snapped some photos of the support crew for the website. It was good to see some team spirit.

Feeling like a fifth wheel, Bec decided to scout around and get some photos of the other teams. Wondering up and down the line of tents, Bec inspected the different carts. She was amazed at the variety. There were mismatches of timber, steel, bicycle wheels, and rope. Finally, she arrived at the top of the hill and saw Fletcher's Hardware's team tent. She nosed around, feeling like a spy in the cold war. Three carts sat on small stands in the tent. Steel frames, racing seats, racing steering wheel, proper wheels. These carts looked built for speed. Bec snapped a couple of shots and hurried back to the Youth Centre tent.

At the tent, Bec asked Ryan, "How could anyone win against Fletcher's Hardware. They've got *real* carts."

"These are real carts, too," Objected Ryan, but as he spoke, he thrust his hands in his pockets and nodded.

"They've got the money, the materials, and the knowhow to build them, but they don't have the heart."

A siren sounded, and the tent bustled with activity - time to go to the marshalling area. Ryan guided the team to a section sign posted with 'Youth Centre. Blue Team, Green Team, Red Team'

Ryan said, "All right, last minute checks. First race starts in ten minutes. Arkell, you're up first, against Sully's Sports Bar." Arkell nodded and checked his cart over.

A cheer erupted in the background. Bec looked about her. A cart had gone too fast around a bend and rolled over, spilling the driver out. Bec looked more closely as the driver stood up and brushed himself off. It was Jerry!

"Yeah, he gets involved," said Ryan.

On the other side of the track, Bec saw someone else she recognized - another photographer with his camera out. It took her a few seconds, but she placed him. Peter Watson. She waved, but it didn't seem like he saw her.

Arkell sat in the blue cart, practicing his steering technique by leaning from side to side. His steering system was a rope tied to either end of the steering bracket. At the green cart, Keysha tested the brakes with a concerned look on her face. She would be in Race two. In the red cart, sat Sally. She had an old motorcycle helmet on. Unlike Arkell, she had a real steering wheel from a scrapped Toyota Corolla. She would be in Race five. Adam Lee crouched next to Sally talking softly. Bec thought how lovely and intense teenage romance could be. She envied Sally and Adam.

"It'll take more than a fresh coat of paint to win this race." It was Steven James. Bec's eyes flickered from Steven to Ryan.

But Ryan merely glanced in his direction, "We re-use old

materials. It's called sustainability. Community spirit is what it's really about."

"World's full of losers talking about community spirit. My money's on Fletcher." He walked off with his head held high.

Bec spoke quietly at Ryan's shoulder, "I can't believe I dated that jerk."

"I can't believe you dated him either." Ryan grinned and Bec gave him a playful thump on the shoulder.

"Hey Adam, why don't you take the photos?" Bec held her camera out to the youth.

Adam stood quickly. "Are you sure Miss Williams? I don't want to mess anything up." Bec smiled warmly and handed the camera to Adam. He grinned and an excited gleam flashed in his eyes.

They were interrupted by yelling a couple of teams downhill. "You stupid homo fuckwit!"

"Settle down son. You're going to win this thing."

"Don't tell me the fuck what to do!" It was Tyler yelling at his father with vehemence. People turned to watch the drama. Bec included. Michael Brooks appeared to notice the extra attention and spoke quietly and intensely to his son. Tyler pushed past his father and stalked down the hill past Ryan and the youth centre teams., "What the fuck are youse lookin' at!" Tyler yelled as he went by.

Ryan turned to his team and said, "Don't worry about him. He might have the best billy cart money can buy, but we built these ourselves and we've got more self-respect."

Nerves rippled through Ryan's innards as the PA system crackled, announcing time for the competitive races. A crowd gathered at the starting mound and another at the finish line. Arkell wheeled his cart and positioned it next to an overweight man with a ruddy-coloured nose representing Sully's Sports Bar. The two shook hands, then adopted a serious posture at the controls of their respective machines. Spectators pushed against the rope to get a better view.

The starter raised his starting pistol in the air, "Ready. Set." *BANG!*

Arkell pushed off with all his might. Ryan imagined the nervous tension in Arkell exploding in release, fueling his energy, senses alive and focused like a flashlight in the night on the track in front of him. The crowd disappearing and so to his opponent, bumping his way down the hill.

On tip-toe, Ryan craned and stretched to see Arkell bounce and bump down the track. The young man was in the lead he when took the first bend and made it around. Arkell made the first jump off the contour bank and the crowd cheered. Safe! Arkell approached the second bend, leaned into it, but he leaned too far, over-corrected, and ran off the course, crashing out. Ryan sprinted down the hill to where a dazed Arkell stood and watched his opponent roll by. Ryan clapped Arkell on the back before helping to drag the cart off the track. Race one went to Sully's Sports Bar.

Next up was Keysha against a team from Fletcher's Hardware. The driver was a young man in a steel frame cart that looked more like a motorised go-kart with suspension than a home-made billy cart. The advantage of having a hardware store behind the team was obvious.

Again, the starter raised the pistol. *Bang!* Keysha flew down the hill. Her friends from school yelling support. She was behind the young man when he hit a contour bank too fast and was bucked out of the cart. He landed heavily and rolled several meters down the hill. His cart flipped and rolled until it hit a tree. Keysha took her time and made it through the finish line a winner. Ryan cheered and hugged Bec. The team's first win. Race Three and race Four went by without incident. Then it was Sally's turn. She was racing against Tyler - fate. Bec and Ryan went with her to the start position. Michael Brooks hovered around Tyler like a blow fly around a sheep's dags.

Sally wheeled her cart into the start position beside Tyler. He smirked at her and said, "Hey sexy. Bet you ride Adam as well as you ride your cart. Oh, I forgot. Your boyfriend's a fag, haha."

Ryan stepped forward, but Bec grabbed his arm and held him tightly. Sally kept her cool, smiling sarcastically. Sally returned her gaze to the track in front of her, but Tyler leaned across and grabbed at the steering bracket of Sally's cart. This was too much for Ryan and he broke free of Bec's hold. Moving forward, Ryan called out, "Tyler, don't you touch that cart!"

IT ALL HAPPENED SO FAST and so innocently. Bec was surprised about what happened. Michael Brooks pushed his way towards Ryan, hand outstretched, pointing in accusation at Ryan. "I want that man removed! He assaulted my son at school. Abused his authority as a teacher. He shouldn't be here and I want him gone."

Bec saw Ryan's face flush red. Could this be any more embarrassing? Ryan faced his accuser. "I have done nothing wrong. Tyler has. I saw him trying to tamper with Sally's cart."

Jerry pushed through the crowd. "Now, Mr. Brooks, why don't you step over here and tell me what the problem is?"

Brooks replied, "I'll do no such thing. This man," he

pointed at Ryan again, "assaulted my son. He should have been arrested, but that weak blouse of a Principal, damn her, did nothing. Now look at what is happening – verbal abuse at a family event. It's a disgrace. A damned disgrace to the community!"

Jerry stood tall amongst the gathering crowd, and Bec wondered how Jerry managed to stay so calm. Jerry interjected, "Mr. Brooks, Janice Heartford informed the police of that incident and no charges were laid. Mr. Anderson is free to go where he pleases."

Brooks eyes began to bulge, "Then I'll press charges!"

The crowd began whispering and people exchanged confused looks. Bec looked around for any form of support. She saw Watson with his camera aimed at Ryan.

Jerry spoke to Tyler now. "Tyler, did Mr. Anderson hit you as you claimed to Miss Heartford? Be honest now."

All of a sudden, Tyler looked like the young boy he actually was. He was a kangaroo caught in the headlights looking from Jerry to his father. Bec almost thought the kid might tell the truth, but then Tyler nodded his head.

Jerry took a deep breath. "Ryan, I'd better take you down to the station. Sort this thing out." Bec could see the anger welling up in Ryan. She wanted to hold him, tell him it would be fine, but Ryan simply walked off with Jerry, shoulders slumped.

It was as if a glacier had split and fallen into the sea. The crowd erupted in a frenzy of gossip. Sally rushed up to Bec and said, "Why did they arrest Mr. Anderson? He didn't do anything!" Suddenly Bec was responsible for these teens. It frightened her, but she decided to her best.

Bec replied, "I don't think he's under arrest. But he did the right thing by going with the police. Now. The best thing to do is go and win that race." Sally nodded. Bec put on her best game face, but secretly, she was scared. Ryan of all people should not be the one answering questions from the police. A voice over the PA system tried to restore order. It took a full five minutes until the race could be started.

Putting her hands on Sally's shoulder and looking directly into the girl's eyes, Bec said, "The best thing you can do is beat Tyler Brooks. Now and go and race. That's what Mr Anderson would want."

Sally's face grew serious. She nodded, then ran off to her cart. The starter raised his pistol. *Bang!*

Sally sped off down the hill. She had a slight lead. Bec jumped up and down on the spot and clapped her hands. Tyler was right beside Sally, a quarter second too slow.

Sally took the first bend in the lead. She was still leading, but only by half a length. The first jump. Yes! The second bend – most people crashed out here. Yes! Still in the lead. The second bend. No! Sally lost control and the cart careened off the course, bumping off the track and over rocks and clumps of dirt. Tyler continued on his way and through the finish line. He got out of his cart and flung his arms up in victory.

24

R yan waved from his veranda as the last of his visitors drove off. All except one. He closed the front door and walked through to the kitchen where Bec sat nursing a cup of tea. Relief mixed with fatigue flooded her nervous system. Ryan was home.

Word of Ryan's 'arrest' had spread quickly. Mark arrived first at the police station. Tony and Paul soon followed, then the students came: Sally, Adam, Arkell, and Angela. After Ryan left the police station, his supporters had escorted him home.

Ryan hadn't actually been arrested. Jerry just took Ryan to the station to calm the situation. Janice had already informed the police of Tyler's accusation and Jerry called her to check on a few things. All said and done, the witnesses reported Tyler had threatened Ryan. On Monday, Ryan would be back in front of a classroom of teenagers.

Now at home, Ryan slumped on the sofa. "I could do with a coffee," he said. "I'm still in shock that Sally lost to Tyler." He grinned.

Bec shook her head. "I don't know how you can joke.

Michael Brooks is really out to get you." Incredulous, Bec wondered how Michael Brooks could be so blind to his son's darkness. Maybe every parent has that blind spot. Some more than others.

Lost in thought, she ran her fingers over the wooden discs of her necklace. They were smooth and soothing to the touch. She looked about the kitchen and dining area of Ryan's home, marveling at the quality of Ryan's renovations. The kitchen was stunning, yet reserved. Much like the man who built it.

Ryan put the water on to boil. He brushed passed Bec as he collected her cup and she caught the scent of his after-shave. Ryan bent down and pulled out a bag of coffee beans. Bec couldn't help but take in his form.

"These are from the Flat Rock Café. They have a great selection of beans." He opened a draw and pulled out his coffee mill. "A medium-fine grind should be about right." Bec stood close to Ryan as he measured the beans on a small digital scale. She went into the kitchen and stood beside him, enjoying the closeness. Ryan said, "Here. I'll show you what to do." Ryan talked through his process and assured her that she would 'get it' in no time.

He rolled up his sleeves as he tipped the beans into the hopper of his hand-mill. He started to grind the beans and Bec looked longingly at the muscles in his forearms. The aromatic small of the coffee reassured and excited her.

After a minute or so, Ryan stopped rotating the handle. He took out a coffee filter and said, "It's a good idea to wash the coffee filter. Gets rid of any paper taste and it sticks to the cone better." Ryan deftly washed the paper filter in sure movements. Next, he emptied the freshly ground coffee into the filter. The scent of the coffee was glorious. A wooden stand sat next to the sink. Ryan set the pour-over cone in the stand and a glass server underneath.

"Aren't you angry about the whole thing?" Bec asked. "I mean, the whole town thinks you hit a kid."

Ryan took the kettle off the boil. "I was at first, but when no one backed up Tyler's story, I knew there was nothing to worry about." Ryan put a small divet in the ground coffee, then poured some water in. He stopped after only a second or two. "Now we wait for half a minute. Here, you pour."

Bec took the kettle and said, "You sure? I don't want to ruin the system you've got going on here."

"Haha, you don't ruin my 'system.' You improve it." Ryan kissed her on the forehead. "I'm a little disappointed in Adam, though. I can't understand why he didn't call Tyler out."

Bec still held the kettle in one hand. "Maybe Tyler has something on him. Something embarrassing. Teenagers are pretty sensitive to that sort of thing."

"Yeah, I wish I knew what it was, then I could help." Ryan rubbed his jaw line with his thumb. "Now, pour slowly and in concentric circles. Don't let the water hit the paper filter. Go slow."

Bec followed Ryan's instructions. He stood behind her and guided her hand as she poured. He was gentle, yet firm. She felt warm and safe.

When the last of the water dripped out of the spout, Bec turned and embraced Ryan. "I've never kissed a jail-bird before." He kissed her, gently at first, then passionately took her lips. "Now you have."

Bec felt heat flush through her and Ryan's hands slid under her clothes and up her soft stomach. But Bec found herself breaking away from the kiss and putting both of her hands against Ryan's chest. What was wrong with her? She wanted this, didn't she? She was drawn to Ryan, yet something seized her on the brink and reefed her back.

"I'm sorry," Bec blurted out.

Ryan brushed her cheek with the back of his fingers and replied, "It's okay. If you're not ready for more, it's okay."

Bec looked down at her feet and Ryan side-stepped her. He filled two cups with coffee and added a dash of cream. "No need for sugar," he said. "This coffee will taste great all on its own." He smiled and went to the table on the other side of the kitchen counter. That simple movement gave Bec space to breathe. And think. What just happened? She was attracted to Ryan. She prompted the kiss, then backed away.

Confused feelings and thoughts swirled in Bec's mind, but she didn't want to leave. Ryan's presence was calming, so she joined him at the table. She sipped the coffee slowly. It was full, rich, and textured. "You make a great coffee, Ryan."

There was a twinkle in Ryan's eyes. Gallahs cackled in the distance and Ryan laughed. "I guess they know something we don't." The awkwardness past. Then Ryan surprised Bec. He said, "We should talk about sex. What our expectations are. I get that it's not easy after a tough relationship. I'm feeling a little vulnerable myself, if I'm totally honest."

Bec looked out the tall windows at the fading light. She sighed, "I don't know. I wasn't expecting to get cold feet, but, I don't know. Just give me some time."

Leaning across the table, Ryan took Bec's hand and said, "Time I can give."

25

It was late afternoon and heavy clouds brought darkness early. July had given way to August and early spring rains washed the streets of Brooksdale clean and flecks of green in the grass lawns began to show.

Bec had the afternoon and the next morning off so she decided to work from home – yes, even Bec worked on her days off. This was rare, though. In the weeks since the Billy-Cart Bash, Paul's Photography Studio had been booked solid, which meant Bec had worked nearly every day for the past three weeks. It seemed like every country couple wanted to get married in early spring. Too bad for her. Bec had barely seen Ryan. She hadn't even worked on the youth centre website, or online petition, and Ryan's presentation to the town council was only a few days away.

The pressure on the Youth Centre built, and to complicate matters, Phil had contacted her -a letter. She just threw it in the bin. Good bye and good riddance.

Bec closed her work laptop with a firm clack, moved to the kitchen and filled her wine glass. She thought about the last few days: a wedding, a maternity shoot, and a sweet sixteen. Plus, her entries to several photography competitions made her life insanely busy.

She took a long, thirsty gulp from her glass. Then there was Ryan. He had messaged her trying to set up another date, but she was never free when he was. Maybe it was best. The whole sex thing was still a little awkward. Was she ready, or wasn't she? How would she know? It's not like she was a virgin or anything. She wasn't embarrassed. She sipped at her wine again. Was she scared? She thought Phil was going to be the love of her life and look what happened. That was it: she didn't trust her feelings.

Keys click-clacked in the door and Jen came in. "It's freezing out there!" Jen said as she threw her keys into the bowl on the table and hung up her winter coat. "Spring is supposed to be here and I can't wait a day longer."

She paused when she saw Bec with a glass of wine in her hand.

"Relax," said Bec. It's my first one for the day."

Jen replied, "Less drink might be good for you. Or maybe more Ryan?" Bec pretended not to hear and poured a glass for Jen, who plopped down on the sofa. Bec's backpack was on the sofa, so Jen moved it. As she put it down, a half-empty vodka bottle rolled out and clinked on the wooden floor. Bec heard the sound and forced herself to keep moving naturally as she walked casually over to Jen. This could be bad.

Jen looked at the bottle, then looked Bec. Her eyes said it all. Accusations, recriminations, shame, and guilt. Bec was trapped. Halfway from the kitchen to the sofa with a glass of red in each hand, her sister's gaze locked onto her.

Bec said, "I just bought it and forgot about it."

Jen stood up. "Are you telling me you bought a half-empty bottle of vodka?" Jen used her teacher-tone and it was powerful. Bec had no words. She looked down at the glass of wine she had poured for Jen.

Jen folded her arms and said, "How long have you been hiding this?"

"Only a week or two." Bec didn't want to make it sound as if she had drank a half bottle in two days.

Jen's eyes narrowed. "Not this bottle. The drinking. Every night I come home and you're guzzling wine. Now I see you're sneaking more booze during the day. What am I supposed to think, huh?" Bec was caught and she felt like a guilty teen. There was only one course of action. Get angry back.

"It's so damn easy for you to stand there and judge, isn't it! Miss 'I have a career.' Looking after your washed-up sister. I bet that makes you feel great, doesn't it? Looking after your poor helpless sister." Bec's temper ran away with her. The boiler of her emotion was stoked and now she let Jen have a full blast of steam.

Bec's voice got louder and louder as she leveled accusation after accusation at her sister. "You must love all the attention, 'Oh Jennifer, she's so great. Looking after her sister like that.' It's just like when Dad died. You were the fucking hero of the family. Looking after Mum, making sure the house ran smoothly. What was I? I was the drop-kick. The waster. Well, let me tell you, Jennifer Williams, I loved Dad, too. I loved Mum, too. But I was out making something of myself, so I could make them proud." Bec didn't notice the tears running down Jen's face until it was much too late.

Jen's reply was low and quiet, "While you were out getting drunk and getting fucked by any boy who'd have you, I was at home helping Mum pick up the pieces of her life."

Bec was gut-punched. Fire ran through her veins

closely followed by ice. She spun on her heels and stalked into the kitchen, hurling the glasses into the sink. They smashed, splashing wine on the floor and across the counter-top.

"Bec, shit!" Jen cried. Bec paid no heed. She stormed across to her backpack, stuffed the vodka bottle in, grabbed her winter coat and wool hat, and left the apartment. She slammed the door as hard as she could and felt the bang vibrate into the corridor.

RYAN STILL HADN'T FIXED the clock in his truck, so he guessed it was somewhere around eight-thirty at night. He was driving home after a solid training session at the gym. His shoulder felt good and he enjoyed wearing his newly earned blue belt after months and months of being a white-belt.

It felt good to be physical and let all the stress of the past weeks come out, especially as he hadn't seen Bec in a while. He wondered if he shouldn't have talked about sex the way he had the last time she was at his place, after the Billy-Cart Bash. Thick drops of rain began to fall, thumping on the roof of the car and splattering the windshield. Ryan slowed so he could see the road better. He saw a woman stumble on the side of the road. He slowed and realized it was Bec walking along Main Street – stumbling would be a better description. She tripped and fell. Worried, Ryan pulled over and got out of his truck.

"Hi Bec, are you alright?" Bec pulled herself to her feet, staggered, then focused on Ryan. She had a bottle of vodka in one hand. "Shit. What happened to you? I'll take you home," Ryan said.

Bec swayed as the wind gusted and rain drops splatted

onto her face. "No! I don-wanna-see Jen." She stumbled and Ryan rushed forward, catching her just in time.

"Whew! Your breath could fuel an ocean-liner," said Ryan as he helped Bec into the passenger seat of his truck. "I'll take you back to Jen's place.

Bec yelled, "No! Not goin.'" Then, "Gonna be sick." She flopped out of the truck using Ryan to lean on, then vomited on the foot path.

The sound and smell of someone throwing up is the most reliable way to induce vomiting in the onlooker. Ryan held Bec's arm for support.

"Finished," said, and she got back into the Ford. Ryan closed her door and wondered what he was going to do. Take her back to his place?

Ten-minutes later, Bec's head rested against the passenger window of Ryan's truck – passed-out. Ryan pulled into his driveway and carried her from his truck to the spare bedroom of his house. He tucked her into the bed, put a bucket beside her, and went out. This wasn't what he had imagined as a reunion with Bec.

He decided to call Jen and let her know where Bec was and that she was safe. "Hi. Jen? It's Ryan. Bec's over here."

Jen sounded drunk and angry. She certainly wasn't making a lot of sense, so Ryan hung up, figuring the sisters had had a big fight and both of them needed to sleep it off. He'd try again tomorrow. In the mean time, Bec would be safe at his place.

26

The next day, the first Sunday of August, Ryan rapped gently on the door of the spare bedroom. Bec had been asleep for twelve-hours, and Ryan worried about her. There was no response to his knocks, so he opened the door and peered in. Bec slept soundly. She reminded him of a bird tucked safely in its nest. She was beautiful.

Ryan stepped into the bedroom and pulled back the curtains, letting sunlight fill the room. It had rained heavily last night and the world outside shined with reflected sunlight. Clean and wholesome. He returned to the kitchen and began making coffee. He boiled the water and ground the beans in his hand-mill.

BEC WOKE with sunlight on her face and the smell of coffee surrounding her. Thank goodness for that coffee smell, because she had a killer headache.

She looked around the room. *Where am I?* Panic burst in her stomach like a water-filled balloon breaking on the street. She stayed under the covers and ran her hands over her body. All her clothes were in place on her body. Had she crawled? There was no pain and no bruising, well aside from the pounding headache.

Bec sat up. Her winter coat was draped over the end of the bed and her socks were rolled and placed neatly on the floor. Swinging her legs off the bed, she knocked the bucket over with a clatter. No spew, lucky. She slipped on her socks and followed the smell of coffee to the kitchen. It didn't take her long to realize where she was.

Ryan stood at the counter in a pair of blue jeans and a white t-shirt. Bec took a moment to take in Ryan's physique. His well-developed arms moved rhythmically as he poured hot water into a coffee cone.

RYAN SENSED SOMEONE WATCHING HIM. He looked up and saw Bec standing at the corner of the hallway. Her hair was messed up and she looked pale, as if she had a bad cold.

"Morning," he said. "You look like crap."

"Thanks." Bec's voice was raspy. It sounded like she had spent the night singing karaoke and smoking cigars. Ryan handed her a glass of water. She took it and gulped the water down. When she finished, Ryan explained briefly what had happened last night. Bec nodded her head, but Ryan wondered how much she really remembered.

"There's a fresh towel in the bathroom and some clothes. Nothing your size, I'm afraid, but they'll cover you up until the laundry is finished."

"Thank you," said Bec and she walked back down the hallway to find the bathroom.

"Last door on the left!" called Ryan.

. . .

BEC RAN the shower and the room was soon full of steam, blessed steam. She stripped off her clothes. She could smell the sweat and booze on them and something else, vomit. *I hope he didn't see me throw up.*

She stepped into the shower and let the hot water run over her body. The steam helped clear her head. She stood there, under the stream of water, like a horse weathering in the rain. Funny, her first night at another man's house and nothing happened.

When she got out, she found two white towels on the vanity. They were soft and fluffy. They felt good on her skin. Who'd have thought a man like Ryan would add softener to his laundry. There was a pile of clothes neatly folded. She put them on and laughed. The flannel shirt hung down to her knees and the jeans were baggy like clown pants. She felt like a little kid playing dress-up with her wood-cutter father's clothes.

She ambled out to the kitchen. Ryan looked up and smiled. Bec melted inside. The sight of Ryan standing barefoot in tight jeans and white t-shirt, in a beautiful kitchen, with coffee ready, was just too much for her hungover mind.

A beautiful red-cedar table sat between the kitchen counter and a floor to wall glass doors that opened out onto a patio. Bec sat at the table, and Ryan place a steaming hot coffee in front of her. Bec smiled, thanked Ryan and said, "I've been a bit silly, haven't I?"

Ryan sat opposite her with a coffee of his own. Bec looked into his face. His clear blue eyes settled on her and she felt safe. He said, "You'll need to talk to Jen about whatever happened."

"No. I mean you and me. I shouldn't have given you the cold shoulder. I'm Sorry."

Ryan nodded.

Bec sipped her coffee. "Do you have any brothers or sisters?"

"Yeah, a brother, Dennis. He moved down to Sydney a while back."

Ryan sipped his coffee. "Do you have to be at work today?"

Bec shook her head. She hoped Ryan had a plan up his sleeve. She wasn't ready to go back to Jen's place, even if Jen wasn't there.

A smile crept onto Ryan's face and he said, "I've got something I want to show you. Actually, it's a place. With this rain, it will be a sight."

After putting her dirty clothes in the washing machine, she followed Ryan outside and hopped up into the passenger seat of his truck. She said, "This wasn't the type of date I was thinking of," she quipped.

Ryan smiled at her and replied, "Sometimes you just have to let chance spin the wheel." It was a sentiment that went straight to Bec's heart.

RYAN DROVE DOWN A SMALL, bumpy dirt road that lead towards the river. The road opened out into a small car park. Ryan's Ford splashed through puddles and Bec felt like she was on a safari. Ryan was glad that Bec had agreed to go with him. This was a beautiful place at any time of year, but more so now given the rain.

They got out and their boots squished and squashed in the mud. Water droplets still clung to the leaves of the eucalyptus trees. The smell of fresh vegetation and budding blossoms filled the air like perfume.

Ryan looked at Bec. Her eyes were bright as she surveyed the area. A huge grin spread across her face. She reminded him of a kid walking into an amusement park for the first time. Ryan was glad that she found joy in this place. He took Bec's hand and lead her down a windy path to the river bank. Steam rose from the river's black surface, and willow trees reached over the water's edge. It could have been a scene from an old black and white film. Ryan squeezed Bec's hand and she returned his grip. Ryan's heart beat a little faster.

Bec was in awe of this place. What had been a cold, moistureless winter with dry browns dominating every garden and every natural area, was bursting in greenness in such a short time. Life was full of surprises.

But what struck Bec the most was the noise. Birds chirped and shared their songs. Insects were out in numbers and frogs croaked. It was as if she had stepped into nature`s opera. Bec's photographer's eye noticed everything, a fluttering in the trees, a fish jumping in the river, and the ripples in the water when a frog jumped. The interesting shadows cast by the trees.

She noticed Ryan. His even breath, confident stride, and his strong hand holding hers. Yes, it was a bit juvenile, but it touched her. It gave her connection.

She pulled Ryan close and faced him. He looked at her with those clear blue eyes and some pink on his cheeks from the coolness. She leaned into him and he responded. She kissed him gently on the lips. At first it was cold, but as they held each other, they embraced, and the kiss grew warmer.

· · ·

RYAN PULLED AWAY FIRST. He wasn't expecting a kiss today, but he certainly was glad it had happened. He looked at the beautiful woman in front of him who was dressed in his over-sized winter coat, jeans, and shirt, and an old wool cap that engulfed her head. She looked so sexy and the kiss had aroused deep sensual feelings.

Bec wandered along the river bank. It was as if they were the only two people left in the world. After ten minutes of exploring, the couple walked back to the truck. The cold was making itself known and Ryan cranked the heat in the truck as he drove Bec back to his place. A curious feeling of anticipation, please, and relief warmed his heart.

Bec's washing was finished and she changed. As she closed the door to the spare room, she winked at Ryan and said, "A kiss doesn't give you permission for anything else, you know."

Ryan thought she might have been teasing and considered pursuing her. Instead, he smiled sheepishly and played on Shakespeare's famous line, "Shall I compare thee to a winter's morning?"

"Points for originality!" Came the reply from behind the closed door, and closed it remained.

27

The sun was out and the sky had crisp blue to it that said no rain. Ryan walked Bec to the door of Jen's flat. They had walked from Ryan's house because Bec wanted exercise to help clear her hangover. Ryan felt good walking with her, he had someone to care for and share his town with.

It was just after midday when they arrived and Bec had to be at work at one o'clock. "Thank you for taking care of me," said Bec. "And for showing me that spot by the river. It really was beautiful."

This time, Ryan leaned in and kissed Bec. When he broke away, she was smiling and she took both of his hands. "Would you like to come over for dinner Friday? I'm busy with photo shoots until then."

"No..."

"Hey. I understand..."

Ryan smiled, "No. I didn't finish. Come to my place. I'll cook."

"It's a date." Bec kissed him on the lips then went inside.

Ryan tried to stay cool, but underneath he was giddy.

Bec was a gorgeous, intelligent woman and things were moving for him.

Feeling lighter than air, he went back out onto the street and strolled leisurely back home. He only paid passing attention to the black Hyundai parked on the street opposite Jen's flat.

INSIDE THE FLAT, Bec stood in the middle of a disaster zone. What had Jen been doing last night? *No.* Bec caught herself. *Jen always cleans up.* Today was Bec's turn. She had thirty minutes before having to go to work. She put clothes away, cleaned up broken glass, took a bin full of empty wine bottles out to the recycling, and threw a bunch of clothes into the washing machine before she left for work.

BEC DIDN'T GET HOME until well into the early hours of the morning because of the photo shoot. So the next morning, Bec awoke to the sound of the TV blaring. It was eleven in the morning and Jen was in the kitchen, spatula in hand.

"Hi Jen."

No reply.

She tried again, louder. "Jen!"

Jen pursed her lips and focused more intently on her cooking.

The smell was enticing and Bec felt good – no trace of hangover. She had only drunk a couple of beers last night. She was serious about taking good photos. She looked at the food laid out on the kitchen counter. "Mmmm. Tacos?"

Jen replied curtly, "Yeah. Pork and cabbage."

Bec opened the fridge. There was no wine and she hadn't bought a replacement bottle of vodka. *Water it is.* Bec leaned her back against the fridge and said, "Listen, Jen. I'm sorry about the other night."

No reply.

Bec continued, "I was in the wrong. I shouldn't have gotten so drunk."

Jen started chopping cabbage.

"C'mon Jen. We're sisters. It's been a tough time. It's not like I'm an alcoholic or anything."

The sound of chopping stopped. Jen looked over her shoulder at Bec and said, "Prove it. No more hiding alcohol and no alcohol for a week."

Bec massaged her fingers nervously, like a toddler trying to explain how the milk ended up on the floor. Jen pushed, "Prove you're not an alcoholic. It's only a week." She went back to chopping.

Her vulnerability suddenly felt exposed, Bec felt as if she were in a fish bowl and each tap of that knife was like some kid thumping on the glass of her life. Now or never. "Done. No alcohol until *Friday* night," replied Bec.

The chopping stopped. Jen spun around and embraced Bec. "I know you can do it!" Bec blushed in response and secretly hoped Jen was right.

Once the cooking was done, the sisters sat down to a wonderful spread of tacos and salad, but Bec fidgeted. She felt the need for a glass in her hand. Jen must have noticed, because she made herbal tea and sat a cup down in front of Bec. "I've just discovered these," Jen said. "I've been trying to kick caffeine at work, so I've been trying camomile and spearmint tea. I'm down from four coffees a day to two."

Bec sipped the tea. As she raised the cup to her mouth, the spearmint wafted into her nose and relaxed her before she even took a drink. Maybe this would help, if she were an alcoholic, which she wasn't.

Jen leaned forward, put her elbows on the table and asked, "So, tell me about your new boyfriend." A cheeky grin on her lips.

"Ryan?" Bec put down the taco she was about to devour. "He's not really my boyfriend, yet. I guess you could say we're 'dating', though. Bec sighed and continued, "I don't know if he's good for me or not. He seems like the marrying kind, and I'm not ready for that."

Jen sipped her tea and replied, "So you keep saying, but look at you. You've changed so much since you got here. No," Jen waved her hand in the air as if she was erasing the words from an invisible whiteboard. "You're the woman you were before you moved to Brisbane with that jerk, Phil."

"You think so? I feel a lot more in control of my life, and I don't want to get stuck again," replied Bec.

It was Jen's turn to giggle, but there was a serious edge to it. Jen said, "You think settling here is being 'stuck?' Well, maybe it is, but I like it."

Bec saw her gaff, "No. Not you, Jen. I can see this place and your work make you happy. It fits you. But I'm not ready to settle down. I want to pursue my art. I want to be the best photographer I can be and that means traveling around. Ryan wouldn't go for that. That just leaves 'casual fling', and I'm just not ready for that either."

Jen put her glass down and it clanked on the wooden table. "So where does that leave Ryan?"

Bec ran her fingers through her hair. "I don't know. I like him. I really like him. He's gentle, confident, and sexy in a carpenter-academic kind of way. A lot of guys seem to have this thing they're trying to prove, like they need to show their manhood, but the more they try the weaker they seem. Ryan doesn't have that. It's like he's achieved everything he's set out to do already."

Jen nodded in agreement. "It's funny. I see the exact same thing with the boys at school as they come out of puberty. Men are forever boys." Jen laughed then added, "But I don't think he's achieved everything, yet." She winked.

Bec said, "Listen to us. It seems like we've reverted back to our high school-selves." Jen laughed. It was a wonderful sound. The sound of family. Bec thought back to those teenage years. In school when she was always getting into trouble with boys, booze, and grades. Especially after her father died. It was Jen who stayed level-headed. Most of the time, anyway. Bec smiled at the memories. "Remember when Mum caught me with William Harvey in my bedroom?"

Jen laughed out loud. "How could I forget! He was halfway out the window when she stormed in."

Bec retorted, "You weren't always so innocent yourself. I seem to remember *you* sneaking *into* the house after spending the night with Liam Graham."

Jen chuckled, "Oh God, if Mum and Dad ever found out, they'd kill me and skin Liam." The sisters fell quiet. Both aware that Jen had talked about their parents as if they were still alive.

Bec broke the silence, "Do you miss Dad?"

"Yeah," Jen sighed.

So did Bec. "It's the scents, you know. The faint scent of wood shavings or varnish..." She trailed off, immersed in memories.

Jen's eyes moistened. "I know. If he wasn't playing with his cameras, he was fooling with saws and drills and things. Haha! Seems silly now."

Bec asked, "I wonder what Mum thought of it all?"

"I'm sure she loved him for it. She loved you, too. Especially for your photography."

Bec scowled. "How would you know that?"

"She told me. She often talked about you."

The revelation struck Bec hard. She peered into her tea and a tear rolled down her cheek. Jen was older and had to take on more responsibility after their father died. To top it off, Bec had run wild and wasn't there right at the end for her mother, or Jen.

Jen moved to the chair next to Bec and put an arm around her. "It's okay. Things will work out. We were all too young to deal properly with losing Dad, then only a few years later Mum." Bec felt the warmth of Jen's arm around her and leaned into her sister. She missed her father. She missed her mother, but she understood completely how lucky she was to have a sister like Jen. Bec wiped her tears with her sleeve and returned Jen's hug.

28

"And after that, hit print," said Bec, as Adam Lee sat next to her in the backroom of Paul's Photography Studio. They were crammed among computers, printers, and stacks of photos where all the editing, printing, and framing was done.

Friday afternoon - was working out well as a part-time trainee. He was smart, hard-working, and asked a lot of good questions. He already knew his way around Photoshop and he began assisting in studio shoots recently. Bec had put him to work on the school photos. She was determined to make waves by getting the photos done in record time. As he worked through the photos, Adam shifted uncomfortably in his seat.

He asked, "Miss Williams, did you ever feel like you couldn't tell your parents something?"

"I keep telling you to call me Bec, or Rebecca. And yes. I fought a lot with my parents when I was your age. It's a pretty normal thing to go through." Bec smiled. Her eyes wandered to the clock. "Shit, I've gotta go. Adam, can you

package those prints after they come out?" Adam said he
would and Bec rushed off to get ready for dinner with Ryan.

SWEAT BEADED on Ryan's forehead as he stirred the peppercorn sauce. Two steaks rested on a chopping board and the
vegetables were nearly done roasting when there was a
knock at the door. "Just a minute!" Ryan moved the sauce off
the heat, wiped his hands with a towel and went to the door.

"Wow! You look great. Come in," said Ryan as he held
the door open for Bec. And he wasn't just being polite. Bec
looked stunning in slacks that accentuated the curves of her
hips and wool jumper that revealed her neck line.

She walked through to the open kitchen – dining area
and took a seat at the table. "Smells good! What are we
having?"

"Steak, peppercorn sauce, and roasted vegetables,"
replied Ryan as he got back to stirring the sauce. "Help yourself to a glass of wine. Everything's on the table."

Bec had seen the wine as soon as she entered the room,
but decided not to touch it until they started eating.

Instead, she hugged Ryan. "How is school going now
that Tyler has been moved to a different class?"

"A mix of feelings. In one sense, I should have been able
to get through to him. Teachers are supposed to teach *all*
their students, but things are much better with him out of
my class." He bent down to the oven and pulled out the
vegetables. He poked at them with a fork. "They'll do," he
said. "Now go and sit down. You're my guest tonight." Ryan
watched as Bec went back to the table. There was a little
sway in her walk and Ryan found it appealing.

"Dinner is served!" Ryan announced. He put the plates
down on the table with a gentle *clack*. The vegetables and

spices had a wonderful aroma that filled the room with anticipation.

Ryan poured two glasses of red. Bec and Ryan clinked glasses and held eye contact as they drank, and he couldn't look away. Bec's fork pierced the steak and juice flowed out. "How did you know I liked medium-rare?"

Ryan simply grinned. Bec put the steak in her mouth. It was delicious and the peppercorn sauce was the perfect complement to it. She tried the roast vegetables. Crisp on the outside and soft inside. "You've done a wonderful job, Ryan."

"Thanks. I think good food is important. In this age of rushing here and there, we've lost something – as a society I mean."

Bec raised her glass. "To good food!" Ryan joined her in the toast and they drained their glasses.

The time slipped by in easy conversation. When Bec finished the last roast potato, Ryan announced, "Dessert!" He went to the kitchen and returned with a sticky-date pudding. The sweet smell was divine.

Bec's spoon broke the crust of the pudding and the sweet sauce enveloped it. She lifted the spoon to her mouth and closed her eyes. Ryan felt pleased she derived so much pleasure from his cooking. A dribble of sweet sauce found its way onto Bec's chin. She raised her eyebrows in surprise and wiped it with her little finger.

"I'll clean these plates up," said Ryan. He stood and stacked the dishes. In the kitchen, Ryan ran hot water over the plates and stacked the dishwasher. He wanted to kiss Bec, to hold her, and he was keenly aware of her presence as she entered the kitchen carrying the salt and pepper. She slid her hand across his lower back and Ryan wondered if now was the time to make a move. *Be confident!*

. . .

BEC STOOD close to Ryan with one hand on the small of his back and the other holding salt and pepper shakers. She put the shakers down and felt the need for physical intimacy. Slipping between Ryan and the sink, she thought there would be no-way Ryan could misinterpret her intention. She was not wrong.

Ryan kissed her gently at first, then more passionately. She felt herself respond and he embraced her tightly. She felt protected, safe, and desire washed over her. She pulled at Ryan's shirt while his hands swept over her chin, neck, then reached down. She ripped Ryan's shirt off and over his head, leaving him in a tight undershirt that showed his lean physique. Ryan's hands caressed her and she fumbled with Ryan's belt. It came loose and his jeans fell to the floor. The belt buckle clattered on the wooden floor.

In a fit of passion, Bec pushed Ryan against the kitchen counter, knocking over some glasses that stood waiting to be washed. They splintered on the floor and Ryan said, "Don't stop. I don't care about the glasses. He lifted her in his arms and stepped over the shards of glass, carrying her to the bedroom.

When she landed on the bed, the coolness of the dooner sent an electric shiver through her body. Ryan collapsed into her and she welcomed him in a thirst for intimacy.

29

B y the middle of August morning frosts had lessened, and for the first time, Bec didn't need her winter coat. She stood in the reception area of Brooksdale High School with boxes stacked on a trolley that were full of student photos. Working with Adam, the photos had been done in record time. When Paul found out, he was furious. "What am I supposed to do next year! Now everyone will expect their photos done in a couple of weeks," he had yelled. But, Bec calmed him down, and in the end, got the job of delivering the photos.

As she approached the reception window, Bec felt confident and relaxed. Gone were the feelings of anxiety she had experienced that first time she visited the school. In fact, Bec was as happy as she had ever been. Her relationship with Ryan was going well. Her worries that sex would change things were unfounded. In fact, things were better. Bec hoped she could catch Ryan before she left the school and set up a little date. She had news to share.

"Yes. Can I help you?" It was Delores Mayfield. Her eyebrows were arched and lips pursed.

Bec discretely cleared her throat before answering. She felt the need to have a strong voice. The town watched. "I'm here to deliver the school photos."

Delores' face softened, "Ah, Rebecca Williams. I thought I recognized you. Changed your hair, have you?"

Bec involuntarily touched her hair as she replied, "Just back to my natural colour."

"Well, it suits you, dear." Delores left the office and joined Bec in the reception area. She said, "So, you're the woman who has put a spring back into our Mr Anderson's step." Bec felt heat rise in her cheeks as she thought about everyone knowing her personal life details. Delores continued, "How lovely for Ryan to be dating such an attractive and talented woman."

Bec laughed uncomfortably, trying to deflect the praise. She replied, "Well, I don't know about that."

"No? Well I *do* know that *you* are certainly lucky to have found a man like Ryan Anderson." Delores reached out a hand decorated with several gold and diamond rings. Bec stiffened, but Delores said, "Relax dear. I've heard good things about you. But you should know, Ryan's a man who takes commitment seriously. Not like his brother at all!"

Delores removed her glasses, letting them hang from the pretty, silver chain that held them around her neck. She continued, "You could hardly do better than Ryan Anderson. I'll call up to Ryan's office – see if he's free to come down."

Delores giggled and grabbed a firm hold on the bar of the trolley with the photos stacked on. For an old lady, she certainly had a lot of energy. All Bec could do was hold the door open as Delores charged forward.

.   .   .

RYAN ARRIVED at reception as Bec finished stacking the boxes in a corner by the photocopier. He saw Bec straining to straighten the boxes and took a moment to enjoy her physicality. She would do well in BJJ. "This is a pleasant surprise," said Ryan to announce his presence.

"Quit staring," retorted Bec.

Delores chuckled. "You have found a wonderful woman, Ryan." Ryan and Bec held each other's gaze, but were interrupted by a loud sigh from Delores. "How is the Youth Centre going?" she asked. Crafty Delores. She could observe the new romance in town *and* get the gossip on the drama of the Youth Centre.

Ryan replied, "As to be expected. Brooks is publishing stuff in the local paper about how the money they'll save from cutting the Youth Centre will be used in other ways; more jobs and less taxes apparently."

Delores nodded knowingly. "Well, I don't know about that stuff, but I know kids need a place to be kids."

With a grim smile, Ryan said, "Don't worry Delores. I'm not giving up. I'm presenting to the council on Wednesday, just before they make a decision." Satisfied with his answer, Delores patted Ryan's hand again and returned to her desk where she shuffled papers.

Ryan looked at Bec. She looked great. He said, "I've got a meeting from four. I should be home around five-thirty. Do you want to come over for dinner?"

"Actually. I've got some news," replied Bec.

"Now I'm intrigued."

"How about I go to your place and I cook. A little celebration." Bec glanced at Delores and added, "Just the two of us."

Ryan grinned. He put his hand in his pocket and pulled out a key fob. "Here's the house key. Can't wait!" Ryan handed over the key, gave Bec a gentle squeeze on the arm, and left for his meeting.

AT FIVE-THIRTY-FIVE THAT AFTERNOON, Ryan left the staff meeting with Mark and Donita beside him.

As they walked through the corridors toward the car park, Ryan said, "I find it hard to believe Tyler Brooks' grades have improved that much."

Mark added, "He's certainly the same lazy, disruptive, impudent child he's always been in my class."

Donita put her hands on her hips and stopped in front of a bank of lockers. Ryan and Mark turned to face her. She said, "Same with me. You can't tell me his turn around is just because of a teacher change – Ryan to Lewis Jones."

Ryan rubbed his chin with his thumb. "I'm sure something is going on between Tyler and Adam, too. Tyler's grades are improving and Adams are falling."

Mark nodded seriously, "Inversely proportional."

Donita said, "I've noticed it, too. Adam's withdrawn and he's just doing the bare minimum. He used to be at the top of the class."

Lewis Jones, another English Teacher in Ryan's department, came down the corridor. "Good news about Tyler, eh? Amazing what the right teacher for the right student can do." He grinned smugly and gave Ryan an awkward 'bro' punch on the shoulder. There was a strained silence, then Lewis continued his way down the corridor.

"Weird," said Donita.

"Yeah. He's gunning for the Head of Department job," said Ryan.

"Surely he won't get it over you!" Mark exclaimed. Two

months ago, Ryan would have thought he was a shoe-in for the job. Now, he wasn't so sure.

BEC LOOKED up at the clock. It was just after six and Ryan was late. *Meeting probably ran over.* The chicken meatballs were going cold in their tomato sauce. The smell of basil and tomato still hung in the air. After work, Bec had slipped into her slim-fit jeans and a blouse that had a neck line that would be hard to resist. She had her hair up. A knock at the door gave her a start, then realized it must be Ryan, since he gave her his house key. Bec went to the door and unlocked it.

"Trying to lock me out of my own house, eh?" Ryan stepped forward and kissed her. His lips were cold from being outside, yet his presence warmed her. His eyes swept over her. "I didn't realize I was supposed to get dressed up. You look wonderful."

Brushing a strand of hair over her ear, Bec replied, "Hurry up. You're letting the chill in."

Ryan stepped inside, removed his shoes in the entranceway and said, "Something smells great. Pasta?"

"Trust a man and his stomach. Chicken meatballs, to be precise. You're late, so they may not be the best." Bec went ahead to the kitchen and put the pasta on. "This will be another fifteen minutes. How about you make me a coffee while we wait?"

"Unconventional. Coffee before pasta, but I'll do it."

Jets of steam erupted from the pot on the stove and Bec dropped the pasta in. Ryan rolled up his sleeves and began making the coffee. Bec watched as he ground the beans. His forearm flexed and a calm concentration descended over his face. The aroma of coffee soon competed with the tomato and basil for dominance in the kitchen. It was intoxicating.

Bec reflected back over the past few months: life had changed so much and although Brooksdale was less glamorous than Brisbane, Bec felt happy and secure here. As she watched Ryan pouring hot water in concentric circles into the coffee cone, Bec wondered what it would be like if she settled down in Brooksdale. And why not? Her sister was here, she had a job in photography, and she had met a wonderful man.

"You all right? Looks like you zoned out for a moment," said Ryan as he handed Bec her coffee.

In reply, she looped her free hand around Ryan's tight waist and kissed him gently on the cheek. "I'm fine, just fine."

TEN MINUTES LATER, Ryan and Bec were sitting down at the table to chicken meatballs and pasta. A bottle of red sat unopened on the table. Bec skewered a meatball and popped it in her mouth. The balance between texture, tomato, and basil was excellent, even if she thought so herself. The whole evening had been excellent. Now for her big news. Bec sat a little straighter and tried to suppress a grin. "I won a contest. A photography contest."

Putting down his fork, Ryan's eyes lit up with excitement. He said, "That's great news! What was the competition?"

"*Photo Boss Magazine*." Ryan looked blank, so she guessed he hadn't heard of it – it didn't matter. Bec continued, "It's a big online magazine. They're based in Bathurst. My photo will get published in their next issue. Do you want to know which photo it was?"

Ryan scratched his head. Bec let him sweat, then she

gave him the answer. "Do you remember our second date? The one to Uriah Brooks' House?"

"How could I forget?"

"Well. One of the photos of Uriah Brooks' House won!"

Ryan grabbed the bottle of wine and opened it. "Well, I guess we need to celebrate."

Bec went to the kitchen and got two wine glasses. She handed them to Ryan, who poured the wine.

"Cheers to success!" cried Ryan. They clinked glasses and drank while holding each other's gaze.

Bec was delighted. Could there be a better way to enjoy a victory than this? Perhaps there was. Ryan put down his glass and swept Bec up in a hug. He twirled her around, just like in an old black and white romance film. He kissed her on the lips and she kissed him back, losing herself in the moment. Ryan ran his hands through her hair and pulled out the pin holding it in place. Her dark hair fell around her shoulders and Bec intensified her kiss. She ran her hands underneath Ryan's shirt and felt the firmness of his chest. She wanted him right there. She pressed hard against him.

Ryan lifted her up and took her in a firm embrace. He carried her into the master bedroom and they collapsed on the soft comforter that covered Ryan's King-sized bed. Bec gasped as Ryan's hands brushed along her stomach. Then he unbuttoned his shirt. She was not so careful, though. Bec ripped Ryan's shirt open and the buttons popped off.

"Hey, that's one of my best shirts," Ryan said in mock horror.

"Fix it later," Bec said.

They made love, passionately, desperately.

Afterwards, Bec and Ryan lay next to each other, holding hands and breathing heavily. "Dinner will be getting cold," said Ryan." Bec laughed, sat up, and pulled on her clothes.

Ryan did likewise, except he pulled on a new shirt. One with all the buttons on.

"Do you think you'll stay in Brooksdale forever?" Bec asked as Ryan put Bec's pasta into the microwave.

"Mum's here. My friends are here. My job is here. *You're* here. So yeah, I guess I'm a lifer of Brooksdale." The microwave beeped and Ryan took out Bec's plate and sat it in front of her.

She looked at Ryan, at his quiet confidence. He had changed since she first met him. Perhaps Brooksdale *was* a good place.

Ryan put his plate into the microwave, but Bec cuddled him from behind and nibbled at his ear. "Not yet," she whispered into his ear. She led Ryan back to the bedroom and they fell into each other's arms once again.

30

The Brooksdale Council Chambers sat in a modern building across the road from the court house on Main Street. The court house was an old brick building with a white façade and hard-wood interior. In contrast, the Council Chambers was steel and glass. The meeting room that Ryan found himself in was furnished with a pine-coloured conference table and new black office chairs. Most of the council members were present tonight, the last Wednesday in August.

Ryan knew most of them; Steven James, Thomas Fletcher, Gene Lewis, Michelle Partridge, Paul Jeffereies, Josephine Brumsfield, Adeline Greene, Benjamin Burnside, and Travis Timson. Greg Lee was absent, but Ryan wished he was there. He knew Adam's father would support the Youth Centre cause.

Finally, Michael Brooks sat at the head of the conference table. Ryan knew this man wanted to funnel more funds into the chamber of commerce and from there into his own business dealings.

It didn't matter. Tonight was his night. The night when

community trumped self-interested business. Ryan waited patiently but confidently for his turn to address the council members. He had been preparing for this moment for a long time. He intended to ask for an increase in funds for the Youth Centre, not just the maintenance of the budget. He counted off the people he thought would support his request; Adeline Greene, probably Gene Lewis and Michele Partridge, and possibly Benjamin Burnside. That was four. Damn. He really needed Adam Lee tonight.

Surely once the members heard his case for an increase in funding they would understand. Students who participated in after school programs typically graduated high school and went on to further studies. There were less juvenile delinquency cases, and participants' attendance at school was higher than those students who did not attend after school activities. It was a win for everyone.

At last, it was Ryan's turn to address the councillors. He stood confidently before the council members and looked each one in the eye as he spoke. "Ladies and gentlemen of the council, I'm here tonight to ask that you: do not cut the Youth Centre's budget."

Some notes passed around the table from council member to council member like bored kids in Ryan's class. Some council members looked through their budget papers. Michael Brooks yawned, whilst Steven James whispered softly to Travis Timson, but the rest seemed to be listening.

Flutters of nerves rolled through Ryan and his confidence flagged, but he kept his focus. "The Youth Centre provides an invaluable resource to this town's young people. The centre keeps youths off the streets after school and provides a place for students to study on weekends. To cut funding would be to hurt our citizens in their most vulnerable years." A bark of laughter from Steven and Timson punctured Ryan's speech. He clenched his fists and continued, "The centre already does a lot on a small budget and with only a negligible increase, a lot more can be done."

Brooks interrupted, "Like the Billy Cart Bash? The one where you were arrested?"

Adeline Greene interjected, "I think this needs clarification; Ryan was not arrested. No charges were-"

"Oh, come on! He was taken away by the cops. If that's not arrested, then I don't know what is." Brooks leaned across conspiratorially and whispered to Steven James, who nodded and smiled gleefully. Fighting down the desire to unleash a verbal tirade at Brooks, Ryan clenched and unclenched his fists. Josephine Brumsfield gestured for Ryan to continue. He directed the councillors to the Youth Centre's budget and the accomplishments for the year.

Another interruption, this time from Timson, "We know all this. Move on."

"Right. The petition, then." Ryan reached into a box he had on the floor and pulled out a pile of papers. He dumped them on the table with a thud. The glasses of water rattled from the vibration.

"6223 people signed the petition. That's a lot of people who want the Youth Centre funded properly."

Ryan glanced around. Fletcher and Burnside nodded. Adeline said, "That's a lot of people. More than who make use of the centre."

"Yes. Yes, but not a majority of our population. Which would only matter if the issue were up for a referendum; which it isn't." Michael Brooks rubbed his eyes. He looked like a condescending parent trying to explain a difficult math problem to a child. "Mr. Anderson, you were invited here as a courtesy to the community. Now stop wasting our time. We're going to vote. Wait outside."

Ryan ran his thumb over his jaw line. "I haven't finished my presentation."

Steven James spoke, "Ryan, come on buddy. You've had your turn. Councillors are busy. Wait outside." Ryan looked about the room, saw the tide had turned, then walked outside.

The double wooden doors closed heavily behind him and he took a seat on a cheap sofa with a view of the court house across the street. He knew the outcome.

Bec waited anxiously at Ryan's place. She felt the same anxiety as Ryan. She had seen the value of the Youth Centre and felt proud to have been involved, if only in a minor way. The TV was on, but she paid no mind to it. She had her work laptop out and tried to keep herself occupied by editing photos.

She heard the jingle of keys in the front door. Ryan walked through the door. He walked heavily with his shoulders bent under an invisible weight. He looked at Bec and shook his head.

"What happened?" Bec asked.

"They voted for a cut in the budget and the sale of the land. We've got one more year of operation and with what they're giving us, we'll have to cut back to three days a week. The Youth Centre is dead."

That was bad news and Bec felt Ryan's disappointment. She went to him, hugged him, and kissed him gently.

She put her hand against his cheek. "I'm proud of you. You did all you could. You didn't let anyone down."

"Hmmph. You'd better kiss me to prove it." At least he hadn't lost his sense of humour. Bec kissed him gently at first, then passionately as she led him to the bedroom.

31

On her hands and knees under the dining table, Bec picked up the papers that had been blown off and scattered across the floor and she needed to find a business card. It was Monday morning and the sun lovingly warmed Jen's flat, so Bec had opened the windows to the world, letting the breeze in.

Her weekend had been productive - with Ryan at the Youth Centre. Ryan's reaction to the funding cut had been to carry on as usual – at least until the money dried up. That pioneer spirit of never giving up and battling onwards caught Bec, and she found herself feeling like part of the struggle, like part of the town. She felt grounded and accepted in the community.

"What are you looking for?" Jen asked.

"I'm looking for a business card. Do you remember I told you about that guy from Smith, Hall, and Townsend?"

"The real estate agent? I think I put the card in the top drawer of the cabinet," Jen replied. She picked up her work bag and headed for the door. Bec crawled out from under the table and went to the cabinet and found it almost immediately. Jen looked suspiciously at her sister, "Are you moving out, or something?"

Bec bit her bottom lip then cleared her throat. "I just want to find out what rents are like. You know, what I could afford, if I were to move out."

Jen put her bag down. "What's wrong with staying here?"

"Nothing. I was thinking what it would be like if I stayed in Brooksdale a bit longer."

Jen raised her eyebrows and smiled. "Really? That's great news. But, you know, we could get a bigger place together."

Bec raised her hand, palm towards Jen, in a calming manner. "I'm only checking prices. And I'm not one-hundred percent sure I want to settle down yet. I mean, work is great, you're great..."

"Ryan's great," Jen added.

The sisters giggled together. Bec continued, "I mean, my dream is to pursue photography. Not just doing weddings and family portraits, but *real* photography. The *art* of it. I'd have to travel. Or, at least move to where the scene is more vibrant."

Jen walked forward and took Bec's hands. "Those aren't bad choices. Besides, why does it have to be all one or the other? Have you talked with Ryan about it?"

Bec looked out the window when she answered, "I know what he'll say, 'You can do all that stuff here in Brooksdale.'"

Jen replied, "There's no rush." Jen gave Bec a quick hug, then left for work, leaving Bec alone in the apartment.

RYAN STEPPED out of the shower. He wrapped a towel around his waist and walked into the kitchen. He looked at the clock: seven-thirty. *Good timing.* He loved his morning routine. Get up at five-thirty, work out, shower, breakfast, coffee, go to work. Perfect. Ryan put on the water for his coffee and put a bowl of oats in the microwave. While they heated, he dried himself and dressed for work.

He still felt defeated about the funding cut to the youth centre and its eventual closure. By now all the students and parents had heard. Some were angry and vowed to write letters until council changed its decision. Most were just sad, but realized there was very little to be done. That's just how things were. Ryan wasn't entirely ready to give up the fight.

The microwave beeped, signaling that the oats were done. Ryan mixed protein powder, frozen blueberries, and Greek yoghurt with his oats, then finished making his coffee. Sitting at his dining table, Ryan looked out the window at his garden and workshop. He looked forward to getting in there and making something, but not today. After work and BJJ training. Life wasn't all bad. Bec helped, too.

He picked up his smartphone and played an audio recording of Nathaniel Howthorne's *The Scarlet Letter.* This was Ryan's world – a small but wholesome world.

A loud knock at the door fractured Ryan's morning. He paused the audio book and wiped the corners of his mouth. He went through to the front door and opened it. Cold air rushed in.

Ryan regretted opening the door almost immediately. Two men stood before him: Phil and another, square-shaped man. Both wore business attire.

"Get off my property," Ryan said in a calm, level voice.

Phil sniffed and replied, "I haven't come for trouble. I could easily hire some people for that."

"Then who is this?"

The other man spoke in clipped tones. "Peter Watson. Private Investigator."

Understanding dawned on Ryan. "How long have you been spying on us?"

Phil interjected, "Not 'us,' Becky. I needed to know if she was okay. Someone like you wouldn't understand how deep love can go."

Ryan rubbed his chin with his thumb. His eyes flickered over Peter Watson, who stood stock-still. Ryan knew he could take Phil, but this other guy? He looked as though he could handle himself. Ryan looked Phil in the eyes. "A person can't own another. You don't have the right, especially after what you've done." The wind blew and Ryan fought the urge to shiver. He couldn't show any weakness here.

Peter Watson reached into his coat pocket and pulled an envelope out. "I have here some incriminating photos of Tyler Brooks," said Watson. "And some others of his father, Michael. Might do some damage to his influence on the town council. Might put an end to any thoughts of revenge on his part. You're causing him some embarrassment, you know." Ryan looked at the envelope, but didn't take it.

Phil held out his hand in a peaceful gesture, "I just want five minutes of your time." Ryan clamped his jaw shut. He stepped back and let the two men inside. Sitting at the dining table, Phil said, "You've done a wonderful job with the renovations."

Ryan retorted, "Your spy has been busy."

Smiling grimly, Phil cast a glance at Watson. "He does what he's paid to do."

"Including stalking innocent women?"

"Ha!" scoffed Phil. "No one's innocent, not even Becky."

Ryan rubbed his chin again and said, "I've got a job to go to. Tell me what you're selling."

Without taking his eyes off Ryan, Watson placed the envelope in Phil's hand. Phil then slapped the envelope on the table. "All your problems with Michael and Tyler Brooks go away with what's in here."

"And you're giving this to me?"

"C'mon Ryan," said Phil as he leaned back in the chair. "You know what this is. You get the envelope and you leave Becky." Ryan's eyes narrowed and he could hear his pulse pound through his head. But Phil wasn't done. "She's not your type. Frankly, I'm surprised the relationship got this far. You're a Brooksdale boy, born and bred. You've always lived here and you always will." Phil thumped the table to reinforce his point then leaned forward like an adult giving advice to a nine-year-old child. Becky's a different animal. She needs excitement, art galleries, concerts. She's going places and she needs me to take her there."

Ryan blew air out of his nose in disgust. "The only thing you showed her was violence and fear."

Phil stiffened and his smile vanished. "Careful country boy."

Ryan stood up. The sound of the chair scrapping on the floor was loud in the tension of the moment. He said, "You and your hound come to my home, throw this rubbish in my face, and expect me to betray the most important person in my life?" Ryan pointed towards the door. "Get out."

Phil smiled wanly. "That's too bad. It really is." Phil folded his arms, "I have Becky's camera equipment – her father's old junk. I'm willing to sell it to you for two-thousand dollars. If she's so important to her, you'll buy it, won't you?"

Ryan felt anger build in his chest. Bec had mentioned

the old cameras and gear that used to be her father's. It was of purely sentimental value and was worth only a few hundred dollars. Only a snake like Phil would do something like this. Ryan suppressed a snarl. "I'm late for work. Take your sleazy deals and go back to Brisbane."

Shaking his head in disappointment, Phil stood up and pulled a business card from his pocket. He dropped it on the table and it glided across the smooth surface. "My card," said Phil. "When you change your mind."

With that, Phil walked out and Watson followed. Picking up the business card, trailed behind, making sure these two intruders left his home without planting anything in his house that could incriminate him later, or stealing anything.

Ryan watched Phil and Watson from the front step of his house. When the pair drove off in a white Mercedes, Ryan breathed a sigh of relief. The sheer arrogance of what just happened shocked Ryan. That son-of-a-bitch actually thought he *owned* Bec. He looked at the business card in his hand, crushed it, then dumped it in the key tray by the front door. About to be late for school, Ryan grabbed his bag and coat and rushed out to his truck.

BEC MADE A COFFEE. She smiled warmly as she set the filter in the stand as Ryan had shown her. Coffee done, she sat down and flicked through a photography magazine. She imagined what her work would look like when it made it on the cover.

A knock at the door interrupted Bec's musings. She looked towards the door. Probably Jen had forgotten her phone or keys or something. The knock came again. Louder and with authority.

That was not Jen.

Thump. Thump. Thump. "I know you're in there Becky. Open up and we'll talk." Bec felt her legs go to jelly. It was Phil. Her breathing sharpened, as if she had just sprinted one-hundred meters. *Control yourself damn it!* Bec tried to speak, but all that came out was a pathetic squeak.

She cleared her voice and tried again, "I'm not letting you in. Last time I saw you, you hit me."

"Ahh! Will you ever let me forget my mistakes? I was angry, hurt, and confused. You hurt me and I needed you, but you weren't there for me. I'm not angry now."

He was doing it again: making Bec feel responsible for the suffering he caused. She could see it now and just that simple thing – seeing it – made her stronger. Finding her legs, Bec strode towards the door and slid the chain on.

"Oh come on! Did you just put the chain on? Open up and let's sort this thing out. It's time you came back to Brisbane with me. To the life you were destined to have." Phil sounded so sweet. So strong. That's what drew her to him: his confidence that everything was wonderful. He had a way of making everyone believe in him.

"Phil," said Bec as calmly as she could. "I'm in a relationship now. I've moved on. I have a job and a life."

"Working at a small-town photo studio? That's no life for you. And that Ryan Anderson guy? He's a teacher; an English Teacher. Everyone knows those guys are just try-hard novelists."

How does he know all this?

Bec put her eye up against the peep hole. She could see Phil, but behind him was another man. She could just make him out. It was Peter Watson! Bec called out, "Peter Watson! You're a liar and con-artist."

Watson replied in even tones, "Miss Williams, I'm sorry

about the deception, but it was the only way to make sure you were okay."

What did that mean? Bec stayed silent. She didn't know how to respond.

Phil filled the silence, "Becky, we all know you have a little drinking problem. I hired Peter to make sure you didn't get into trouble. Come back to Brisbane and we'll book you into a clinic."

That arsehole!

"I DO NOT have a drinking problem. I have an ex-boyfriend problem. Now both of you leave before I call the cops."

"Don't be like that." It was Phil again. "Hey, I saw your new boyfriend this morning. He invited me in for coffee. We had a good chat about things - about you."

"Liar! Ryan would never let you into his house." But the fire had been snuffed out of her voice. What if Ryan didn't recognize him as the man who had assaulted her? What if Ryan was being his usual, friendly self? And what would they have to say about her?

Phil broke into her thoughts, "He agrees with me. He knows he can't keep you satisfied here in Brooksdill- Brooksdale. He wants to settle down with someone reliable. Someone who'll look after his babies, cook his meals, wash his clothes. That's not you Becky."

Running both hands through her hair, Bec could hardly believe what she was hearing. Or could she? That idyllic lifestyle seemed to suit Ryan. And wasn't that why Tammy ran off? No. She wouldn't believe Phil's crap. "Get out of here Phil. I'm calling the police."

"Alright, alright. I'm leaving. But I'll come back. I love you, Rebecca Williams. We're meant to be together." The sound of footsteps grew faint. Bec slid down the door and crouched on the floor where she remained there for a full fifteen minutes.

When she finally stopped shaking, she went to the window and peered out. No cars. She went back to the door and opened it until it banged against the security chain. No one there.

She gently closed the door, as if scared the noise would bring Phil back. Looking at her hands, Bec saw them trembling. Somehow, they weren't her hands. She needed a drink.

32

Bec walked as quickly as she could along the footpath not noticing the spring flowers budding in the brick flower beds that lined Main Street. She sent two messages: one to Ryan and one to Jen. Both messages said the same thing:

Phil came. Don't feel safe. Going to Ryans.

As she walked through the warm spring sun of late August, she felt chilled. Bec checked her phone to see if anyone had replied, nothing yet. She looked over her shoulder to see if anyone was there, but the street was empty. At this time of morning, all the kids were in school and all the adults were at work.

She turned on to Rock View Street. Bec's phone buzzed. It was from Ryan.

Be home in 45. Organizing cover for classes.

That was a relief. Bec continued on her way, quickening

her pace. She turned onto Granville Street, and Ryan's home was just there. Fumbling in her bag for the keys, Bec let herself in to his house. She kept a set of work clothes, weekend clothes, and toiletries here. She could stay for a couple of days.

Once inside, there was nothing to do but wait. The desire for a drink itched. Bec paced in the living room, then began opening and closing cupboard doors, Bec swept through the kitchen and the pantry. Each cupboard revealed tins of food, boxes of oats, protein powders, instant noodles - man food. Each time she opened a door, she closed it progressively harder until she really slammed a door closed and the cups rattled inside.

"What am I doing?" Bec said out loud. "This is not who I am. This is what Phil wants, not me."

Bec went back through the kitchen, tidying up. It took her mind off things for a moment. Next, she prepared coffee. While she ground the beans, she heard Ryan's Ford pull up. The door banged open, slammed shut, and heavy footfalls ran up the back of the house. Ryan burst in through the back door. Looked around, saw Bec, and breathed a sigh of relief. "Thank goodness you're all right. I thought maybe..."

Bec knew she should have felt relieved and grateful that Ryan had left work halfway through the day, yet a fit of anger flashed across her emotions. "You thought what? I'd be a blubbering mess on the floor waiting for my white knight to save me? Or that I'd be passed out drunk, in a pool of my own urine and vomit?"

Ryan strode forward confidently and enveloped her in a loving embrace. At first she tried, with clenched fists, to beat on his arms and chest, but Ryan held firm. He knew what she needed and the anger passed like a freak wave that rolls and pitches a boat at sea and then is gone. melting into the safety of Ryan's body, great sobs jerked out of her.

"Let it all out," said Ryan in a soothing voice and she did just that. Two or three minutes later, Bec regained her composure and said, "I was making a coffee when you interrupted me." Ryan chuckled and gave her a gentle kiss on the forehead. "Thank you for coming, by the way. Was it difficult to get cover for your classes?"

"You're welcome and no, it wasn't too difficult. I haven't had a day off for two or three years and I never say no to other teachers when they need a hand. So, Janice okay'd it straight away, and once I'd written up my instructions, I came home."

Pouring coffee into the filter cone was meditative for Bec. That, combined with Ryan's presence, calmed her immensely. The itch she'd been desperately needing to scratch with booze had vanished.

"SO, WHAT HAPPENED WITH PHIL?" asked Ryan with genuine concern. He felt guilty that he hadn't gone to Bec's place straight after that mongrel left Ryan's own place. That's what Ryan should have done, but like a self-absorbed fool, he had gone to work instead of to Bec's place.

Bec answered, "He actually came to the apartment with a scum bag private investigator. Can you believe it? He actually thinks I'd go back to him." Bec shook her head as she spoke. "He said that I belonged with him, not here. And he said he talked with you about it. I told him to stop lying and go."

Ryan's thoughts went to Phil's business card that sat crumpled in the key tray by the front door. Thankfully Bec hadn't noticed it. She must have been too distressed to pay close attention on her way inside. Ryan made an excuse, "I'm just going to put my keys back, otherwise I'll lose them." Bec nodded and returned to making the coffee.

Standing by the front door, Ryan un-crumpled Phil's business card. He knew he should tell Bec the truth, but wouldn't that just upset her all over again? That prick Phil was clearly adept at weaving truth and lies together so it was impossible to pick apart which was which. Would Bec think Ryan actually felt she was better off without him? Ryan knew he was taking too long. Bec would become suspicious, so he walked back into the kitchen.

Placing the coffee mugs on the table, Bec asked, "He didn't really come here, did he? Phil, I mean."

Ryan hesitated. He didn't want to make things worse. Lying usually made things worse. "He did come here. As I was about to leave for work."

Bec froze. In a monotone she said, "Go on."

Ryan told her what had happened. About the envelope and Peter Watson. About the 'deal' Phil proposed and Bec's father's photography equipment. Ryan hung his head in shame. He had no idea about how Bec would react. He waited in the silence. He heard Bec's chair scrape on the timber floor. He looked up and saw Bec coming towards him and she sat next to Ryan. She took his hand in hers. "I'm sorry that you got mixed up in all this. Phil is a manipulative arsehole."

She smiled and Ryan's heart leapt. Everything would be okay. Ryan said, "You know I'm not taking Phil up on his deal - about the photos and Michael Brooks.?" He gave Bec an encouraging smile. "I think we need to get the authorities involved. I'll get Jerry over and see what he says." He gave Bec's hand a squeeze.

"I don't know about getting the police involved. I just want Phil to let me go."

Pulling his phone out of his pocket and sitting it on the table, Ryan said, "He has attacked you before. What's to say he won't do it again? It's been months since you left Brisbane and clearly he hasn't moved on. He's got issues, Bec. Serious ones. You're not the problem here. He is." Bec nodded solemnly.

TWENTY MINUTES LATER, Jerry was sitting at the table across from Bec and Ryan as they recounted the events of the morning. Ryan hoped the police could do something about Phil. Jerry nodded his head and took notes in a pocket notebook. The pen looked like a toothpick in his meaty hands.

"Sounds like you've been through a lot, Bec. I'm sorry that this happened."

As she wiped a tear from her face, she asked, "What can you do?"

"Showing up to your homes is not a crime, and Ryan, you invited him in," replied Jerry.

"I didn't have much choice. He..."

"He'll say you invited him in and that private investigator of his will confirm it." Jerry slowly exhaled. He seemed to be taking time to choose his words. "The assault in Brisbane will be hard to prove. His word against Rebecca's. And the photography gear, also tough, since Rebecca left it at Phil's residence." There was silence as everyone waited for someone else to speak first. Jerry prompted, "Is there anything else?"

Ryan and Bec exchanged a long look. Ryan knew what she was thinking: the incident in the Flat Rock Café. But Bec remained silent. Ryan would have to give her a nudge in the right direction. "Jerry, could you excuse us for a moment. Bec and I need to have a little conversation."

"If that's what you need. But if there's anything else, you really should tell me." Jerry stood up. "I'm going out to the car to request a check on this guy. I'll be back in a few minutes."

When Ryan heard the front door close, he said to Bec, "You need to tell him about that day in the Flat Rock Café, when Phil went for you and had a go at me."

Bec looked out the window and replied, "I don't have to if I don't want to." She sounded a little bit like the teenagers Ryan was so used to dealing with. It was frustrating with them, and it frustrated Ryan now. "What are you going to achieve by *not* reporting it?"

Bec faced Ryan with fire in her eyes. "I don't want to go back to the person I was at that time. It's not me anymore."

Ryan took up both Bec's hands in his and kissed her lovingly on the lips. He said, "You won't go back. And I didn't think you were that bad anyway." He smiled and Bec laughed half-heartedly.

"You are trying to charm me. It's not working," said Bec and her phone buzzed. "It's Jen," said Bec. "She's coming over now."

"Plenty of people here support you and love you."

"Ryan. Don't. Not right now. I'm still all mixed up from this morning."

Jerry walked back in. "Anything else to add, Rebecca?"

Ryan felt Bec give his hand a squeeze under the table. She said, "Actually. Yes. There is." She told Jerry the whole story and he took down more notes. Ryan knew it must have been difficult for her to re-live that day and he felt proud that she could recount it now.

After Bec had finished, Jerry said, "I have enough to

arrest him, but a witness besides Ryan would be helpful. Do you remember who was on shift at the time?"

Shaking her head, Bec said, "I didn't know anyone in town at that time."

Ryan knew someone. "Bradley Westerfield."

Jerry wrote the name down and made the appropriate goodbyes as a concerned friend and officer of the law. As Jerry left, Jen arrived. She exchanged a 'hello' with Jerry then rushed up to Bec, giving her a huge hug. She began peppering Bec with questions the way a mother might a child. Ryan retreated to the kitchen and put the water on for another coffee.

33

Tuesday morning break time and the staffroom at Brooksdale High was a hive of activity. Ryan busied himself catching up with all the teachers who covered for him yesterday while he was with Bec. Through the room of teachers, Ryan caught sight of Donita and went over to her. "Hey, thanks for covering for me yesterday." Ryan wasn't sure how much more to say, but Donita was a friend. "Bec's ex-boyfriend showed up. He had some private investigator keeping tabs on her."

Donita's eyes widened in disbelief. "Oh my goodness! What happened?"

Ryan told Donita the quick version of events. When he finished, Donita said, "That guy should be locked away! Is Bec getting a restraining order?"

"I hope so. She was supposed to go to the police station today to find out more. Jerry is leading her through the process."

"Jerry? I know him. Well-built and big, eh? He's got a kind heart that one." She smiled and touched Ryan's forearm in a warm, friendly way. The bell rang and the room emptied. Ryan picked up his bag and made his way to the next class, British Literature, which had now become his favourite class since Tyler had been moved to Lewis Jones' class.

As he passed the toilet block, Ryan heard loud sobs come from the girl's toilet. He stopped and called out, "Hello? It's Mr. Anderson. Are you OK?"

The reply came through bursts of crying, "I'm OK. Go away."

It sounded like Sally, normally level-headed and articulate, so Ryan felt concerned. He knew that teens rarely told an adult what was bothering them the first time they're asked, so he persisted, "Sally. Is that you? Why don't you come out and tell me what's bothering you."

"I'm fine."

"You don't sound fine. Is there anything I can help with?"

A cubicle door squeaked opened and slammed shut. Sally appeared at the entrance. Her eyes were swollen and the end of her nose was red. "I look terrible," she said.

Ryan knew that it didn't help lying to teenagers either. "You don't look great. Walk with me to class and tell me what's happening." Stragglers who cared about their classes ran past Ryan and Sally. Stragglers who didn't care about their classes meandered to class, chatting and laughing. A few students peered at Sally and Ryan's direction, but few paid much attention.

"Adam dumped me." Sally said it so quietly and quickly that Ryan wasn't sure he had heard it.

Ryan kept walking and Sally kept up with him. Ryan replied, "That's terrible. I'm so sorry. You two seemed like such a great couple."

A sob resurfaced and Sally tried to hold it back, but she

was unsuccessful. "I don't know what happened. I guess I should have seen it coming. Adam just - just. Like, he became distant or something. He spent more and more time alone, or with Tyler and his gang. He just became someone else. I don't know what I did wrong."

With the classroom only a few paces away, Ryan stopped walking and faced Sally. They were already late for class, but the students had work to go on with and this was important. "Sally, teachers have noticed a change in Adam, too. I don't think you did anything wrong. People grow and change. But what's happening with Adam is troubling. Is there anything that could have triggered Adam's behaviour?"

Sally looked at Ryan imploringly. "Mr. Anderson, I just don't know. He's not active online much. He doesn't talk to me anymore. I just don't know." Sally cried again.

Ryan could see the rest of the day would be a right-off for Sally so there was no point sending her to class and suffering the embarrassment of stares and awkward questions from classmates. He told her to go down to the front office where students who were ill were sent. Delores was there and she could offer unofficial emotional support - the best type. After all, how many teachers went to her for unofficial counseling? As Sally walked towards the office, Ryan entered the class, and noticed Adam was absent.

34

Bec sat in an old interview room in Brooksdale Police Station. The room was sterile with a brown desk and four office chairs - two on each side. A water cooler and paper cup dispenser stood in the corner of the room. The door opened and the horizontal blinds clattered with the disturbance of air. Bec felt like she was in a cop drama, except she was the victim. Jerry walked in with another officer and both of them took a chair across from Bec. Jerry started, "This is Sharon Burgess. She works with victims of domestic violence."

Sharon leaned across and shook Bec's hand. "Call me Sharon."

Swallowing back her anxiety, Bec shook Sharon's hand. Her grip was firm. Bec tried to relieve some of her nerves by making chit-chat. "Brooksdale seems like such a happy town. I didn't know it needed a domestic violence specialist, haha."

Sharon, obviously used to such nervous and incompetent conversation, gave a warm smile and answered, "Domestic violence is not just about arresting a husband after he hits his wife. Women, as well as men, are perpetrators of domestic violence. I also do a lot of preventative education and community awareness."

Bec felt a little embarrassed at her lack of knowledge of how the system worked. "I didn't know that even existed. But, I wouldn't really call myself a *victim* of domestic violence. I just want Phil to leave me alone so I can get on with my life."

"That's understandable. From what Jerry told me of your story, you've had a tough time. I want to talk about Philip Mansfield, your former partner." Shifting in her chair, Bec looked from Jerry to Sharon. She really wanted all this to be resolved with as little fuss as possible. Sharon continued, "We've checked with the airline. Philip Mansfield boarded a plane for Brisbane yesterday afternoon."

Bec breathed a sigh of relief, but there was more. Sharon continued, "We checked his police history. Philip Mansfield was arrested three years ago for assault of his then girlfriend. The charges were later dropped."

Bec could hardly believe what she was hearing. She hadn't known anything about Phil's past. He had seemed so sweet and kind when they first met. Sharon said, "Rebecca, we have enough to charge Philip Mansfield for assaulting you at the Flat Rock Café. Bradley Westerfield, the barista at the café at the time, remembered what happened and Jerry took his statement. I recommend that we proceed with this. We can arrest him and bring him to trial. We can also get a restraining order issued."

This all seemed too much. Did Phil really deserve all this? Bec said haltingly, "I don't know. It seems like a lot of hassle to put everyone through. Besides, Phil was just upset about the break-up. He'll be fine given more time. And there's his business and all the people he employs..." Sharon nodded patiently as Bec rattled of a bunch of reasons why she didn't want to proceed. In the end, Bec was glad she had the chance to sound off. Once out in the open, each of her reasons seemed petty.

Sharon said, "Rebecca. It is normal for people in abusive relationships to feel guilt or shame. But this is not a hassle to me, or anyone else. It is important that you have your independence and live in safety. No one has the right to take that away from you."

Bec knew Sharon was right. "Okay, show me what I have to do."

An hour later, Bec left the station with a restraining order against Phil and shaky hands. Despite the tension, Bec felt in control again. It was three-o'clock in the afternoon. Bec knew she had to keep herself busy otherwise the booze-itch would return. Jen would be in the middle of class and Bec didn't want to tell Ryan before she told Jen. Jen was family, and family was first. Instead, Bec went to the photo studio. Although her boss had given her the day off, she had to edit a shoot she did last week. Also, Adam came in on Tuesday afternoons. He had seemed a bit down lately and helping the young man learn about photography would take her mind off her own issues.

At the photo studio, Bec busied herself with the task of processing and editing her last photo shoot. A cover of Photo Boss Magazine with Bec's winning photo was framed and hung in the foyer. A copy of the magazine sat by her desk. She glanced at it occasionally to help re-focus her attention. Her phone buzzed with a message. It was from Ryan:

How did it go?

She wasn't ready to answer just yet. She put her phone down and went back to the photo she was editing. *Bzzz, Bzzz.* Her phone again. This time it was Jen:

I'm finished school.

That's what she had been waiting for - Bec wanted to talk with Jen first. She was about to hit the green phone icon to call Jen when a voice called her attention away. "Hi Rebecca, Paul told me to come back here and help you."

Bec put her phone down, pushed her chair back and looked up at Adam Lee who stood in the doorway of the little editing room. He was a handsome young man who, until recently, had been happy and hard working. Now, he seemed to just go through the motions. Bec thought she could get Adam going on the editing and then meet Jen "You can help me edit these photos of the shoot I did on the weekend."

Adam nodded and sat down next to Bec. He seemed distant and Bec noticed some redness in his eyes. She said, "I want you to go through these photos, adjust the exposure and crop the images down a bit. Hey, are you listening?"

Adam stared blankly at the computer screen making no indication that he had heard Bec's instructions. Bec placed her hand on his shoulder, "Adam, something's wrong. You need to tell me or take the afternoon off."

He swiveled in the chair and faced Bec. "I broke up with Sally today. She was really hurt."

Bec wasn't surprised. Adam hadn't talked about her for the past few weeks. This was big news for the teen, so Bec decided to place her own wants on hold, and hear this young man out. "Do you want to tell me what happened?"

Adam fidgeted, picking at his finger nails. "It wasn't like

she did anything wrong or anything. It was just, I don't know. It was me. The problem is me."

Leaning forward and giving Adam a comforting pat on the arm, Bec said, "No, The problem is not you. There's nothing wrong with you, or her. Relationships change. People change. When they change in different directions, sometimes they break."

Blinking away tears, Adam's voice fell to a whisper, "You don't understand. No one does." He pulled a tissue from the box on the table and blew his nose. He looked directly at Bec. His startling blue eyes nailed her to her chair. She couldn't look away. He said, "Can I tell you something? But you can't tell anyone else, okay?"

Bec put her hand up to her forehead, but she couldn't break Adam's eye contact. She replied, "I can't make that promise, Adam. If you or someone you know has committed a crime or in danger, then I have to tell someone."

"I haven't broken a law or anything. I wish it were that easy. I'm..."

"Go on."

"I'm gay."

Bec exhaled slowly. This was serious for Adam, but in Bec's mind it was a relief; all manner of gruesome thoughts had been floating around. "How do you feel about that?" Bec asked.

"I don't know. I want to like girls. I like Sally, but I also have these feelings for guys. I'm just all mixed up."

"Is that why you broke up with Sally?"

"Yeah, it wasn't fair on her."

Bec took Adam's hands in hers. "Adam, you should tell her. It's more unfair if she doesn't know the truth. She's probably thinking that she did something wrong. She'll understand, maybe not at first, but she will. And she'll support you. You're going to need that support." She smiled encouragingly and Adam responded with a smile of his own.

Bec remembered Ryan saying that Adam had been hanging out with Tyler Brooks and how odd that was. Bec asked, "Is that also why you've been hanging out with Tyler Brooks?"

Adam stiffened and pulled his hands back into his lap. "No. Yes. Like, well Tyler knows and I wanted him to keep quiet, so I've been like, you know, helping him with stuff."

Bec detected incomplete truths. "Is that all you're doing, helping?"

"Yeah, I promise. Don't tell anyone, okay? I'm not ready for that yet."

Bec smiled again and said, "All right. But if you have trouble, or feel really bad about yourself, you tell me. Don't keep it to yourself. You tell me, you hear?"

"Yes Rebecca. I feel a bit better already." He turned back to the computer screen and got to work. Bec messaged Jen:

Everything's OK. Be home around 5:30.

35

"And so, we'll have much better tracking of students' reading abilities – and the strategies that work – for students as they move from Year Seven to Eight and so on." There was polite applause from the teachers and Ryan sat down.

Janice stood in front of the room full of teachers at the weekly staff meeting. "Thank you, Ryan. I'm looking forward to seeing what your team comes up with."

Ryan didn't hear what she said next. He looked across the room at Jen. He desperately wanted to ask her what happened yesterday at the Police Station with Bec. All he had received was a text message that she was okay and she'd tell him more when she saw him next – after work today. Mark, who was sitting next to Ryan elbowed him in the ribs. Mark must of noticed Ryan was zoned out.

Janice spoke, "The last item on today's agenda is positions for next year." The room fell silent, "We have some teachers moving on. The head of the English and Mathematics Departments are both moving down to Newcastle – congratulations. That means those jobs are vacant. Please check the Department of Education's website for application details."

A murmur of hushed conversations erupted. Mark nudged Ryan and leaned close, saying, "Imagine us as Head of Departments!"

"Stranger things have happened before," quipped Ryan as Janice closed the meeting and the noise level increased as teachers streamed out of the room.

Mark and Ryan were moved along by the flow of bodies. Mark said, "Damn! I forgot to bring the *Ultimate Fighting Championship One* DVD for you."

"I'm not in a hurry, we can go get it now."

"*You're* not in a hurry, but *I* am. I'm meeting up with Angela."

"Angela? Bryce Tremblay's ex?" Mark was incorrigible and Ryan worried his friend might be biting off more than he could chew. Angela was a feisty woman with an off-again-on-again relationship with one of the biggest, toughest men in town.

Mark seemed oblivious to the danger. "Bryce is cool with it. Those two are definitely over and Angela is hot. Anyway, the DVD is right on top of my desk. I sat it on a textbook or something. Just go up to the Math staffroom and grab it." Mark rushed out towards the car park. Ryan shook his head in wonder. It seemed like Mark dated someone new every month or so. Surely Brooksdale didn't have that many eligible women.

Walking up to the Mathematics Department staffroom, Ryan felt calm and relaxed in the nearly deserted school. Except for the cleaning staff, Ryan and a few other hard working teachers remained. As he walked, Ryan could hear the rustle of plastic garbage bags and the high-pitched whirs of vacuum cleaners.

At the Maths staffroom, Ryan tried the handle. It clicked open. As he pushed through the doorway, a sound of rustling papers and something crashing on the ground startled him. "Oh! Adam. You gave me a fright!"

Adam Lee stood next to Mark's desk with a folder of papers in one hand. The desk was messy – not Mark's style. Ryan's gaze went from Adam to the desk, to the papers in his hand, then back to Adam. "Adam. I think you had better explain to me what's going on here."

"I... Ahh... Mr Strathfield told me to pick up an assignment that I missed yesterday."

Ryan folded his arms across his chest and said, "You were here yesterday. Show me those papers." Adam stood stock still as if he had been caught in the headlights of a truck. Ryan repeated the command and Adam stepped forward unwillingly, handing the papers to Ryan. "I think we need to go and see the Principal. Don't you?"

Adam walked out of the room with his head hung shamefully. As he passed Ryan, Adam asked, "Will you tell my parents?"

"That is likely, very likely." Ryan quickly went over to Mark's desk, found the UFC 1 DVD, and slipped it into his coat pocket. He pulled the door closed and escorted Adam to the Principal's office.

In the principal's office, Janice sat back in her executive chair and peered at Adam while Ryan recounted what had happened. Adam sat with his head lowered and Ryan was beside him. Ryan felt his role should be to support the young man rather than condemn him.

When Ryan finished, Adam looked imploringly at Janice. "Are you going to call my parents?" Adam asked.

Janice replied, "Yes. You were caught stealing test papers. That is a major incident."

Adam's head dropped. Ryan still felt a sense of disbelief mixed with concern. So much effort went into making school fit the likes of Tyler Brooks, but who was here for Adam? Adam Lee. Star student - a cheat?

Janice added, "Then there is the cheating. We'll have to award you an 'N' in Mr. Strathfield's class."

Adam's head jerked up. "I didn't really cheat, though. I didn't *use* the answers. I just..."

"You just what, Adam?" Janice's voice as calm, level, but carried authority. Ryan was discovering a new side to Janice. She was being direct, but caring with Adam. She must suspect there is more to the story, and so did Ryan.

"I..." Adam's gaze returned to the floor. "I can't tell you if you tell my parents."

"Adam," replied Janice. "I can't promise that. If there is a legal or safety issue, I am bound by law to report it."

Adam looked to Ryan. The trouble with teenagers was that sometimes the problem was easily fixed, other times it was life-altering and it could be hard to determine which was which. Ryan reflected on that thought a moment. In one's teen years, everything was life altering.

In his best calm, caring voice, Ryan said, "Whatever the problem, it is affecting you in a very negative way. You aren't dealing well with this on your own. You need to tell someone. Is it Sally? She told me you two broke up."

A sob burst forth from Adam and tears formed in his eyes. His face grew red. He was struggling with a decision. Ryan and Janice both waited. There was no need to fill the silence with chatter.

Adam rubbed his eyes with the back of his hand and sniffed. He looked around the room, then at Janice. He said, "I'm gay."

Janice nodded and she said, "Adam, I can see that was

very difficult for you to say. Neither myself nor Mr. Anderson are obliged to inform your parents of your sexuality. That is up to you, but we are both here to help you if you need it. There is something more, isn't there?"

Adam seemed to find his composure. "Yes. Tyler, Bayden, and Foster found out. They said they'd tell everyone if I didn't do some favours for them." Ryan leaned back in his chair and thumped his thigh with his fist. He couldn't believe how callous those three could be.

Janice leaned forward and folded her hands together. "Adam. That is a serious accusation. I'll need to investigate it. Do you have anything that proves this?"

Adam flushed a deep red and started crying again. "I was so stupid. So, so, so stupid." He cried, so Ryan pulled a tissue from the box on table and gave it to Adam. "I got an e-mail from Foster saying he thought he was gay and he found me attractive. I was curious, you know? Someone else was like me. Having the same conflict as me. So, I thought, like, here was a way to find out if I'm really, you know, like that. But it was just a stupid trick. Tyler got involved and the threats started. Oh God! I'm so stupid!"

Adam's shoulders shuddered with his crying. Ryan said, "Do you still have the e-mails or messages?"

Adam looked at Ryan and nodded. "There are some messages on my phone."

Janice took over, "Adam. I need to call your parents and have them come in. This may also be a case of cyber-bullying, so the Police could get involved." Adam simply nodded. The strain of the past months must have been incredible on the poor kid. Ryan sympathized deeply with him. Janice added, "Don't worry, Adam. You haven't done anything wrong. We'll work together so you can be safe from harm, and still earn the grades you deserve in Maths."

Ryan could have hugged Janice. She was going to help Adam, not crucify him, which would be the easy thing to do, especially as the culprit in all this was Tyler, who had the backing of a wealthy, well-connected family.

Adam seemed to collect himself. He looked directly at Janice and asked, "Are you going to tell my parents about, you know, my sexuality?"

Shaking her head, Janice smiled kindly. "That's a conversation you need to have with them."

Adam breathed in deeply, then exhaled. He looked to Janice, then Ryan. "Finally someone knows."

36

Ryan arrived home just after six o'clock and the sky in the west reflected orange sun light off the high cloud. He walked into the kitchen and he could smell a Thai curry and his stomach grumbled, but more than that, Ryan wanted to know what had happened at the cop shop yesterday.

Ryan walked into the kitchen, saw Bec at the sink and went to her. He wrapped his arms around her waist and kissed her gently on the cheek. "It was a tough day. Sorry I'm late home."

"What happened?"

Ryan poured himself a glass of water, sculled it, then said, "A student problem. A good student having a rough time. What happened with you yesterday?"

"Pass me the plates," said Bec. She made Ryan wait for the news he wanted to hear while she dished up a beautiful Thai green curry with Jasmine rice. They sat at the table and Ryan spooned some of the curry into his mouth.

"Mmm, Bec, this is good. Just what I needed. Now are you going to tell me about yesterday?"

"You first. Tell me what's got you so down." Tit for tat.

Ryan kept eating. Between spoonful's he said, "I can't really say much. Student confidentiality."

Bec put her spoon down and clinked loudly on the edge of the plate. She said, "Like doctor – patient confidentiality? Really?"

Ryan detected a hint of sarcasm in her voice and he was stung by it. "I take my job seriously. A lot of people don't take young people seriously. They should."

Bec's posture became more erect. She said, "I take young people seriously."

Now Ryan put his spoon down. Gently. "I didn't mean *you*. I just meant..."

"I know what you meant."

"Listen, Bec. You can't expect me to tell you everything. Some of this stuff is serious for students and you know some of them. It wouldn't be right for me to gossip."

"So, I'm a gossip now?"

Ryan shook his head. "No. Look, did yesterday go badly? Did Phil try to contact you or something?"

Bec crossed her arms and leveled her gaze at him. She said, "I just thought we were getting close. I confided in you. I thought you might confide in me. And keeping teenagers' secrets doesn't usually help them."

Ryan felt defensive now. He felt the urge to bite back. He said, "Confide in me? I've been waiting in agony for you to tell me about yesterday. But you've kept me waiting. I'm worried as hell!"

"Don't bring that up. That's different. I needed to tell Jen first. She's family..." Ryan knew he should stop. He was crossing a line, but his urge to hit back clouded his mind. He cut Bec off. "And I'm what? Your recovery guy?"

As soon as the words tumbled out, Ryan knew he had

hurt Bec. For an instant, she looked deflated. Then she stood, tall and strong. She strode out to the living room and sat down on the sofa. She turned on the television and crossed her legs.

Ryan cleaned up in the kitchen. After he was done, he said, "Look I'm sorry. That wasn't a helpful thing to say. I'll drive you home if you want." No reply. "Well, I'll be out in the workshop." And with that he went out in the cool spring night to wallow in his own stupidity.

AFTER AN HOUR OF MINDLESS TELEVISION, Bec's anger faded. *Men are such jerks!* Then again, she had pushed him when he didn't want to talk about school. *Damn it.* Bec went to the fridge and took out an ice-cream. She sucked on it noisily. Outside, a light shone from the window of Ryan's workshop. She finished the ice-cream, put on her coat and hat, then went outside.

RYAN FELT a cool draft of air on the back of his neck as the workshop door opened then closed. He turned and saw Bec standing behind him. He put down his sandpaper and opened his arms, palms out. "Look, I'm sorry about before. I shot my mouth off without thinking."

Bec's face was stony. Ryan couldn't tell what she was thinking. She took a step forward and said, "I was angry. A lot has happened this past week. I guess I need to learn to trust you more." She rubbed her eyes with her hand and continued, "I finally feel part of life here. My sister, you. Everyone has been so supportive. Then Adam Lee confided in me at the studio." She flapped her hands by her side, searching for words.

Ryan interjected, "Wait. Adam said something to you? Adam is the one I'm worried about."

Understanding dawned on both of them at the same time. Ryan said, "He's going to need support. I know his parents. They're conservative."

Stepping forward, Bec embraced Ryan. She snuggled her head into his chest and Ryan stroked her hair lovingly. He could think of no better feeling in the world. "Let's go back into the house. We need to celebrate," Ryan said.

Bec looked at him quizzically, so Ryan added, "We just had our first fight and made up. This is a landmark occasion." Bec pinched him on the shoulder and lead the way out of the workshop and up to the house.

Inside the house, Bec pulled Ryan by the hand towards the bedroom. Ryan stopped. "Tell me about yesterday. I need to know everything's okay."

"I got a restraining order against Phil. Also, charges were laid against him for the Flat Rock. I think I'm finally done with him."

Ryan embraced her fully. "That must have been tough to go through. I'm proud of you." They kissed and Bec lead Ryan into the bedroom. As they went, they pulled off their clothes. Entangled in each other's kisses and embraces, Bec felt love, safety, and excitement all at the same time. Was this what real love is supposed to feel like? Exhausted and content, they lay like kittens snuggled in a shoe box. Bec felt a strange sense of ease and serenity. She rolled over to look at Ryan. His eyes opened and he met her gaze. The world was in that gaze. She closed her eyes and fell into a peaceful slumber.

37

August gave way to September with a cold snap that had people talking about how winter was back for a second bite. The farmers hoped the change would bring rain with it. Ryan looked out the window of the English department staffroom. A thunderhead brewed on the horizon - the farmers might be right this time. He returned his focus to the stack of essays left to grade. Bec had messaged him earlier and wanted to meet at five o'clock in town. She had news. It was four-forty now. Ryan packed away the essays with a sharp thump. They could wait until Monday. He rushed out to his Ford - it started on the third attempt after a long *whir*.

Parked behind the supermarket, Ryan walked through the shop and onto Main Street, where He saw Bec sitting on a bench. She looked wonderful rugged up in parka, winter jeans, and long brown boots. This was winter's last breath.

She saw him and went to him, wrapping her arms around his waist. "Well this is nice," said Ryan.

"I just like seeing you. Let's walk down the street. I just want to enjoy these old brick buildings." The past week had been wonderful. Ryan felt as giddy as a teenager in the midst of first love. He felt blessed to have Bec. They looped arms and headed south past old red and yellow brick buildings with red awnings and gold signage on the windows. Ryan said, "You had something to tell me?"

"I'm going to Melbourne!" She was excited, but the news brought Ryan to a halt.

She looked at him with amusement. "Not permanently, just for a week."

He relaxed and resumed walking while peppering Bec with questions. Her cover photo in Photo Boss Magazine had caught the attention of a gallery in Melbourne. They were doing an exhibition on small country towns and invited her to hang some photos. She left next week. "That's wonderful," said Ryan. "How are you getting there?"

"Bus. I'll only get paid a royalty if my work sells. I need to go on the cheap."

"Don't take the bus. I'll pay for a flight."

Ryan felt Bec squeeze his arm. It felt good. But she said, "No. I can't accept that. This is my thing, so I need to make it happen."

Ryan nodded. "When do you leave?"

"Monday."

They strolled on past brick flower beds. The flowers that had bloomed but now closed their petals against the recent cold weather. The beds would come to life again once the rain passed over.

Bec and Ryan approached Adeline Greene's café, *Books, Cake, and Coffee.* It was a beautiful red-brick building with classic gold signage and timber-framed windows. A chalk board out front had today's special and those quaint sayings that are supposed to make you feel better. This one was, "Today's leg-iron is tomorrow's gold."

Bec thought how silly such sayings were. She said, "Isn't this Arkell's mother's place?"

"You're becoming a local after all," teased Ryan. Bec grinned. She was starting to appreciate how valuable having a connection to a place was.

"Let's go in," said Bec. "You can buy me a coffee and a cheese cake instead of the airfare." Ryan laughed and the sound pleased her. Secretly, she had been worried Ryan wouldn't be so supportive of the trip to Melbourne. Bec couldn't tell if his reaction to her news was genuine or not. He seemed pleased, but Bec knew he didn't like the big city.

They stepped towards the door, but it opened from the inside and a middle-aged man dressed in a business suit and winter coat stepped out. Michael Brooks.

Bec felt Ryan stiffen. Brooks stopped in his tracks. His eyes shifted from Ryan to Bec, then back to Ryan. A smile slipped onto Brooks's face. Bec felt like she had just met a snake-oil salesman. "Well, good afternoon Mr. Anderson. I see our finest teachers are cutting work early to spend time with their sweet hearts."

Ryan stood firm and replied, "Good afternoon to you, Mr. Brooks. You'll have to excuse me, I'm getting coffee for my friend here."

Brooks said to Bec, "Watch out young Miss. This man'll ruin you. Has he told you about how he neglected the learning needs of my son? I bet he hasn't. Well, don't you worry. He'll get his." Brooks looked at the sky. "It's going pour down. Mark my words." He pushed past Bec and Ryan, and he walked up the street towards the council chambers. Bec looked at Ryan and saw the muscles and sinew in his jaw strain. "Was he for real? He blames you for Tyler's problems?" asked Bec.

"Yup. Let's get that coffee and cheese cake." Warm air and the smells of cake and coffee blasted Bec when Ryan pushed the heavy glass door open and walked into the shop.

"Well, hello Mr. Anderson!" It was Adeline Greene. "And Rebecca Williams, I've heard a lot about you from Arkell." Adeline extended her hand over the counter and shook Bec's hand. Adeline continued, "Mr. Anderson here is the best English Teacher we've got in Brooksdale, maybe even New South Wales!"

Bec couldn't suppress a smile as she glanced around the shop. The walls were lined with bookshelves and they were packed full with paperbacks from best-sellers to literary fiction. Ryan replied to Adeline, "Now Mrs. Greene. That is quite the exaggeration. And you *can* call me Ryan you know."

"I'll call you Mr. Anderson, same as my Arkell does." Adeline's face turned serious. "I am sorry about that Michael Brooks. He was in here poking around, pretending to be interested in how the business is doing. He even had the audacity to say that it was pretty quiet for a Friday afternoon."

"What did you say to that?" Bec asked. She was drawn to this woman, who seemed like everyone's favourite aunt.

Adeline replied, "I told him it was noisy enough with just him in here. He is a mean-spirited man, that one. And Ryan, I am so sorry about the Youth Centre."

Ryan replied, "I haven't given up yet. There's always next year."

Adeline nodded. "Now you two take a seat and I'll bring your coffees and a little something. On the house."

Ryan refused Adeline's offer, but she insisted and in the

end, Bec and Ryan were shepherded to a table by the window. Adeline brought coffee and a delightful cheesecake with a huge dollop of whipped cream on the side. She picked up her dessert fork and sliced off a section of cake, placed the piece of cake on her tongue, and all her worries melted away in that simple moment. It was the best cheese-cake Bec had ever tasted.

As Bec and Ryan talked, thunder clapped and rain poured down, turning the street dark.

38

B ec slipped off her shoes and sunk down into the sofa. It had been a long day. She had been in the studio alone while Paul was out at a wedding shoot. She had put up with screaming babies and moody kids from nine till five and if Ryan thought she was going to jiu-jitsu with him tonight, he had another thing coming. The was a knock on the door. Bec groaned then answered it. It was Ryan and he had his gym bag. "Hi. You ready to go?"

He was serious, and she was not ready to go. She was tired and she wanted an early night because tomorrow she caught the over-night bus to Sydney, then on to Melbourne. Bec ran her hand through her hair and sighed. "I'm not going."

Ryan behaved as if he hadn't heard her. He walked through to the living room and dropped his gym bag on the floor. "Bec," he said. "You need to come. One lesson will prepare you for trouble. Melbourne is the big-smoke, you know. Not everyone has the best of intentions down there."

Bec couldn't help but roll her eyes. She strode up to

Ryan and put her arms around him, but she did not smile. "I used to live in Brisbane, remember? I'll be fine."

Ryan broke away from her embrace. "Just one lesson. For me. I'll feel better knowing you've had some training. Besides, I told Tony you'd be coming so he's going to do a special self-defence class."

Bec's eyes narrowed. "Great, so I'll be the reason why your BJJ buddies don't get their 'roll-time.'"

Ryan laughed, which fanned Bec's anger – and her determination. "Fine! I'll go, but don't ask me again." A look of victory appeared on Ryan's face and she wanted to kiss him, but her pride wouldn't allow it. He bent over, unzipped his gym bag, and pulled out a present about the size of a kid's picture book. "Here, this is for you."

Bec's anger drained away and was replaced by excitement. She slipped her thumb nail under the tape and carefully unwrapped the gift. The paper crinkled as she slid a photo frame out of the wrap. It was made of a fine red-wine coloured timber that was heavier than it looked. Ryan said, "It's for your magazine cover. Sorry it took so long. I had to order the timber from Perth."

He knew how to melt her heart. She had to give Ryan that. "Come here," she said and they embraced lovingly. Thirty minutes later, Bec stood barefoot on the mats at Brooksdale Gym. Saturday evening was a busy time, so the gym was packed full with people. Photos of well-known MMA fighters lined the wall and there were a few of Tony from his recent fights, too. Bec watched as Tony demonstrated how to escape an attacker who grabs you from behind.

Ryan acted as the attacker. Tony narrated the moves as he went. "The key thing is to react quickly. If you let your attacker get a good grip, it's too late," instructed Tony. He looked like a WWF wrestler in a karate uniform.

Bec felt that this was a waste of time for her and this comment cemented it. There was no way she would be fast enough, or strong enough, to get out of an attack like that. To make matter worse, she was partnered up with Angela.

The demonstration started. Ryan stood behind Tony, then grabbed him from behind, slipping his arm around Tony's neck and trying to pull backwards. Ryan was well-built, but Tony barely moved under Ryan's attack. "As soon as you feel someone is there, drop your weight and rotate your whole body towards them, like this," stated Tony, and he dropped, like he was doing a squat. At the same time, he spun around, so his face was level with Ryan's navel. "From here, punch or kick the attacker in the groin. Push your hand into his or her face. You want to try to get'em in the eyes."

Tony demonstrated on Ryan, who stepped backwards. Bec chuckled quietly to herself. Then it was time for Bec to practice. She partnered up with another woman, Angela, who seemed to have forgotten their past rivalry over Ryan. At first, Bec felt uncomfortable being the attacker. Tony walked up to her and said, "You can be a bit stronger, otherwise Angela won't get good practice."

The next time, Bec went a bit faster and a bit stronger. Angela emitted a half-choke, half—cough sound and failed to get out of Bec's grip. Eventually, Angela tapped on Bec's arm. They swapped. Bec felt distinctly uncomfortable knowing Angela was behind her and about to grab her. She waited. Nothing. Then, bang. Angela hit hard and Bec was pushed forwards, then yanked back. Bec tried to escape, but couldn't. She coughed and spluttered until Angela released her.

Tony walked up. "You gotta move faster. As soon as she grabs you. Or, stomp on her toe, then escape. She won't release you when you stomp on her toe, but it'll make her think of something else for a moment. Use that moment to escape."

Bec felt flustered. She couldn't do this. She was a photographer. She was supposed to take photos of the action, not be in the action. Again, Angela grabbed her. Bec missed the first opportunity to escape, so she stomped on Angela's toe. "Ouch!" yelped Angela. Bec dropped her weight, swiveled, pushed Angela in the stomach, and she stumbled back.

Tony grinned. "That'll do, Bec. That'll do the job." Bec could barely suppress a grin of satisfaction and she began to understand why Ryan liked BJJ so much.

The lesson lasted another forty-five minutes and they covered some other escapes from common attacks. By the end of it, Bec was lathered in sweat and breathing heavily, but she felt light and a bit more confident in herself.

As Ryan drove back to Bec's flat, they held hands. It was gentle and intimate. They had been through the same experience tonight and they didn't need words. The physical contact was enough.

When Ryan pulled up, Bec said, "I'm leaving tomorrow."

"I know."

Bec felt physically tired. It wasn't fatigue. More like a feeling of contentment. She wanted Ryan tonight. "Stay tonight?"

Ryan nodded, but said, "What about Jen?"

Jen? How could he think of Jen at a time like this? They weren't kids and Jen wasn't her mother, for goodness sake! Still, Bec wanted to respect Jen's space. "Can I stay at your place?"

A smile spread across Ryan's face. He turned the truck around and drove back towards his house. As he drove, he said, "I worry about you going to Melbourne."

So Ryan wasn't entirely okay with the trip. Bec wondered if he still had an open wound about Tammy leaving for a holiday, but actually leaving him. She decided to comfort Ryan rather than start a fight. "I'm coming back. It's just for a few days." She kissed him gently on the cheek and Ryan smiled.

"I know," he said. "I know."

39

Melbourne. The big smoke. Bec looked out of the tram window as she rode towards the art gallery. The Yarra River reflected the city lights in a dazzling array of blues, reds, and yellows. Restaurants did a brisk trade with outdoor gas heaters warming the diners who sat out on the street and well dressed couples strutted their fashions.

Even though Spring time was warm, Melbourne's weather could turn bitingly cold within an hour, accordingly, Bec walked down a side-street with her winter coat zipped up to her chin and covering her evening-dress. A flutter of nerves rolled across her stomach and she reminded herself that there was no need to be nervous. This was a Wednesday night opening – only those with a keen interest in the arts, or the social connections, would be in attendance. At least that's what Margery said.

Bec squinted at the building names and numbers on the dark buildings that towered over here. When she found the right one, she had walked through the double glass doors and into the heated lobby, which was somewhat like an up-market hotel's lobby, except much smaller.

She rode the elevator up to the third floor and got out. People were already there. Men wore black suits and ties, while women wore evening gowns. Small tables were placed throughout, with glasses of champagne, wine, or water with a slice of lemon. Bec felt a bit ordinary in her black sleeveless dress.

Glass panes hung from the ceilings. They created artificial corridors. This exhibition focused on life in rural Australia, yet the gallery had a distinct modernist feel to it. A few of the male guests wore Akubra hats to show they had roots in the countryside - the bush. Bec doubted any had really spent more than a night out of a five-start hotel. Bec turned a corner and there were her photos. Self-awareness and embarrassment consumed her and she felt heat rise in her cheeks, as if she didn't deserve to be here. Her photos were framed and hanging on the white-washed walls with small pin-lights illuminating the images. A woman in her mid-fifties stood before the images. She had a blank expression on her face and her head was cocked slightly to the left.

That can't be good. Bec turned to go back in the opposite direction, but Margery Nederfield, the owner of the small gallery, glided up to Bec's shoulder with a champagne flute in each hand and wearing a red evening gown with a revealing neckline. She passed one of the champaign flutes to Bec.

"Oh Rebecca! These images just love this space," said Margery. She took Bec by the elbow and lead her to where the woman was standing. "Olivia darling," began Margery. "I do want you to meet the artist to whom these images belong."

The woman named Olivia faced Bec, "These are delightful photographs, dear. The light creates a sense of hopeful energy, wouldn't you say Margery?"

"Certainly. It is such a relief to have representations of rural life that aren't based on the romanticism of Australia's pioneering past." Bec was taken aback. She hadn't expected such a critique of her work, or such praise.

The older woman extended her hand and Bec shook it. She had a firm grip, and Bec decided there was metal in the woman. She said, "Rebecca Williams, photographer."

"Olivia Fraser, business woman."

Margery added, "Not just a business woman. Olivia also sits on the school board of Penkhurst Girls." Bec hadn't heard of it, but she smiled and nodded. Margery continued, "Weren't you saying that your artist in residence up and left for South America?"

Olivia rested a hand on Margery's forearm. "I'm so glad you mentioned it. Rebecca dear, Penkhurst is looking for an artist in residence. I don't suppose you would be interested?"

Bec's hand went to her chest, covering her heart. This was her chance. An artist in residence position would allow her to teach *and* pursue her line of artwork. And in Melbourne? She'd be crazy not to take it. But, what about Jen? What about Ryan?

Olivia must have noticed her hesitation. She said, "I know dear, it's a terrible thing to spring on you. You must already be established someplace else, what a pity. For Penkhurst, I mean." She smiled.

Bec glanced at her photos then looked back to Olivia. "Actually, I think I can be available from next month."

Olivia's face cracked into a smile. "Oh darling, wonderful. Listen, send me your portfolio so I can show it the Board and the Principal. She will definitely want a say in all this. I'll have a firm answer for you by the end of the week. Margery will give you my contact details."

Margery gave Bec's arm a firm squeeze. Just like that, Bec had gone from a small-town photographer to artist in residence at Penkhurst Girls School. She could barely contain her excitement.

As soon as Olivia had moved on, Bec downed the champagne, quickly found a replacement, and downed that one, too. She couldn't stop herself from grinning.

AT A TABLE in the Black Rock Bar Pub, Ryan checked his phone. He had a message from Bec,

Opening night went well. Lots to talk about. C U Sunday.

He showed Jen the message, since Jen had, yet again, forgotten her phone. "I'm glad the opening went well for her. I think she was pretty nervous, more than she let on." Ryan nodded his agreement and drank from his glass of beer.

Wednesday nights at the Black Rock were generally quiet affairs. On the TV screens mounted in the corners of the ceiling, highlights from weekend sports played silently. A few workers from the meat-works sat at the bar and talked loudly. A few farmers in jeans and flannel shirts played pool.

Mark and Donita were with Ryan and Jen, as was Angela. They were out to celebrate and commiserate. Mark got the Head of Maths job. Ryan had missed out on English.

Donita shook her head. "I still can't believe that idiot Lewis Jones got the Head of English over you, Ryan."

Ryan finished off his beer and said, "I felt sure I was going to get it. I was the most experienced candidate, I lead some school initiatives, community involvement. I don't get it."

Angela, who was sitting next to Mark, sipped her cocktail through a straw, then leaned forward. "I heard that Michael Brooks has something over Janice Heartford. Maybe he pressured her? It's no secret he hates your guts, Ryan."

Jen chimed in, "That's ridiculous. What could Brooks have over Janice? She's a career educator and not from Brooksdale." Angela shrugged her shoulders in response and sipped her cocktail.

Mark stood up, "I don't want to listen to that sort of gossip. You up for another beer, Ryan?"

Ryan looked at his empty glass. He'd had five already. So much for the two-by-two rule. "Yeah, one more."

Ryan was glad he had friends like Mark, Jen, and Donita. Left alone, he'd probably drink himself to sleep and skip work. Well, perhaps not skip work.

Before coming to the pub, Ryan had bought a carton of beer and put a six-pack in the fridge. He could still drink himself to sleep when he got home. Then there was Mark. He had gotten the job – Head of Maths. And Bec, she was having some success. *Time to stop feeling sorry for yourself, Ryan.* He decided to put his disappointment away and celebrate.

"Hey! It's my favourite English Teacher. I'm looking forward to having you on my team, Ryan." Unbelievable. It was Lewis Jones. He had just entered pub and seemed oblivious to the mood of the party. Lewis patted Ryan on the shoulder. Ryan tensed at the touch. Was this guy deliberately being a jerk, or was he genuinely clueless?

"Congratulations on the job, Lewis. You must be very happy," mumbled Ryan.

Amazingly, Lewis sat down in Mark's chair. "Well, I kind of knew I'd get the job, so no surprises really. I just applied for the Head of English job in Brooksdale in case I didn't get the one down in Musswellbrook - just in case." Ryan gripped his empty beer glass tightly. His jaw clenched tight. *So the cocky bastard got two jobs and nothing for me.*

Mark returned and put the full glass down in front of Ryan. "Well, Lewis. I didn't expect to see you here," Mark said. "You're in my seat. Shift it."

Lewis looked up at Mark and extended his hand for a handshake. "Hey Mark! My colleague. Congrats on the new appointment."

Mark put the beers down and shook Lewis's hand. Disdain flooded through Ryan. It was an ugly feeling that surprised Ryan. Lewis wasn't a bad guy, he just didn't deserve the job. Ryan imagined throwing Lewis to the ground and choking him out. Just for fun. Sliding the untouched beer that Mark had delivered across to Lewis, Ryan said, "Congratulations on the job, Lewis."

"Thanks, man. Appreciate it."

Ryan stood up. "It's past my bed-time. I want to get an early start tomorrow." Out on the street, Ryan on foot, meandered his way home. He stopped outside his old family home. It was dark and empty. The front lawn had quickly become overgrown with the rain and warmer weather. Remembering the good times and fantasizing about doing the place up usually made him feel better, but not tonight. He carried on past the Youth Centre. Again, he stopped, but it too was empty of everything except memo-

ries. Important memories, but there was no comfort there
tonight.

Finally, at home, Ryan opened the fridge and pulled out
a beer. He opened it with a crack-pop and took a swig before
closing the fridge door.

He put on UFC One and sank into his sofa, prepared to
drink himself to sleep.

40

Bec dropped her backpack on the floor next to the sofa in Jen's flat. The mid-morning sun lit the place up and Bec felt warm - she had just hiked down from the bus station at North Brooksdale Service Station - an hour walk. Bec didn't mind, even after her epic bus journey from Melbourne. If anything, the sojourn had restored more of her self-reliance - but it was good to be home.

After giving Bec a sisterly hug, Jen turned on the kitchen light and put the kettle on. "Coffee?"

"Forget coffee. Give me a wine."

Jen raised an eyebrow but Bec could barely contain her excitement. Like a tomato about to split after heavy rain, Bec blurted, "I got a new gig!"

Suspended in the middle of pouring the wine, Jen might as well have been caught in a spider's web. "What does that mean exactly?"

Bec squealed when she spoke, "I got a job offer! Artist in residence at a prep school."

It was Jen's turn to squeal. She rushed forward and embraced Bec. They jump-hugged and clasped each other's arms at the elbow. "That's wonderful news!" Breaking away, Jen rushed to the kitchen and finished pouring the wine. "Cheers to opportunities!" The sisters clinked glasses and drank deeply. Jen said, "Sit down and tell me everything."

"Only if you bring that bottle over here," laughed Bec.

Sitting on the sofa, Bec told Jen about Margery, and the flighty artist in residence that had passed Bec the opportunity of a lifetime! "So, what are you going to do? Are you seriously going to take it?" Jen asked.

There was a hint of trepidation in Jen's voice. Bec noticed it and realized this decision would affect Jen's life, too. They had become best friends over the last few months and that wasn't something to simply throw to the wind. Bec replied, "I really want to take it. The schedule is light, so I'd still have time for my own art. And the school covers accommodation - it's a boarding school. The pay is much better than here, and it's a chance to learn more skills and take my art to the next level." Nodding gently, Jen let Bec continue. "I really love it here in Brooksdale, too." Bec turned and looked Jen fully in the face. She grasped Jen's hand. "We've never been closer, you and me. My job is fine, and then there's Ryan."

"He is a great guy."

Bec exhaled and looked at the TV, blank and showing the reflection of the sisters sitting on a sofa. "He could come with me. There are a lot of good schools in Melbourne. I'm sure he'd find something."

The sisters sat quietly for a moment. Finally, Jen spoke, "You have to decide what you want. But, just so you know, I'm always your sister, and Ryan will have to make his own choices."

Bec leaned across and hugged Jen. She had the best sister in the world.

41

Ryan pulled in at the river-side car park and got out of his old F-150. He had come here during spring with Bec and she had been transfixed by the beauty of this small nature reserve on the Black Rock River. Now it was slipping into summer and the area was bursting with wildflowers and the sounds of nature. He breathed deeply and caught the scent of wattle blossoms. The sweet richness of the beautiful yellow-ball blossoms was like a switch that turned the world from winter into spring.

Along the river bank and through the bush, explosions of yellow were like fireworks against the browns and greens of the Australian bush. For the first time since Wednesday night, his head cleared. The past few days had been tough. Missing out on the promotion really sent Ryan for a loop. The maddening thing was that he knew it shouldn't have. The resulting feeling of anger with himself had lead him into a spiral of drink. That hadn't happened since Tammy left.

Ryan thought back over the train-wreck of a week he had had. On Thursday, Ryan had such a bad hangover that he had to take the day off sick. That was a first. At home on Thursday, he drank all day while watching K1 and UFC, and passed out before six. On Friday, he managed to go to work, but it was a fog in his memory. An automatic response. Ryan hadn't even gone to Jiu-jitsu.

On Saturday, he talked to Bec on the phone. She sounded excited and her enthusiasm warmed him, like sunlight breaking through on an overcast day. Her exhibition went very well, she said. She had exciting news to tell him, she said. Let's meet on Sunday, at the river.

By Sunday, the warmth had left Ryan and anxiety replaced it. What was it with the depressed mind that turned normal events into occasions for fretfulness. The odd thing was that Ryan knew what he was experiencing. He had felt it before when Tammy had left him.

This awareness did little to assuage his worry. Had Bec met some hipster down in Melbourne? Had she decided to up stumps and lead the traveling artist life? These concerns whirled around and around in Ryan's mind as he trudged along the path to the river. A kookaburra cackled in the distance. At least someone found all this funny.

Ryan wandered along the path of the nature reserve and reached the picnic area by the river bank by mid-afternoon. There was a teenage couple sitting on a bench, feeling the summer love. Ryan recognized them from school. They were good kids and Ryan was glad they had found romance together. Further long, Ryan saw Bec with her camera pointed out over the water.

.   .   .

DOWN BY THE water's edge, Bec stood with her camera trained on a spot across the water. A bird flew up from a low hanging branch. Her camera click-whirred as she snapped off rapid photos. Lowering her camera, she saw Ryan approaching. A smile spread across her face. "Hi," she said.

"I saw that bird take off. Did you get some good shots?"

Bec stood on her tip-toes and kissed his lips, stopping his words. She detected reluctance in his kiss. Was that alcohol on his breath? He was holding something back. After the kiss, Bec looked at Ryan and took both of his hands in hers. "I love it down here, Ryan. It's so tranquil and the wild life is amazing. Can you hear the bees? The birds? It's nearly a roar. So different from Melbourne."

"It is a beautiful place. That's why the teenage Romeos come here." Ryan smiled, but Bec could tell it was forced.

Undeterred, she grinned, "Did you bring your teenage sweet-heart down to the river?"

"I certainly did. It was compulsory for the times." Bec laughed at Ryan's response and she saw his smile soften. That was the Ryan she remembered. Maybe he knew what was coming.

They held hands and walked along the bank. Bec said, "Ryan, these last couple of months have been truly wonderful. I didn't think I'd feel like this again after leaving Phil." She looked out over the water as she said that man's name. Bec stopped walking and faced Ryan. There was a touch of anxiety in his eyes. She said, "The exhibition went well, really well. I sold some photos. I actually got paid for my work!"

RYAN FELT RELIEVED. Was that it? The big news? Ryan took her in his arms, lifted her off the ground and twirled on the spot. Bec giggled with delight and Ryan felt light again. He said, "That's great news!"

Bec hesitated, then added, "And... A school offered me a job. Their artist in residence took off to South America and they need someone in a hurry. I'm moving down there. I'm moving to Melbourne." Ryan felt winded. The same way he did when he realized Tammy wasn't coming back. Abandoned, again. He let go of Bec, stepping away from her. He walked a few paces off the track, then sat down on a fallen tree. Its bark had long since rotted off and the timber had weathered smooth, leaving a grey skeleton of a gum tree.

BEC FOLLOWED HIM. She saw the hurt on Ryan's face, but she knew there was no easy way to do this. Hurting Ryan was the risk, and she had known it from the start. "Ryan. This is an important opportunity for me. A better job. A chance to focus on my art. A chance to be me. Ryan. I want us to go together. Come with me to Melbourne."

He ran his hands over his head as if he had just walked through a spider web and was trying to get rid of it. Then he rubbed his chin with his thumb, a gesture Bec had come to know and love. "I don't know. My life is here. I can't just up and leave. Who would take care of Mum? Who would run the Youth Centre? Bec searched Ryan's face, but he wouldn't, or couldn't, make eye-contact with her. Ryan continued imploringly, "Your sister is here. Are you ready to leave her? Then there is your job at the studio. You're doing really well there. You have a life here, too."

Bec sighed. She knew Ryan had been around this area all his life, but there was no way she would give up on her creativity for a man ever again. "Ryan, come with me." She touched his cheek lovingly. He looked at her. His eyes were sad.

Ryan reached out and put both hands on her shoulders. "Bec. There is no need to run off chasing dreams." That stung. Bec stepped away from him. Her gaze hardened. "My dreams are worth chasing. This place will always be here, but dreams float away and stay just that – dreams, unless you go after them. You have to take a risk sometimes, take a chance."

With that, Bec walked back up the track towards the car park. At the crest of the rise, she turned and called out to Ryan, "I'm leaving next weekend. You can come with me, or you can stay. Your life." And that was it. She walked away feeling hurt, upset, excited, and scared all at the same time. Above all, she hoped Ryan would come with her.

RYAN WATCHED in a semi state of shock as Bec walked away. *What did women want anyway? They say they want stability, then turn around and run off on some whim!*

He didn't really know how long he sat on that fallen tree. His thoughts were disturbed by a dog and its owner out for an afternoon walk. Ryan said hello, then walked back towards the car park. The crunch of tires on gravel as cars pulled into the river-side car park followed by the shouts and yells of teenagers alerted Ryan to impending danger. Ryan didn't want to embarrass his students, or himself, by being around while the teenagers kissed and fondled by the river, so he took a different path that wound around to the back of the car park.

As he walked, he tried to clear his mind. Organize his thoughts and feelings. He felt confused and hurt. Things had been going so well with Bec, despite them both coming out of long-term relationships.

A shout jolted Ryan out of his thoughts, "Mr. Anderson's out havin' a perv!" followed by derisive laughter. Ryan stopped and looked to his left. Tyler and his gang sat on the hood of Tyler's black Holden ute, about fifty meters from Ryan. Tyler had a blue can in his hand. He lifted it to his mouth, tossed his head back, then threw the can on the ground.

One of the boys, Bayden, called out, "Enjoying the *bird* life, Mi-s-ter Anderson?" Bayden laughed at his own joke.

Ryan called back, "Don't drink-and-drive and don't get in a car with a drunk driver. You'll end up killing someone or yourself. You hear?"

Foster called back, "Bit hot under the collar there Mr. Anderson?" More laughter.

Tyler slipped off the hood of his truck, "You ain't got no power out here. Fuck off back to your little books in your little house, and your little woman. Oh, I forgot, she left you because of your little dick!" That brought the house down and Ryan's discomfort turned to anger. Had they overheard? They couldn't have. They arrived well after Bec left.

Their attitude wounded Ryan deeply. Not just because of the words, but the thoughtlessness behind them. Education was a ticket to a better job, a better life. Why couldn't these kids see that? Why did those kids reject something as precious as their own minds and waste their lives burning brain cells? Didn't they know there was a whole world out there waiting to be discovered? A world where people can make a difference? Ryan wanted to walk right up to them and tell them how foolish they were being.

Folly. Instead, Ryan got a hold of his emotions and walked on. Anger, frustration, and sadness clouded his mood like a summer thunder storm. He got into his truck and drove off, not really thinking about where he was going. Ryan eventually found himself outside his old home. The one his father died in.

Standing on the street with his old Ford idling roughly behind him, Ryan faced his family's old house – his history. Muscles twitch in his neck, and he glared at the old house. The street was quiet; people were out for the weekend. The only sound was the rustling of eucalyptus leaves in the breeze and the rumble-throb of the Ford engine.

Suddenly striding across the road, Ryan found himself picking up a rock and hurling it at the old house. The rock bounced ineffectually off the wooden wall and fell through some broken planks that once formed the veranda. *Thumph.* The rock landed with a barely audible thud on the ground.

The tension built and built and his breathing became heavier and faster. Ryan picked up more rocks and hurled them one by one at the old fallen down house. *Thump, thwack, smash!* The rocks flew and hit their target until Ryan's energy was spent.

Placing his hands on the wobbly, half-fallen down fence, Ryan exhaled slowly in an attempt to alleviate his restricted breathing. He felt as if he had just sprinted one-hundred metres. Ryan swallowed heavily and felt dryness in the back of his throat. *How did I end up here?*

Ryan's thoughts went from his parents, to Brooks, to Tyler, to Tammy, his job, then Bec. He had given so much of himself to the things he cared about and in the end, it was as good as this rotting house in front of him.

Backing away from the fence, and the house, memories of Christmases past ran through Ryan's mind; playing back-yard cricket with his father in the summer, kicking a football in winter, and fighting with his brother, came back. They were good memories. But that's all they were.

Ryan tried to think of all the things that needed doing to the house: a fresh coat of paint, federation-style windows, new kitchen, new roofing. But it was no use. The house, once an imaginary shrine to an old dream, had now lost its radiance. It was as if Ryan had stepped behind the stage of a magic show, and for the first time, he saw things for what they were.

42

On Monday morning, Ryan arrived at work with a two-day beard and a hangover. He told himself it wasn't too bad, since he had left one six-pack unopened – one out of four ain't bad – and was determined not to buy another. Yet, as he slipped through the school, Ryan avoided eye-contact with those he passed.

When he got to his desk, he checked his e-mail. There was a message from Janice asking him to see her period one this morning. Lewis would cover his classes for him. Lewis bloody Jones.

"Hey Ry!" It was Lewis. "I got your class this morning. What do you want me to do?" Ryan grimaced. If he were honest with himself, his plan was to be flexible and responsive to student needs. In other words: wing it. Composing himself, Ryan looked up into Lewis's face. "Exam essay practice. I'll write down the questions for you."

Pulling out a scrap piece of paper, Ryan scribbled down five exam style questions for the students to choose from. He gave the scrap of paper to Lewis, who said, "Thanks man. Oh, and again, really enjoyed working with you this year."

Ryan inhaled sharply through his nose. What was it with this guy? He couldn't be this clueless, surely? Everyone is entitled to a safe workplace free from the harassment of idiots.

Sulking through the halls of Brooksdale High, Ryan arrived at Janice's office. He knocked. She replied, "Hi Ryan. Come in." Janice held her door open for Ryan. The room was tidy and Ryan appreciated a clean workspace. Tidy space, tidy thinking was Ryan's motto. He tried not to think of the mess of beer cans and pizza boxes at home.

Janice gestured to a chair opposite her desk. "I'm sorry I couldn't tell you this earlier." She began. What was this? Was he losing his job, too? "I had to leave suddenly on Wednesday. Family matter. I didn't get to tell you the news and I didn't want to do it over e-mail These things are best done face-to-face, I find."

Ryan nodded his sympathy, but he was perplexed. What was the damn news?

"Ryan, I want to offer you the Curriculum Coordinator position. I know it's a tough job and you'll still have some teaching duties, but I've arranged the timetable so you'll have at least one period a week for meeting with the other Heads of Department." Ryan was speechless. He did get a promotion – a step above Head of Department. Well, up a bit and sideways a bit, but it was still a step in the right direction.

Janice waited for Ryan to speak. When he didn't, she added, "You don't have to say yes. A lot of good teachers are good teachers because they love the classroom. And you *are* a good teacher. I would say, though that this is an opportunity to have an impact beyond your classroom. A lot of the staff look up to you."

Ryan cleared his throat and replied, "I wasn't expecting

this. It's a bit of a surprise." He felt acutely uncomfortable. What an idiot he had been to let his world collapse into drunkenness. He wanted to say 'yes.' He knew this was a good proposition, but something held him back. "Can I think about it? I want to talk with my family."

"Certainly. Shall we say Thursday?"

Ryan agreed. He stood and shook hands with Janice. She showed him out of her office, holding the door for him. He went directly to his classroom. Through the glass slit in the door, he could see Lewis in front of the class. He was animated and the students were paying attention.

So, Lewis wasn't a jerk after all. He had just known that Ryan would be Curriculum Director. Ryan had been wrong all along. He took a deep breath and stepped into the classroom ready to start the day a rejuvenated man.

43

"I'm done. I'm done," said Ryan as he desperately tapped out on the mat. Ryan sat up, breathing hard.

Paul, who stood over him, said, "Damn man, you're easy tonight." Ryan had been getting his tail handed to him all through training. No doubt a result of boozing it up for a week. But, the job offer had helped kick him out of his self-pity and Ryan wasted no time getting back into his routine, yet his thoughts kept getting dragged back to Bec.

After training, as everyone left the gym and got into their cars, Jerry approached Ryan. "You seemed off your game tonight."

"Yeah. Tough day."

"Something happen?"

"Just the usual," replied Ryan without making eye-contact.

Jerry said, "I'm heading over to Sully's for a late dinner. Come along."

. . .

Sully's Sports Bar and Grill was nearly empty on Monday nights, and tonight was no exception. There were a few people from the meat works playing pool and a farmer, wearing a sun-faded John Deer hat, was throwing darts at an old board.

Jerry and Ryan found a seat at the bar in the dining area. When the beers arrived, Jerry clinked glasses with Ryan and drank deeply. "Ahh, that's good. It's been a long week." Ryan only nodded. Jerry continued, "You gonna tell me what's got you so wound up, or do I have to beat it out of you?"

After taking a drink from his beer, Ryan decided to tell Jerry about the job offer, but not everything else.

"Sounds like a no-brainer to me. Take the job. Unless there's a certain lady that's complicating matters," replied Jerry.

There was no fooling a copper. Holding his glass with two hands, Ryan peered into it, trying to build the courage to talk. Finally, without looking up from the glass, Ryan said, "She's moving to Melbourne."

"Damn. We'll need some more beers, then." Jerry ordered another round.

Once the bartender poured the drinks and sat them on the table, Ryan said, "I thought we had something special, you know. Me and her here in Brooksdale. Family and friends around us. It would have worked out really well."

The corners of Jerry's mouth deepened. "You can't decide what's good for another person. It's Bec's life, too." A cheer went up in the background from a small group of punters. Someone won some money on the TAB. Jerry added, "If you like her so much, go with her. Brooksdale is not going anywhere."

"It's my home, Jerry. She needs to understand that,"

"But it's not her home. You need to understand that," retorted Jerry.

Ryan looked up into the big man's face. "I've worked so hard here. School, the house, the Youth Centre. I can't just leave it all. Who would look after that stuff?"

Jerry breathed in deeply through his nose. The sound added weight to what he said next, "That's martyr syndrome right there."

Ryan ran his thumb across his chin before knocking off half of his beer in one gulp. He slammed his glass down. "You mean I haven't done anything worthwhile here?" His voice was louder than he he intended it to be.

"Nope," replied Jerry as he put both hands flat on the counter, palms down. "I'm sayin' someone else will step up. What good is all that stuff if it's dependent on you?" The sting came out of Ryan's argument and he sat quietly, pondering Jerry's point. It hurt to think that the town didn't need him. Who would stand up against the likes of Michael Brooks?

Jerry said, "Well. I think I'm done. I'm walkin' home tonight. Doesn't do any good for a copper to be seen drinking and driving." Ryan finished up and wobbled as he slipped off his stool. Jerry looked at Ryan then clapped his large hand on Ryan's shoulder, "You should walk, too. Clear your head a little."

Outside, the air was cool and crickets chirped. Summer was coming. Ryan and Jerry parted ways. Ryan started walking and decided to go past his old home. The one his father had bought. The one his father had died in. The one which Michael Brooks cheated his mother out of. He strolled along the familiar streets. The same ones he had been walking for nearly three decades. He saw the same drunken arguments, the same couples kissing in the shadows. The same Holdens and Fords lapping the town. He didn't see the black Hyundai Sonata cruise past. He was too focused on his inner thoughts.

PETER WATSON WAS WORRIED. He didn't like to feel worried, but he couldn't shake the feeling that something bad was going to happen to that lovely girl, Rebecca Williams. Watson had kept Rebecca Williams under surveillance for over two months. In that time, he got to know her, albeit from a distance. What he saw just didn't add up to what his employer claimed.

Two weeks ago, Philip Mansfield failed to make payment for Watson's services. When Watson called him on it, Philip reacted angrily, saying that Rebecca hadn't come home yet, and that he wouldn't pay until Watson 'got Becky home.'

Watson did a little checking on Philip Mansfield. It didn't take long to find the assault charge and the restraining order. Watson cursed himself for not conducting due diligence on this client before taking the job in the first place. He didn't feel he had enough to go to the police. What would they do anyway? They couldn't give her a police guard. That was movie stuff, and he couldn't guard her, someone had to pay the bills. In the end, he decided the boyfriend, Ryan, was the best option.

Watson wrote a short note explaining his concerns. But when he eventually located Ryan Anderson, the guy was clearly drunk and in an emotional state standing outside an abandoned house crying into the night. Not good timing to talk about your girlfriend's stalker.

So, Watson had driven past Ryan, planning to leave the note under the door before Ryan got home. The note was anonymous. No point risking questions from the police, especially in his line of work.

So that is what Peter Watson did on Monday night. He went to Ryan's house, left an anonymous note warning of a threat from Philip Mansfield, then he left. He wanted to make it back to Brisbane by morning. Another job done.

RYAN STOOD outside his old house like a young man rebelling against his father. The good memories felt distant. The dings and dents from the rocks Ryan had thrown the other day were barely visible. A rumble of rage and confusion swirled inside Ryan. His father had gambled in business and lost, ultimately sending him into a deep depression followed by suicide. Ryan spoke out loud to the empty house as if it could be hurt by his words, "Why did you do it Dad? Everything would have been fine if you'd just stayed here and kept going."

Stagnation. The word came to Ryan and he was surprised to feel tears burn in his eyes. Stagnation. Ryan looked at the house and it was just a house. He saw the paint peeling from the walls like burnt skin. The fence had fallen and the flyscreens hanged from the windows like laundry drying on a line, but left far too long. The front door was peeled and cracked with weather damage and the guttering had collapsed.

Decay. Suffocation. Fear.

Mum was scared. She still is. So am I. The realization stung. Ryan turned his back on the house and started jogging. He didn't stop at the Youth Centre, either. He felt the urge to move his body. He ran faster and faster until he was sprinting in a drunken tumble, barreling forwards.

When he got to his house, Ryan panted hard and his shins hurt.

He fumbled his keys in the lock, then pushed and flung the door open, nearly falling through. He didn't see the note get crushed between the door and the inside wall.

Rushed through to the kitchen, Ryan opened the fridge door and pulled out the remaining six-pack of beer. Taking a deep breath, he cracked open the first bottle and tipped the beer into the sink. It felt good. He did it again, and again, until all the beer was gone.

Relieved and refreshed, Ryan felt back in control. Wobbly and vulnerable, but in control. He pulled his phone out of his pocket. It was just after ten o'clock. Bec might still be up. He texted:

Can we meet tomorrow?

44

The morning sun lighted up Ryan's kitchen revealing an orderly scene. The beer bottles were all in the recycling bin. The pizza boxes cleaned up and in the garbage. It was seven o'clock and Ryan stepped out of the shower feeling energized. He was meeting Bec this morning.

He made a protein drink, poured cereal and yoghurt into a bowl, and sat down to eat. Meeting Bec wouldn't be an issue. He had two free periods this morning and the following two were senior classes. They were practicing exam essays again. No problems there. At seven-thirty, he dialled the number for the office. Delores answered, "Brooksdale High School."

"Hi. Delores? It's Ryan. Listen, I won't be in this morning. The tap in my kitchen's broke and I need to get it fixed."

"Mmmhuh. Trying to get things tied up before Bec leaves?"

Ryan swallowed. How could she know? But then again, Delores knew everyone's business. Ryan replied, "Yeah. She's leaving this weekend, so busy time, you know."

"I'll tell Janice. Anything else you want me to tell Janice?"

Damn. Delores knew about the promotion, too. "No. I need to see Janice this afternoon anyway. Thanks Delores."

"You take care Ryan."

He hung up thinking how many people actually knew what was going on. Small towns. He looked at the clock. Seven-forty-five. He was supposed to pick up Bec at eight-thirty.

Last night he had messaged her, then she called him. They talked about Melbourne, Brooksdale, jobs, and their relationship. In the end, Ryan had decided it would be better to talk face-to-face. Bec had agreed. Now, Ryan just had to wait. He decided to vacuum the house – something to do for thirty minutes.

The whirr of the vacuum cleaner released the tension of waiting. Under the table, the bedrooms, the hallway, and the entrance to the house. Ryan pulled the machine around behind him, totally focused on sucking up dirt, dust, and mites from the carpets of his home. He reached the front entrance. The security screen door let a refreshing breeze into his house, but he knew dust monsters lurked behind the heavier wooden door.

He swung the door closed and rammed the vacuum cleaner head into the corner. The sound of crunching paper and the increased whine of the electric motor alerted Ryan to a problem, so he switched off the cleaner and inspected the cleaner head. He found a crumpled note half sucked into the mouth of the cleaner. Pulling it out, he didn't recognize the writing but the message was clear. Ryan grabbed his car keys, and bolted out of the house.

45

P hil sat in a rented Toyota Tarago. He waited. He knew the patient hunter was the victorious hunter. Country music came through the car radio. How Bec could possibly choose to live here instead of Brisbane was beyond him. He turned off the radio. Better to wait in silence than listen to that rubbish. It was just more confirmation that Bec needed his help to get back on the right path. Phil had it all planned out. He would go up to the flat, present Bec's father's camera gear as an apology for past sins – girls liked that sort of thing – explain his case, then drive Bec home to Brisbane.

He didn't need Peter fucking Watson anyway. That guy proved to be loyal only as far as the money stretched. He shouldn't have been surprised, really. Over the past few months, some business dealings had fallen through. Then Phil's business partner sold out. The bank started asking questions. All this had happened after Bec left, and Phil realized that he needed Bec as much as she needed him. She was his lucky charm – his secret sauce. What was the saying? Every great man had a decent woman behind him? Something like that.

Sure he'd had a few girls in the meantime, but that was only fair. Bec was seeing other guys. It balanced the equation. All in all, Phil rationalized, Bec was his princess and he was her knight in shining amour. They belonged together. Her Guinevere to his Sir Lancelot.

Jen's little blue Honda pulled out of the car park and drove off down the road. Phil checked the photos and schedules Peter Watson had given him at their last meeting. At least *they* were reliable. Bec didn't usually leave the apartment until nine-thirty. He had time on his side. She was probably still asleep. Bec always slept late. It was one thing that annoyed him about her. How could she sleep so late? The morning was the best time of day. It was probably the tequila. She never could handle her drink. Phil was a caring man – he would give her time to sleep.

INSIDE THE FLAT, Bec rummaged through her things. She had only five days to prepare for her move to Melbourne. As she opened and closed draws, she thought of her talk with Ryan last night. They hadn't reached a consensus, but she sensed all he needed was a little security and to maintain a foothold in Brooksdale, and he would come with her. *Perhaps Jen would agree to rent his house?* That was a nice thought – keep it all in the family.

Bec picked up the necklace that Ryan had made for her. She hadn't worn it since their meeting at the river. Now, she held it for a moment, then put it on. Things would work out just fine, she was sure. The bedroom clock read: eight-ten. Time for her morning coffee. In the kitchen, she noticed Jen's phone on the counter. Bec shook her head. Everyone had their faults and she knew she would miss Jen's habit of leaving her phone or her car keys lying around.

A knock at the door startled her. She put down the coffee pot. "Just a moment!" It was probably Jen back for her phone. Bec shook her head as she swung the door open. A strong hand pushed her in the chest and she stumbled back several paces.

Phil. In front of her. He closed the door and locked it. Reacting to the shock, Bec dashed to the sofa where her mobile phone sat on a cushion. Phil was faster. He grabbed her, lifting her off the ground. Bec kicked into the air like a toddler having a tantrum. she felt a white flash of panic burn across her mind and adrenaline flooded her body.

She screamed.

Phil flung her to the ground and Bec rolled onto all fours and crawled away. She screamed again hoping someone would hear and come to her aid, but a sharp pain reverberated through her skull and she fell flat on the floor. Her head pulsed and she had trouble collecting her thoughts. She saw Phil's feet in front of her, then felt his hands under her armpits as he lifted her up and sat her on the sofa.

Phil's glare cut right through her. "Why do you make me hurt you? Just sit there and there won't be a problem." Bec couldn't help it. Tears came and she gasped for breath. The shock, the blow to the head, and the fear broke through like a water bursting through a crack in a damn wall.

"Damn it!" Phil said louder. "Stop this shit. I'm here to bring you home." He went to the kitchen and returned with a box of tissues. Bec took some, wiped her eyes and blew her nose. While crying and wiping her eyes with the tissue, Bec shuffled closer to the edge of the sofa so she could make a grab for her phone. Perhaps she could get a message away.

Phil had a gym bag slung over his shoulder. He slipped it

off and it fell to the floor. He took his eyes off Bec for an instant. She made a grab for her phone, and stuffed it between her leg and the arm of the sofa.

Phil faced her and pulled out her father's old camera. "Here," he said. "I want to give this to you. It's your father's camera."

"I know what it is," replied Bec. She had all but given up on the camera, assuming Phil had sold it or thrown it away. He had never understood her attachment to it.

"Well? What do you say when someone gives you a gift?"

The fear left Bec, pushed out by rage. She felt the muscles in her neck twitch, but she knew she was in a dangerous place. She had to temper her anger with caution. "Thank you," she mumbled.

Phil seemed to relax. He dragged a chair over and sat in front of Bec. He still held the camera. "I have the other stuff, too. Your father's stuff I mean. I wanted to give it to you as a welcome home present. I know I haven't been the best to you of late. But, I'm sorry. There. I said it. I'm sorry." He ran his fingers through her hair and looked her in the eyes. He seemed to be searching for something.

Careful not to show any fear, Bec composed herself, "Phil, my father's gear was mine to begin with. It is not yours to give."

He sighed and said, "Why do you do this to me? You always make things more complicated than they need to be. I just want you to be happy." He shook his head and his mood shifted like a cloud passing over the sun. "Get your stuff. We're going back to Brisbane."

Bec tried to swallow, but found her mouth was dry. A lump welled in the back of her throat. She was worried her voice would come out as a croak, but she held her nerve. "Phil," said Bec. "I don't live in Brisbane anymore. We broke up. Our relationship doesn't work." Bec pulled more tissues from the box with one hand and jammed the other hand down the side of the sofa where her phone was. If she kept talking, may be Phil wouldn't notice. "You deserve someone better than me. Someone more... more entrepreneurial. Someone with the same drive as you."

Phil leaned over her. He said, "Don't you get it? That *is* you! *You* need to see what you mean to me. Do you know how hurt I was when I found out about the restraining order and the assault charge?"

He began pacing back and forth. He held the camera by the strap and started swinging it. Around and around. He wasn't looking at her, so Bec started typing a message. Years of typing single-handed with her thumb paid off now as she mashed the keypad without looking at the screen.

Phil's volatility undid her. "Here! Have the damned camera!" Without warning, Phil flipped from pacing thoughtfulness to anger. He threw the camera at Bec, forcing her to pull her hands up in front of her face in protection, but the camera hit the sofa, then bounced onto the floor.

There was a moment of stunned silence. Bec peeked out from behind her hands and realized her mistake. She was still holding her phone.

"God, damn it, you bitch!" Phil yelled. He ripped the phone out of Bec's hands, threw it on the floor and stomped on it. The crunch of glass and plastic under the heel of Phil's boot was as loud as a car crash in her mind.

Bec said, "Okay. Okay. Maybe I should think about things again. Do you want a coffee? You must be tired. You drove here, right?"

"Yeah I drove here! I couldn't risk taking the plane in case I got picked up in this shit-town airport."

Legs feeling like jelly, Bec stood, wobbled, then walked to the kitchen. Jen's mobile phone was somewhere in the kitchen, or maybe she could grab a knife. Ryan always said that if someone has a knife and starts slashing wildly, it doesn't matter if the other person knows Jiu-jitsu or not.

"I don't want a damn coffee," said Phil. "You make the shittest coffee I've ever tasted."

Bec kept walking and said, "Well I need one."

She was halfway there. Halfway to a second chance of escape when her head jerked backwards, feeling as if her hair was being ripped from her head like weeds from a garden. She fell backwards to the floor, grabbing at Phil's hands as he dragged her back towards the sofa. "I don't want a damn coffee! Get your stuff. We're going."

All Bec wanted was for the pain to stop. She would have agreed to anything. She whimpered, "Okay, okay." Phil released her and Bec lay on the floor panting and sobbing from the pain and stress.

A key clicked in the lock in the front door. Bec couldn't believe what she was hearing. For an instant her heart soared with hope. Had someone heard the violence in the flat? Had that person called the police?

"Hi! I forgot my phone and I need it today."

It was Jen. Bec had to warn her. She croaked a warning, "Phil!"

It was too late. Phil strode to the door as it opened, grabbed Jen, pulled her in, and threw her to the floor.

He pulled a pistol from inside his jacket and pointed it at Jen. "Move and you're dead."

46

Ryan sped through the streets of Brooksdale. The contents of the note he had found behind the front door fresh in his mind. Phil was still a danger and had possibly planned a kidnapping. The note was anonymous. It could be that Phil or that private investigator were trying to pressure Ryan into leaving Bec or make him over-protective. If that was true, they couldn't be more wrong. Ryan was determined to stand by her.

He pulled up outside the block of flats just as a black mini-van accelerated away. Ryan's only thought was to check on Bec. He jumped out his Ford without locking it and ran across the street. He got to the door and knocked. No answer. He tried the door knob and it opened. Ryan took a deep breath. It was unusual for either Bec or Jen to leave the door unlocked.

With his heart pounding, Ryan pushed the door open. The lights were on. The floor was strewn with papers and clothes. A chair was overturned, a glass lay broken on the kitchen floor, and Bec's phone was smashed into the carpet by the sofa. Ryan ran his hand through his hair and swallowed hard. He pulled out his phone and called Jerry.

THE BLACK MINI-VAN accelerated away from the curve. Phil recognized Ryan in the Ford F-150 and gripped the pistol he had by the side of his leg. When he saw that Ryan hadn't recognized him, he laughed. "You see Bec? Your boyfriend isn't very observant. He mustn't care enough about you."

Bec turned her head until her neck ached, trying to get a view of Ryan. Hoping Ryan would see her. But she was limited in movement by the rope around her neck and hands. In any case, the windows were so heavily tinted that Ryan wouldn't have seen her even if he looked straight at her. Jen was tied and gagged in the very back. Her body rolled with the motion of Phil's driving and Bec could hear Jen's body thump against the interior of the car.

Bec sat in the middle row of seats. Her hands were bound and the rope around her neck bound Bec to the head rest. Each time Phil braked, she choked.

There was one chance left. In the confusion of Jen's return to the apartment, Bec managed to slip Jen's phone into her pocket. Now, she desperately swiped at the screen, trying to send a message for help.

"Fucking idiot!" Phil shouted as he accelerated through an intersection. Bec looked out the window and recognized Paul's Holden ute speeding away from her. When Phil returned his gaze to the road, Bec took her chance, she glanced at the screen as best she could and hit send.

STANDING HELPLESSLY in the wreck of Jen's living room, Ryan hung up the phone after talking with Jerry. His mind flew in several directions: stay here, run out onto the street, or drive out off in search of Bec. But how to find her? Ryan had no idea what car Phil would be driving nor which direction. Ryan calmed himself and forced his mind to think. If Phil thought he were rescuing Bec, where would he take her? Back to Brisbane!

Ryan raced out of Jen's flat knowing he had to get on the highway heading North to Brisbane as quickly possible. Just as Ryan got into his F-150, his phone buzzed. It was from Jen. Frantically, Ryan read the message,

Phil. Black minivan North Main Str.

Beautiful! Now he knew what car to look for. But why had this message come from Jen's phone? Unless the psycho had kidnapped Jen, too. Ryan jammed his key into the ignition and floored the accelerator. The old Ford revved and jumped forward into action. His tyres squealed as he rounded the corner. Another driver honked angrily behind him.

Steering with one hand, Ryan called Jerry with the information. "God damn it Ryan! I told you stay where you were," yelled Jerry. "How do you know Phil didn't send that message to throw us of the trail?" In the background, Ryan heard the police siren come on.

PREDICTIVE TEXT WAS a bitch and all Bec could do was pray she sent the message correctly. She could see Phil's eyes in the rear-view mirror. Without warning, Phil swerved, braked, then accelerated, choking Bec against the rope around her neck and desperately tucked her chin in to fight against the biting rope like Tony had showed her in jiu-jitsu when someone is trying to choke you. The phone fell from her grip and bounced on the seat, then dropped on the floor with a thud.

Phil twisted in the driver's seat and saw the phone. "You God damned bitch!" He tried to pick the phone up off the floor, but Bec kicked at his hand and Phil momentarily lost control of the vehicle, running the van up onto the curve. Phil jammed the brakes on. The rope bit mercilessly into Bec's neck as momentum pushed her forwards. When the vehicle came to a stop, she dry-heaved.

A police siren sounded in the distance. Phil heard it because Bec could see fear in his eyes as they widened in the rear-view mirror. The car bumped and rocked as Phil drove it off the curve and back onto the road. A few cars honked playfully at the black minivan's misfortune. Drivers waved as they went past. Bec, helpless, looked out the tinted windows. If only they knew.

As Phil picked up speed, a horrible grinding noise sounded from under the car. "God fucking damn it!" Phil yelled. He took the next left and pulled over. Perhaps some good fortune. As Phil unbuckled his seat belt, he said, "You stupid cow. What have you done?"

Bec looked around in an attempt to orientate herself. They were just outside Uriah Brooks' House. Phil got out of the car, went around to the side and opened Bec's door. He held the pistol in one hand. With the other, he pulled the rope tight around her neck.

Bec's lungs fought to get oxygen in and she made horrible gargling sounds. She felt her eyes bulging and her muscles straining. She kicked out, but only hit the car seat in front of her. Phil released her and she coughed and spluttered as she sucked air into her burning lungs. She wanted to throw up right onto her tormentor as he reached down and grabbed the phone and threw it onto the footpath.

The wave of anger seemed to have passed by him. He stood beside the car, breathing heavily. The smoother talker returned and he ran his hand through Bec's hair, he said, "I'm sorry babe. If you'd just do what I say, there wouldn't be any problems. Trust me, okay?"

Phil's hand on her head was as soothing as a snake slithering over her skull. She had to fight hard to control her reactions. She croaked a response, "Okay, okay." Police sirens sounded again in the distance. If she could buy some time, maybe. Just maybe... *Cough. Cough.* "Phil. I can't breathe. Loosen the rope. Please."

He looked at her with what she thought was tenderness. He put the pistol into his waist band and began untying the rope around her neck.

IN THE DISTANCE, Ryan saw the black minivan swerve. That was it. Ryan knew it in his guts, so he accelerated, overtaking several cars. He was gaining. One more set of lights. A semi-trailer pulled onto Main Street right in front of Ryan. He moved over to try and overtake and stuck his head out of the window to see if the road was clear, but cars were coming quickly in the opposite direction.

At the lights, Ryan drove up onto the footpath and around the semi. As he bounced down and back onto the road, Ryan caught a glimpse of the black minivan make a left turn. Ryan crept out across the intersection, then accelerated as the light turned green. Down at the next light, he swung left and saw the van parked in front of Uriah Brooks' House.

He pulled in diagonally across the front of the minivan,

just like he had seen in cop films. Jumping out, he saw that the driver seat was empty.

Ryan felt a twinge of nervous energy pulse through his body. He saw the smashed phone on the ground and fought down panic. What if Phil swapped vehicles? The sound of thumps coming from the back of the minivan brought Ryan back to the moment. He opened the back of the vehicle to reveal Jen frantically kicking at the side of her prison.

"Agh, agh." Jen coughed as Ryan pulled the gag from her mouth and untied the rope binding her.

The sirens grew louder and Ryan could see the flashing lights of Jerry's patrol car making the turn. "Don't worry," said Ryan soothingly. "Jerry's on his way."

Pop! Pop!

Ryan and Jen froze. The shots came from the direction of Uriah Brooks' House. Jen pushed Ryan away from her. "Go!" she orders. Ryan obeyed, sprinting into the Uriah Brooks House.

Moments later, Jerry's patrol car pulled in behind the black minivan as Ryan bolted across the road, through the front garden, and into Uriah Brooks' house.

Inside, it took a moment for Ryan's eyes to adjust to the dim lighting. Groans came from behind the information counter. Ryan forced himself to walk over and look. He felt like his feet were encased in clay. Angela lay on the floor, her back against the wall. Her breathing was short and her face pale. Her hands clasped her abdomen and blood oozed through her fingers. "Angela!" Ryan knelt beside her. She looked at Ryan and her face was pale. A glaze of sweat was on her brow.

"That guy shot me." She winced in pain. "He dragged Rebecca in here, and I shouted to stop. He shot me."

Ryan searched under the counter for the first aid kit. He

found it, ripped open a bandage and pressed it against the entrance wound.

"Ryan! You in here?" It was Jerry.

"Over here," replied Ryan. "Angela's been shot. Phil has a gun and he's got Bec."

Jerry radioed in about Angela's gunshot wound. He had his Glock 22 out and readied. Sirens echoed in the distance. Ryan could feel his heart thump in his chest. His senses were alive and alert – he could feel the tension in the air like seeing a heavy fog on a winter morning.

A scream sounded from deep in the house and Ryan watched as Jerry advanced towards the sound, glock pointed forward like a wolf hunting. Ryan didn't hesitate, he followed several paces behind Jerry, then broke off to go around through another direction. Ryan figured Phil would run from Jerry and Ryan would be there to close the gap.

As Jerry entered the next room and Ryan lost sight of him, a shot rang out and Ryan heard the crash of a body falling to the floor. Ryan dashed ahead – he had to get this right.

BEC FOUGHT DOWN PANIC. Didn't these stand offs usually end in the hostage getting shot? She tried to remain calm and keep the tension out of her body as Tony had shown her in the jiu-jitsu class she went to. When Phil shot at Jerry, Bec noticed that his grip loosened ever so slightly. She decided that the next time an opportunity like that presented itself, she would act.

Bec couldn't see Jerry, but she heard him call out and she was glad he didn't seem hurt. "Mr. Mansfield, isn't it? Look, I'm not pointing my weapon at you. We can talk through this if you release Rebecca Williams."

"Bullshit! As soon as I let her-" Phil didn't get to finish his sentence. When he started speaking, Bec felt her captor's attention shift, so she dropped like a sack of potatoes and rotated her whole body towards Phil's chest, just like Tony had taught her. The movement caught Phil off guard, causing him to stumble. Bec broke free. She was free!

She took two steps away from Phil, but her legs felt like led - she could not make them move fast enough. Then, Phil grabbed her by the wrist, yanking her back towards him.

MOVING AS QUIETLY AS he could, Ryan gently pushed open the door in front of him. He was nearly certain that Phil, Bec, and Jerry were in the next room. The door gave way a fraction, giving Ryan a crack through which to peer through. He witness Bec's failed escape when Phil grabbed her and pulled her back.

Adrenaline took over forcing Ryan to make a snap deci-sion. Just like in jiu-jitsu where decisive actions can win you the match, Ryan leapt forward like a one-hundred meter sprinter chasing gold at the Olympics.

Phil looked up, his eyes widened in surprise. The pistol rose up so that Ryan could see the end of the barrel like a gaping mouth that spat a tongue of flame. The bullet grazed Ryan's shoulder that felt more like a sharp burn one might get from oil spitting out of the pan.

Ryan's legs pumped harder. *Smash!* Ryan slammed into Phil before the other man had time to get off a second shot. The pair fell to the ground and Ryan immediately mounted Phil, wrestling hard to choke his opponent out. Phil was much stronger than Ryan had anticipated. He heard Jerry swear and say, "Get out of the way Ryan, damn it!" But Ryan knew he couldn't give up now. And where was Bec? If Ryan backed off now, Phil could have a second attempt at getting Bec. It was all or nothing.

Phil pounded Ryan in the face with his fists, sending pain across Ryan's vision and opening up some space and more opportunities for punches and slaps to land on and around Ryan's head. Phil was fighting for his survival. Despite the pain and the stinging in his eyes, Ryan refused to let the barrage of punches distract him from his goal of getting a choke on Phil.

Ryan managed to slip behind Phil, wrap his arm around his opponent's neck, and secure a rear-naked choke. Phil struggled, slapping and clawing at Ryan's arms... nine, ten, eleven. Out. Phil went limp.

Ryan heaved and rolled Phil's unconscious body out of the way. Next, he looked about for Bec, but his vision was blurred from blood and sweat. She called to him, then felt her hand take his, helping him off the floor. Ryan embraced Bec in a hug asking, "Are you okay? Do you need an ambulance?"

Bec shook her head and Ryan felt her squeeze him. She asked, "Jen?"

"She's fine. A little shaken, but she's fine."

Meanwhile, Jerry pulled out his cuffs, rolled Phil into the recovery position, checked his breathing, and cuffed him.

47

The fluorescent lights reflected off the polished linoleum covered floors and the smell of disinfectant lingered. Once, Brooksdale hospital served the numerous villages in the surrounding area as well as Brooksdale's fifteen thousand people. But over the years, changes to funding had seen a wing closed and most of the specialist services moved to Armidale.

Today, the hospital served as a halfway house for elderly patients who had suffered a stroke or had a serious fall and could no longer look after themselves. The occasional moan echoed through the stark corridors. The emergency department still operated and dealt largely with farm accidents and car crashes. Today they had something different.

Ryan had already given his statement to the police, been checked by a doctor, had his bullet wound seen to, a graze, and was finally free to go home at six in the evening.

He wasn't ready to go home.

The door to Bec's room opened and Sharon Burgess stepped out and clapped Ryan on the shoulder. He nodded in recognition and stepped inside. The room was sterile white with grey blinds over the windows. It was good Bec had a window. There was a bed with those metallic sides that prevented patients falling out - or escaping. A plastic chair, television, and a night stand with drawers and a mirror were next to the bed.

Lying on the bed, Bec had her head turned towards the window through which the evening twilight cast a blue shadow over Brooksdale. The town lights twinkled as they came on. She shifted and looked at Ryan. She croaked, "You could've given a girl a chance to get made-up." Her neck was bandaged and Ryan imagined the raw flesh underneath. He hoped it wouldn't scar her. She had a black eye and her bottom lip was swollen. Ryan rubbed his chin and stood awkwardly halfway between the door and the bed. He wanted to sit beside her and hold her hand. But he wasn't sure where their relationship was. Instead, he said, "Angela's going to be fine."

"That's a relief. I was worried about her. Is she here?"

"They took her to Armidale for surgery. Not life-threatening, though."

"Good. It wasn't fair that she got shot because of me. How about you?" Bec's eyes moved to the bandage around Ryan's bicep.

"Just a scratch. I didn't even need stitches." Ryan stepped forward and put his hands on the aluminium bars of bed. When Bec didn't say anything, Ryan guessed she felt responsible for the injuries caused to people she cared about. Ryan said soothingly, "Hey, none of this was your fault." But Bec simply looked at him. Ryan continued, "I haven't heard anything about Jen."

Bec gestured towards the chair. "She saw me before Sharon came in. I guess you were still talking to the police.

She's okay. Bruising where she was tired up. A cut on her head. She told me she was going to go home."

Ryan nodded. He had been worried about Jen. "Any news on Phil?"

"Sharon said he's been taken into custody and charged with a host of things including kidnapping, unlawful imprisonment, assault, and I don't know what else. She says he'll be put away for a long time and not to worry."

"Will you have to testify?"

Bec nodded and her gaze wandered back to the window.

Ryan reached out and held her hand. He gave it a gentle squeeze and felt Bec return the pressure. He relaxed and said, "Jen can stay at my place. She might not feel safe in her flat after today."

"That's good. I'll message her."

"You can stay at my place, too. Until you leave."

Bec let go of his hand, leaving it stranded on the white bed sheet. This was the elephant in the room. She said, "I have to thank you. What you did was really special. Thank you."

Ryan ran his hand through his hair and looked out the window. He felt uncomfortable with the praise. Besides, he had something else he wanted to talk about. Now or never. "I wanted to talk with you..."

Bec cut him off. "Ryan, if this is about us, it's okay. I get it. You belong in Brooksdale. But don't try to talk me out of going to Melbourne. Even looking like this!" She waved her hand over her face, smiled, coughed, then winced at the pain.

"Just let me talk, will you?" He took a deep breath. "I did a lot of thinking. You're the best thing that's ever happened to me. I... I realized I love you and I want to share my life with you. I want to go to Melbourne with you, or wherever you go. I want to go on that journey."

BEC COULDN'T BELIEVE her ears. She had been sure Ryan was going to stay in Brooksdale, especially after getting the promotion. She blinked away tears. This was all too much. Emotions flooded through her, swirled, then were pulled out again with the tide, leaving her in waves of emotional volatility, numbness, love, confusion, fear, then settling firmly on love.

She grasped Ryan's hand and pulled it towards herself, saying, "Okay. Yes, come with me." Tears trickled down her cheeks and through the blur she could see wetness on Ryan's face, too. He leaned over and hugged her, kissing her gently on the cheek as he did so. In this place, with all that had happened, such a simple form of human contact was the most intimate touch she had ever experienced.

48

B ec and Ryan watched as Jen drove off. The couple stood on the pavement in front of North Brooksdale Service Station, their bags at their feet, waiting for the bus that would take them to Sydney, then Melbourne.

The summer morning was calm as the sun rose above the beautiful red and yellow brick buildings that Bec loved so much. The smell of country summer was in the air. It smelled warm and fresh. Bec took Ryan's hand in hers. She kissed him on the cheek. "Nervous?" she asked.

"A little. I'm glad Jen decided to move into my place. Makes things a bit easier."

Bec hugged Ryan. She knew he was feeling anxious about leaving his home town, his life. She also knew what it meant to him, but they would be back. Jen was settled here, and Ryan's mother was here. Then there was the trial. Phil's trial was in three months. Both Ryan and Bec would need to return from Melbourne for that.

The wind rustled the Spring flowers, filling the air with a dusty-sweet smell of rural Australia. Bec pulled closer into

Ryan. His warmth and strength comforted her. Ryan checked his watch. Eight o'clock in the morning. The bus was due to arrive. Jen had dropped them off and stayed for only a few minutes.

After a lot of hugs between the sisters and promises to phone everyday, Jen had pulled away, got in her car, and went to work. Life went on. Ryan looked at Bec and a wave of fear and responsibility rolled through her. Had he made the right choice? Quitting his job, leaving his mother to his brother's care, leaving his friends, his Youth Centre? He was leaving it all behind for her.

That was no way to think. Ryan had made his choice the same as she had made hers. They were free of their past and beholden to no one. Besides, None of that stuff was actually Ryan's - it was Brooksdale's and the town would have to decide whether to keep the Youth Centre and all the benefits it brought or not.

The whir of the bus broke Bec's thoughts. The Greyhound Bus's air brakes hissed and its suspension groaned as it went up the lip of the footpath to the service station and bus stop. Bec's gaze shifted back to Ryan and she saw excitement in his eyes like bright lights in the windows of her heart.

The bus swayed as it came to a stop and Ryan handed the bus driver their tickets, then hefted their bags into the luggage bay of the bus. Bec turned about, looking at the town she was leaving. Brooksdale had been good to her after and she could say goodbye on her own terms. Ryan brought her out of her thoughts. "Having doubts?"

"I was just thinking that this is where one part of my life ended and another is starting."

Ryan got up onto the steps of the bus, then extended his hand towards her, like an English nobleman helping a lady across the street. Bec took his hand and he pulled her swiftly yet gently towards him and he kissed her sweetly on the lips. Her heart fluttered with excitement.

The bus driver looked at them with deep lines of amusement crinkling his eyes, "C'mon you two. On the bus with you; we've got places to go!"

The End

REWARD

I would like to offer you, the reader, the opportunity to redeem a cash award for introducing this work to any literary agent, publisher or producer that offers an acceptable contract to me, the author, for this work. I am offering 10% of any initial book advance or option contract for film up to a maximum of $10,000 Australian Dollars.

Why am I offering this reward?

Crowd sourcing is a wonderful way to bring creative projects into the world. With your help, this story can get in front of agents, publishers, and film makers.

This reward works on the principle of six degrees of separation - any person in the world is connected to any other person through a chain of no more than five intermediaries.

If you would like to help take this book to the next level:
    - Think about who you know in publishing (literary

agents, editors, readers, executives, etc.) and pass this volume on to them.

- Think about who you know and who they might know in publishing.

- Think about who you know that reads and would enjoy this book.

Send any leads, or opportunities, or introductions to: jdunderwood@jdunderwood.net

Thank you in advance for your help,

J.D. Underwood

SUBSCRIBE FOR UPDATES

Want updates on new releases and special deals?

Staying in touch with readers is one of the pleasures of being an author. As such, I occasionally send out updates on new books and special deals. If you would like to stay informed and get notified when a new book is released or sale is on, please sign up for updates! You can stay up to date by clicking this link.

Thank you!

Use the Q-Code to visit jdunderwood.net

PLEASE LEAVE A REVIEW

Enjoy this book? You can make a big difference!

Reviews are the most powerful way for me to get my stories out into the world. Honest reviews help spread the word and get the attention of other readers who would enjoy my books. If you enjoyed this story, please leave a review!

ALSO BY J.D. UNDERWOOD

The Banker of Brooksdale

Maria's hard-charging career in banking gets derailed when her ex steals a coveted promotion. When she confronts the local muscle about bad business debts, she begins to realise he might be the only one she can rely on.

Maria Henderson finds herself straightening out bad loans in rural Australia. Assuming her city-smarts will win the day, Maria is sure she'll be back in Sydney within a year. But when she uncovers an avaricious ring of corruption, Maria must decide how far she will go to advance her career.

Tony Carpenter is back in town and trouble has followed him. Managing the local gym and helping troubled youth seems like a good way to leave his enforcer days behind. But when the new bank manager starts calling in bad debts, this former bike gang member is faced with a choice: confront his past or slide back into a life of crime.

If you like resolute heroes, intrigue, and enduring spirit, then you'll love the first book in the Brooksdale series.

Start reading The Banker of Brooksdale today!

ABOUT THE AUTHOR

J.D. Underwood is the author of the breakout *Brooksdale* series. An Australian country town native, he lives and works in Japan with his three daughters. He writes stories for his daughters to read when they grow a little older; stories he hopes will bring Australia into their imaginations.

J.D. Underwood makes his digital home at jdunderwood.net

 facebook.com/JD-Underwood-Author-104629131076343

 instagram.com/jasonu1712

ACKNOWLEDGMENTS

Cover Design by

Books Covered

Editing by

https://oneloveediting.com/